Richard Doddridge Blackmore

Cradock Nowell, a tale of the New Forest

Vol.3

Richard Doddridge Blackmore

Cradock Nowell, a tale of the New Forest
Vol.3

ISBN/EAN: 9783337024406

Printed in Europe, USA, Canada, Australia, Japan

Cover: Foto ©Andreas Hilbeck / pixelio.de

More available books at **www.hansebooks.com**

CRADOCK NOWELL

A Tale of the New Forest.

BY

RICHARD DODDRIDGE BLACKMORE,

AUTHOR OF "CLARA VAUGHAN."

"You have said: whether wisely or no, let the forest judge."
As You Like It, Act III. Sc. 2.

IN THREE VOLUMES.
VOL. III.

LONDON:
CHAPMAN AND HALL, 193, PICCADILLY.
1866.

LONDON:

PRINTED BY C. WHITING, BEAUFORT HOUSE, STRAND.

CRADOCK NOWELL.

CHAPTER I.

Upon the Christmas morning the parish flocked to church, and the church was dressed so beautifully that every one was amazed. Amy and Eoa made the wreaths, the garlands, and rosettes; there was only one cross out of the lot, a badly-bred Maltese one; and Eoa walked over the barbarous pew-screens (like the travisses in a stable), springing from one to another, with a cable of flowers and evergreens, as easily and calmly as she would come down-stairs to dinner. Of course she had never heard of that sort of thing before, but she took to it at once, as she did to anything pretty; and soon she was Amy's mistress, as indeed she must be every one's, unless she could not bear them.

The sons of the Forest looked up with amazement as they shambled in one after other, and an old woodcutter went home for his axe, lest the ivy should throttle the pillars. On the whole, the

parish attributed this great outburst of foliage to
the indignation of the pixies at Parson John's
going to London, and staying there so long.

The prayers were read by Mr. Pell, for the
rector was weary and languid; but he would not
forego his pleasant words to the well-known flock
that day. While the choir was making a stu-
pendous din out of something they called an
" anthem," Octave slipped off to his Rushford
duty, through the chancel-door. Then, with his
silken gown on—given him years ago by subscrip-
tion, and far too grand for him to wear, except at
Christmas and Easter—John Rosedew mounted the
pulpit-stairs, and showed (as in a holy bower of
good-will and of gratitude) the loving-kindness of
his face and the grandeur of his forehead. As he
glanced from one to the other with a general welcome, a genial interest in the welfare both of soul
and body, a stir and thrill ran through the church,
and many eyes were tearful. For already a rumour
was abroad that " Uncle John " must leave them,
that another Christmas Day would see a stranger in
his pulpit.

After dwelling briefly on his favourite subject,
Christian love, and showing (by quotations from
the noblest of heathen philosophers) how low and
false their standard was, how poor a keystone is
earthly citizenship, the patriotism of a pugnacious
village, or a little presumptuous Attica, to crown
and bind together the great arch of humanity;
after showing, too, with a depth of learning wasted

on his audience, how utterly false the assertion is
that the doctrines, or rather the principles, nay, the
one great principle of our New Testament, had
ever been anticipated on the banks of the Yellow
River—eloquently he turned himself to the application of his subject.

With some unconscious yearning perhaps, or
perhaps some sense of home-truth, he gazed towards the curtained pew where sat his ancient
friend, brought thither (it was too evident) by
tidings of his absence. As the eyes of the old men
met, for the first time after long estrangement—
those eyes that had met so frankly and kindly for
more than fifty years, during all which time each
to the other had been a "necessarius"—and as
each observed how pale and grey his veteran comrade looked, neither heart was wholly free from
self-reproach and sorrow.

John Rosedew's mild eyes glistened so, and his
voice so shook and faltered, that all the parish
noticed it, and wondered what harm it had done
last week. For none of them had ever known his
voice shake, except when some parishioner had
done the unbecoming; and then the village mourned
it, because it vexed the parson so.

The next day, as soon as Parson John had found
that all parochial matters were in proper trim, and
that he might leave home again without neglect of
duty, what did he do but order a fly, no less than
a one-horse fly, from the "Jolly Foresters;" which
fly should rush to the parsonage-door, as nearly as

might be, at one o'clock? Now why would not
Coræbus suffice to carry the rector and valise,
according to the laws of the Medes and Persians,
a distance of two parasangs?

Simply because our Amy was going, and had
every right to go. Beautiful Amy was going to
London, great fountain-head of all visions and
marvels, even from white long-clothes up to the
era of striped crinoline. And who shall object,
except on the ground that Amy was too good
to go?

If Amy were put down now in Hyde Park, Piccadilly, or Regent-street, at the height and cream of
the season, when fop, and screw, and fogey, Fri-
volus and Frivola, Diana Venatrix, Copa Syrisca,
Aphrodite Misthote, yea, and even some natural
honest girls moderately ticketed, are doing their
caravaning—if Amy were put on the pathway
there, in her simple grey hat and feather, and that
roundabout chenille thing which she herself had
made, and which followed the lines of her figure
so, fifty fellows, themselves of the most satisfactory
figure (at Drummond's, or at Coutts's), fifty fellows who had slipped the hook fifty times apiece
(spite of motherly bend O'Shaugnessey) must
have received their stroke of grace, and hated
Cradock Nowell.

Although the South-Western Railway had been
open so many years, our forest-child had never
been further from green leaf and yellow gorse
than Winchester in the eastern hemisphere, and
Salisbury in the western. And now after all to

think that she was going to London, not for joy,
but sorrow. Desperate coaxing it had cost; every
known or new device—transparent every one of
them, as the pleading eyes that urged it—every bit
of cozening learned from three years old and upward, every girlish argument that never can hold
water, unless it be a tear-drop; and, better than a
million pleas, every soft caress and kiss, all loving,
all imploring—there was not one of these but
came to batter Amy's father, or ever he surren-
dered. For John's ideas were very old-fashioned
as to maidenly decorum, and Aunt Eudoxia's view
of the matter was even more prim and grim than
his. Yet (as Amy well remarked) if *she* could see
no harm in it, there certainly could be none; and
how could they insist so much on the καλόν and the
πρέπον, as if they over-rode τὸ δέον!

It is likely enough that this last stroke won the
palm of victory; for, though Miss Amy knew
little of Greek, and her father knew a great deal,
she often contrived, with true feminine skill, to
take his wicket neatly, before he had found his
block-hole. And then her father would smile and
chuckle, and ask to have his bat again; which
never was allowed him. To think that any man
should be the father of such εὐστοχία!

Therefore, that father was compelled to throw
himself, flat as a flounder, on Eudoxia's generosity;
for the leech-bottle now was dry.

" Darling Doxy, you know quite well you are
such a wonderful manager; you have got a little
cash somewhere?"

He put it with a twist of interrogation, a quivering lever of doubt, and yet a grand fulcrum of confidence, which were totally irresistible. No wonder his daughter could coax. Oh that I were like you, John, when I want a bit of money!

Hereupon Aunt Doxy smiled, with the perception of superior mind, and the power of causing astonishment. Never a word she said, but went to some unknown recesses in holy up-stair adyta: she fussed about with many keys, over sounding boards and creaking ones, to signify her caution; and at last came back with a leathern bag, wash-leather tied with bobbin. Putting up her hands to keep Amy at a distance, she pursed her lips, as if to say, "Now don't be disappointed; there is really nothing in it. Nothing, at least, I mean for people of your extravagant ideas."

Then, one by one, before John's eyes, which enlarged with a geometric progression of amazement, she laid a gorgeous train of gold, as if it were but dominoes, beginning with half-sovereigns first, then breaking into the broader gauge, until there must have been twenty pounds, and John thought of all his poor people. Verily then she stopped awhile, to enhance her climax; or perhaps she hesitated, as was only natural. But now the pleasure of the thing was too much for her prudence. Looking at John and then at Amy, and wanting to look at both at once, she drew from a little niche in the bag, with a jerk (as if it were nothing) a dainty marrowfat ten-pound note of the Bank of England, with a name of substance upon the back, and an authenticity of grease grander than any water-mark. She tried very hard to make light of it, and not wave it in the air even; but the tide of her heart was too strong for her, and she turned away, and cried as hard as if she had no money.

Who may pretend to taste and tell every herb in the soup of nature? There is no sovereign moly, no paramount amellus; even basil (the herb of kings) may be lost in garlic. Blest are they who seek not ever for the forced-meat balls, but find some good in every brewis, homely, burnt, or overstrained. John Rosedew, putting on his boots for the road to London, felt himself, at every tug, quite as rich as Megacles—that man of foremost Athenian blood, but none the more a gentleman, who walked capaciously into, and rapaciously walked out of, the gold-granaries of Crœsus. A delightful sense of having gotten great money out of Eudoxia—a triumph without historic parallel—inspired him, away with that overdone word!—aerated him with glory. Thirty pounds, and some odd shillings, wholly at John Rosedew's mercy (who never gave quarter to money, but hewed it as small as Agag when anybody asked him),—thirty pounds, with no duty upon it, no stamp of responsibility, and a peculiar and peppery piquancy in the spending of every halfpenny, to wonder what sister Doxy would think if she could only know it! He gave careful Amy the note to keep,

and 15*l.* to go inside it, because he had promised
to do so, for Doxy knew his nature.

In that noble fly from the "Foresters," which
had only two springs broken, John and his daughter went away to catch the train at Brockenhurst.
Out of the windows dangerously they pushed their
beautiful heads—the beauty of youth on one side,
the beauty of age on the other—although the
coachman had specially warned them that neither
door would fasten. But what could they do, when
Aunt Doxy was there by the great rhododendron,
with a kettle-holder over her mouth because it was
so cold; fat Jemima too, and Jenny, and Jem Pottles leading Coræbus to shake off his dust at the
shay-horse, and learn what he might come to?

Some worthy people had journeyed up from the
further end of the village, to bid an eternal farewell to Amy, and to take home the washing. They
knew she would never come back again ; she would
never be let go again; folks in London were so
wicked, and parson was so innocent. Evil though
the omens were, as timidly blushing she went away,
tearfully leaving her father's hearth, though a daw
on the left hand forbade her to go, and a wandering chough was overheard, and a croaking raven
whirled away into the wilds of the woodland—for
whom shall I fear, I the cannie seer, while Amy
smiles dexter out of the cab, and wraps her faith
around her?

Make we not half our life here, according as we
receive it? Is it not as the rain that falls, softly

when softly taken, as of leaves and grass and water; but rattling and flying in mud and foul splashes, when met at wrong angles repulsively?

My little daughter, if you cannot see your way in that simile—a very common-place one,—take a still more timeworn and venerable illustration. Our life is but a thread, my child, at any moment snappable, though never snapped unwisely; and true as it is that we cannot spin and shape it (as does the spider) out of our own emotions, yet we have this gift of God, that we can secrete some gold along it, some diamonds fetching the sunlight. Knowing, then, in whose Hand we are, and feeling how large that Hand is, let us know and feel therewith that He will not crush us; that He loves us to rejoice therein, and tamely to regard Him; with confidence in adoration, a smile in every bow to Him.

CHAPTER II.

POLLY DUCKSACRE was sitting in state behind
the little counter, and opposite the gas-jet, upon
her throne—a bushel basket set upside down on
another. It was the evening of Boxing Day, and
Polly was arrayed with a splendour that challenged
the [strictest appraisement; so gorgeous were her
gilt earrings, cornelian necklace, sham cameo brooch
—Cupid stealing the sword of Mars—and Ger-
man-silver bracelets. The children who came in
for " ha'porths of specked " forgot their errand
and hopes of prigging, and, sucking their lips with
wild admiration, cried " Lor now! Ain't she
stunnin ?" " Spexs her sweetheart in a coach and
four," exclaimed one little girl of great penetra-
tion ; " oh give us a ride, miss, when he comes."
That little girl was right, to a limited extent.
Polly did expect her sweetheart ; not in a coach
and four, however, but in a smallish tax-cart,
chestnut-coloured, picked out with white ; on the

panel whereof was painted, as the Act directs, "Robert Clinkers, Junior, Coal-merchant, Hammersmith." Mr. Clinkers, whose first visit had been paid simply from pity for Cradock, and to acquit himself of all complicity in Hearty Wibraham's swindle, had called again to make kind inquiries, after finding how ill the poor fellow was, and that his landlady sold coals. Nor was it long before he ventured to propose an arrangement, mutually beneficial, under which the Ducksacre firm should receive their supply from him. Two or three councils were held, but the ladies were obliged to surrender at last, because he was so complimentary, and had such nice white teeth, and spoke in such a feeling manner of his dear departed angel. On the other hand, their old wharfinger would come blustering about his sacks, loud enough to make the potatoes jump, and he kept such impudent men, and bit his nails without any manners, and called them both "Mrs. Acreducks."

During this Clinkerian diplomacy, Polly showed such shrewdness, and such a nice foot and ancle, and had such a manner of rolling her eyes — blacker and brighter than best Wallsend—that the coals of love were laid, the match struck, the fire kindled, and drawing well up the hearth-place, before Robert Clinkers knew what he was at. And now he came every evening, bringing two sacks of coal with him, and sat on a bag of Barcelonas, and cracked, and gazed at Polly.

" Miss Ducksacre, you should sell lemonade,'
he had said only Saturday last, which was Christmas Eve, " it is such a genteel drink, you know,
when a chap is consumed with internal fires, as
the great poet says—him as wrote the operas, or
the copperas, bless me, I never know which it is;
likely you can tell, miss?"

" Lor, Mr. Clinkers, why, the proper name is
hopperas ; we shows the boards, and we gets a
ticket, when nobody else won't go."

" Oh now ! Do you, though ? Ah, I was there,
afore ever I knew what life was. A tricksome
thing is life, Miss Polly, especially for a 'andsome
female, and no young fellow to be trusted with it.
Valuable cargo on green wood. Sure to come to
shipwreck."

" Lor, Mr. Clinkers, you don't mean me ! I am
sure I am not at all handsome."

" Then there isn't one in London, miss. Coals
is coals, and fire is fire—oh, I should like some
lemonade, with a drop of rum in it. Would you
join me in it now, if I just pop round the corner?
It would make you feel so nice now."

" Do I ever feel anything else but nice?" Oh,
Polly, what a leading question !

" I wishes it was in my province now, with the
deepest respect, to try !" Here Polly flashed away,
though nobody was pursuing her, got behind some
Penzance broccoli, and seized a half-pottle to defend herself. Mr. Clinkers, knowing what he was
about, appealed to a bunch of mistletoe, under

which, in distracting distraction, the young lady
had taken refuge.

"Now nobody else in all this London," said the
coal-merchant to the berries, "in all this mighty
Baal, as the poet beautifully expresses it, especially
if a young man, not over five-and-thirty, not so
very bad-looking but experienced in life, and with
great veneration for females, and a business, you
may say, of three hundred a year clear of income-
tax and increasing yearly, and a contract with the
company, without no encumbrances, would ever
go to think of letting that beautiful young lady
enjoy the sweets of retirement in that most in-
witing position, without plucking some of the pearls
off, and no harm done or taken.   And nothing at
all pervents me, no consideration of the brockolo—
could pay for it to-morrow morning — but my
deepest respects, not having my best togs on,
through a cruel haxident. Please pigs they'll come
home to-morrow morning, and I'll do it on Monday,
and lock up yard at four o'clock, if tailor has made
a job of it.   Look nice indeed, and feel nice ?   I
should like to know how she could help it!"

This explains why, when the wheels at the door
proved to be not of the sprightly tax-cart, but a
lumbering cab, Polly was disappointed. Neither
was her displeasure removed when she saw a very
pretty girl get out, and glide into the shop, with
the loveliest damask spreading over the softest and
clearest cheeks. Though Polly had made up her
mind about Cradock as now a bad speculation, it

was not likely that she should love yet any one
who meant to have him.

Amy shrunk back as her nice clean skirt swept
the grimy threshold. She was not by any means
fidgety, but had a nervous dislike of dirt, as most
upright natures have. Then she felt ashamed of
herself, and coloured yet more deeply to think that
a place good enough for Cradock should seem
too sordid for her, indeed! And then her tears
glanced in the gas-light, that Cradock should ever
have come to this, and partly, no doubt, for her
sake, though she never could tell how.

The little shop was afforested with Christmas-
trees of all sorts and of every pattern, as large as
ever could be squeezed, with a knuckle of root to
keep them steady, into pots No. 32. The coster-
mongers repudiate larger pots, because they take
too much room on a truck, and involve the necessity of hiring a boy to push.

Aucuba, Irish yew, Portugal laurel, arbor vitæ,
and bay-tree, but most of all—and for the purpose
by far the most convenient, because of the hat-peg
order — the stiff, self - confident, argumentative
spruce. All these, when they have done their
spiriting, and yielded long-remembered fun, will
be fondly tended by gentle-hearted girls on some
suburban balcony; they will be watered enough to
kill lignum vitæ; patent compost will be bought at
about the price of sugar; learned consultations
will be held between Sylvia and Lucilla; and then,
as the leaves grow daily more yellow, and papa is

so provoking that he will only shake his head (too sagaciously to commit himself), an earnest appeal will be addressed to some of the gardening papers. Or perhaps the tree will be planted, with no little ceremony, in the centre of some grass-plot nearly as large as a counterpane; while the elder members of the family, though bland enough to drink its health, regard the measure as very unwise, because the house will be darkened so in a few short years.

Meanwhile the editor's reply arrives—"Possibly Sylvia's tree has no roots." He is laughed to scorn for his ignorance, until little Charley falls to work with his Ramsgate spade unbidden. *Factura nepotibus umbram!* It has been chopped all round the bole with a hatchet, and is as likely to grow as a lucifer-match.

Through that Christmas Tabraca John Rosedew led his daughter, begging her at every step to be careful of the trees, whose claims upon her attention she postponed to those of her frock.

" Lor bless me, sir, is that you now, and your good lady along of you! How glad I am, to be sure!"

" Miss Ducksacre, this is my daughter, Miss Amy Rosedew, of whom you have heard me speak;" here John executed a flourish of great complacency with his hat; " my only child, but as good to me as any dozen could be. Will you allow her to stop here a minute, while I go up-stairs?"

Amy was trembling now, more and more every

moment, and John would not ask how Cradock was, for fear of frightening his daughter.

To be sure she can stay here," said Polly, not over graciously; for if Mr. Clinkers should come in the while, it might alter his ideal.

" Ah, so very sad; so very sad, miss, ain't it now ? "

" Yes," said Amy, having no desire to pursue the subject with Polly. But Polly's tongue could no more keep still than a frond of maiden-hair fern in the draught of a river archway.

" Ah, so very sad! To think of him go, quite young as he is, to one of them moonstruck smilems, where they makes rope-mats and tiger rugs! As 'andsome a young man, miss, as ever I see off a hengine; and of course he must be such, being as he is your brother."

Before poor Amy could answer, Mrs. Ducksacre came to fetch her, and frowned very hard at Polly, who began to look out of the window. In spite of all her faith and hope, the child could scarcely get up the stairs, till her father came to meet her.

" There is no one with him now, dear; Mrs. Jupp is in the sitting-room, so very kindly lent us by the good landlady. Only two more pairs of stairs, and there our Cradock lies, not a bit worse than he was; if anything, a little better; and his faithful little Wena with him : she won't leave him, night or day, dear. Give me your hand, Amy. Why, I declare, it is rather dark, when you get too far from the windows! Madam, come in with us."

But Eliza Ducksacre, though little versed in mintage, and taking pig-rings for halfpence, knew when her presence had better be absence, as well as a sleeping partner does at the association's bankruptcy. So, after showing them up to the door, she slipped away into the side-cupboard which Mr. Rosedew had called a " sitting-room."

Then John took Amy's bonnet off (after ruining the strings), and stroked her pretty hair down, and took her young cheeks in his hands, and begged her not to tremble so, because she would quite upset him. Only she might cry a little, if she thought it would do her good. But when she put her hand up, and gave a dry sob only, the father led her very tenderly into the little chamber.

It was a wretched little room, like a casual pauper's home, when he gets one, only much lower and smaller. Amy took all of it in at a glance, for in matters of that sort a woman's perception is, when compared to a man's, as forked lightning compared to a blunt dessert fork.

She even knew why the bed was awry; which her father could sooner have written ten scolia than discover. The bed was placed so because poor Cradock, jumping up all of a sudden in an early stage of illness, and before his head grew soft, had knocked a great piece of plaster away from the projecting hip-beam.

Now Craddy was looking away from them, sitting up in the sack-cloth bed, and trying with the sage gravity of fixed hallucination to read some

lines which his fancy had written on the glazed
dirt that served for a window. That window perhaps pronounced itself more by candlelight than
by daylight, and the landlord had forbidden any
attempt at cleaning it, because he knew that the
frame would drop out. Two candles, the residue
of two pounds which. Mr. Rosedew had paid for,
only helped to interpret the squalid room more
forcibly.

While Amy stood there, shocked and frightened,
and her father was thinking what to say, the poor
sick fellow turned towards them, and his eyes met
hers. She saw that the tint of her lover's eyes
was gone from a beautiful deep grey to the tone
of a withered oak-leaf, the pupils forthstanding
haggardly, the whites dull and chased with blood
veins, the sockets marked with a cloudy blue, and
channeled with storms of sorrow ; the countenance
full of long suffering—gaunt, and wan, and weary.

Amy could not weep, but gazed, never thinking
anything, with all the love and pity, devotion and
faith eternal, which are sure to shine in a woman's
eyes when trouble strikes its light there. How
different from the shy maid's glance which, only a
month or two ago, would have met his youthful
overtures ! And how infinitely grander ! Something of the good All-Father's power and mercy
in it.

She kept her eyes upon him. She had no power
to move them. And they changed exactly as his
did. The pale glance wandering into her gaze,

with an appealing submissive motion, eager to
settle somewhere, but too faint to ask for sympathy, began to feel its way and fasten, began to
quiver with vibrant light and sense of resting somewhere, began to quicken, flush, and deepen—from
what fountain God only knows—then to waver
and suffuse (in feeble consciousness of grief),
retire and return again, fluttering to some remembered home, as a bird in the dark comes to his
nest; then to thrill, and beam, and sparkle with
the light, the life, the love.

So with a weak but joyful cry, like a shipwrecked man at his hearth again, he stretched out
both his wasted arms, and Amy was there without
knowing it. She laid his white cheek on her
shoulder, and let her hair flow over it; she held
him up with her own pure breast, till his worn
heart beat on her warm one. Then she sobbed,
and laughed, and sobbed, and called him her world,
and heart, and heaven, and kissed his nestling
forehead, and looked, and asked, oh, where the
love was. All she begged for was one word, just
one little word, if you please, to know who was to
come to comfort him. Oh, he must know her—
of course he must—wouldn't she know him, that
was all, though she hadn't a breath of life left?
His own, his faith, his truth, his love—his own—
let him say who, and she never would cry again.
Only say it once, his own—

    " Amy ! "

"Yes, your Amy, Amy, Amy. Say it again, oh! say it again, my poor everlasting love !"

Suddenly the barriers of his frozen grief were loosened. With a feeble arm staying on her, although it could not cling to her, he burst into a flood of tears, from the fountain of great waters whose source and home is God.

Then John, who had stood at the door all the time, with his white head bowed on his coat-sleeve, came forward and took a hand of each, knelt by the bed, and gave thanks. They wanted not to talk of it, nor any doctor to tell them. Because they had an angel's voice, that God would be gracious to them.

"Darlings, didn't I tell you," said Amy, looking up at them, with her rich curls tear-bespangled, like a young grape-leaf in the vinery; "don't you know that I was sure our Father would never forsake us; and that even a simple thing like me might fetch back my own blessing? Oh, you never would have loved me so; only God knew it was good for us."

While she spoke, Cradock looked at her with a faint far-off intelligence, not entering into her arguments. He only cared to hear her voice; to see her every now and then; and touch her to make sure of it; then to dream that it was an angel; then to wake and be very glad that it was not, but was Amy.

CHAPTER III.

SLOWLY from that night, but surely, Cradock's mind began to return, like a child to its mother, who is stretching forth her arms to it; timid at first and wondering, and apt for a long time to reel and stagger at very slight shocks or vibrations. Then as the water comes over the ice in a gradual gentle thaw, beginning to gleam at the margin first, where the reeds are and the willow-trees, then gliding slowly and brightly on, following every skate-mark or line where a rope or stick has been, till it flows into a limpid sheet; so crystal reason dawned and wavered, felt its way and went on again, tracing many a childish channel, many a dormant memory, across that dull lethargic mind, until the bright surface was restored, and the lead line of judgment could penetrate.

Mr. Rosedew quartered himself and his Amy at the Portland Hotel hard by, and reckless of all expense moved Cradock into Mrs. Ducksacre's

very best room.   He would have done this long
ago, only the doctor would not allow it.   Then
Amy, who did not like London at all, because
there were so few trees in it, hired some of the
Christmas-grove from the fair greengrocers, and
decked out the little sitting-room, so that Cradock
had sweet visions of the Queen's bower mead.   As
for herself, she would stay in the shop, perhaps
half an hour together, and rejoice in the ways of
the children.   All her pocket-money went into the
till as if you had taken a shovel to it.   Barcelonas,
Brazils, and cob-nuts she was giving all day to the
"warmints;" and golden oranges rolled before her
as from Atalanta's footstep.

It is a most wonderful fact, and far beyond my
philosophy, that instead of losing her roses in
London, as a country girl ought to have done,
Amy bloomed with more Jacqueminot upon very
bright occasions—more Louise Odier constantly,
with Goubalt in the dimples, then toning off at any
new fright to Malmaison, or Devoniensis—more of
these roses now carmined or mantled in the delicate turn of her cheeks than ever had nestled and
played there in the free air of the Forest.   Good
Aunt Doxy was quite amazed on the Saturday
afternoon, when meeting her brother and niece at
the station—for it made no difference in the out-
lay, and the drive would do her good—she found,
not a pale and withered child, worn out with
London racket, and freckled with dust and smoke-
spots, but the loveliest Amy she had ever yet seen

—which was something indeed to say,—with a brilliance of bloom which the good aunt at once proceeded to test with her handkerchief.

But before the young lady left town—to wit, on the Friday evening—she had a little talk with Rachel Jupp, or rather with strapping Issachar, which nearly concerns our story.

"Oh, Miss Amy," said Rachel that morning— "Miss Amy" sounded more natural somehow than "Miss Rosedew" did—"so you're going away, miss, after all, and never see my Loocy; and a pretty child she is, and a good one, and a quiet one, and father never lift hand to her now; and the poor young gentleman saved her life, and he like her so much, and she like him."

"I will come and see her this evening, as you have so kindly asked me. That is, with my papa's leave, and if you don't mind coming for me to the inn at six o'clock. I am afraid of walking by myself after dark in London. My papa has found some books at the bookstalls, and he is so delighted with them he never wants me after dinner."

"Dear Miss Amy, would you mind, then— would you mind taking a drop of tea with us?"

"To be sure I will. I mean, if it is quite convenient, and if you can be spared here, and if— oh nothing else, Mrs. Jupp, only I shall be most happy." She was going to say, "and if you won't make any great preparations," but she knew how sensitive poor people are at restraints upon hospitality.

So grand preparations were made; and grander still they would have been, and more formal and uncomfortable, if Amy had finished her sentence. Rachel at once rushed off to her lord, whose barge-shaped frame was moored alongside of his wharf, dreaming as stolidly as none except a bargee can dream. He immediately shelled out seven and sixpence from the cuddy of his inexpressibles, and left his wife to her own devices, except in the matter of tea itself. The tea he was resolved to fetch from a little shop in the barge-walk, where, as Mother Hamp declared, who kept the tobacco-shop by the gate, they sold tea as strong as brandy.

"If you please to excuse our Zakey, miss, taking no more tea," said Mrs. Jupp, after Issachar had laboured very hard at it, the host being bound, in his opinion, to feast even as the guest did; "because he belong to the anti-teatotallers, as takes nothing no stronger than gin, miss."

"Darrn't take more nor one noggin of tay, miss," cried Mr. Jupp, touching his short front curl with a hand scrubbed in quick-lime and copperas; "likes it, but it don't like me, miss. Makes me feel quite intemperant like,—so narvous, and queer, and staggery. Looey, dear, dad's mild mixture, for to speak the young lady's health in. Leastways, by your lave, miss."

Dad's mild mixture soon made its appearance

in a battered half-gallon can, and Mr. Jupp was amazed and grieved that none but himself would quaff any. The strongest and headiest stuff it was, which even the publicans of London, alchymists of villainy, can quassify, and cocculise, and nux-vomicise up to proof. Then, the wrath of hunger and thirst being mollified, Issachar begged leave to smoke, if altogether agreeable, and it would all go up the chimney; which, however, it refrained from doing.

Now, while he is smoking, I may admit that the contents of Mr. Jupp's census-paper (if, indeed, he ever made legal entries, after punching the collector's head) have not been transcribed to the satisfaction of the Registrar-General or Home-Office, or whoever or whatever he or it is, who or which insists upon knowing nine times as much about us as we know about ourselves. Mr. Jupp was a bargee of Catholic views; "it warn't no odds to he" whether he worked upon wharf or water, sea or river or canal, at coal, or hay, or lime, breeze, or hop-poles, or anything else. Now and then he went down to Gravesend, or up the river to Kingston or Staines; but his more legitimate area was navigable by three canals, where a chap might find time to eat his dinner, and give his wife and nag their'n. Issachar's love of nature always culminated at one o'clock; and then how he loved to halt his team under a row of alders, and see the painted meadows gay, and have grub and pipe accordin'.

His three canals, affording these choice delights unequally, were the Surrey, the Regent's, and the Basingstoke.

That last was, indeed, to his rural mind, the nearest approach to Paradise; but as there is in all things a system of weights and measures, Mr. Jupp got better wages upon the other two, and so could not very often afford to indulge his love of the beautiful. Hence he kept his household gods within reach of the yellow Tibers, and took them only once a year for a treat upon the Anio. Then would Rachel Jupp and Looey spend a summer month afloat, enjoying the rural glimpses and the sliding quietude of inland navigation, and keeping the pot a-boiling in the state-cabin of the *Enterprise* or the *Industrious Maiden.*

Now Amy having formed Loo's acquaintance, and said what was right and pretty in gratitude for their entertainment and faithful kindness to Cradock, was just about to leave them, when Issachar Jupp delivered this speech, very slowly, as a man who has got to the marrow and pope's-eye of his pipe :—

"Now 'scuse me for axing of you, miss, and if any ways wrong in so doing, be onscrupulous for to say so, and no harm done or taken. But I has my raisons for axing, from things as I've a 'ear'd him say, and oncommon good raisons too. If you please, what be the arkerate name and dwellin'-place of the young gent as saved our Loo? Mr.

Clinkers couldn't find out, miss, though he knowed as it warn't 'Charles Newman.'"

"Don't you know his story, then?" asked Amy, in some astonishment. "I thought you knew all about it, and were so kind to him partly through that, though you were kind enough not to talk to me about it."

"We guesses a piece here and there, miss, since he talk so wild in his illness. And that's what made me be axing of you; for I knowed one name right well as he out with once or twice; not at all a common name nother. But we knows for sartin no more nor this, that he be an onlucky young gent, and the best as ever come into these parts."

"There can be no harm in my telling you, such faithful friends as you are. And the sad tale is known to every one, far and wide, in our part of Hampshire."

"Hampshire, ah!" said Mr. Jupp, with a very mysterious look; "we knowed Mr. Rosedew come from Hampshire, and that set us the more a-thinkin' of it. Loo, child, run for dad's bacco-box, as were left to Mother Richardson's, and if it ain't there, try at Blinkin' Davy's, and if he ain't got it, try Mother Hamp."

The child, sadly disappointed, for her eyes were large with hopes of a secret about her "dear gentleman," as she called Cradock, departed upon her long errand. Then Amy told, as briefly as possible, all she knew of the great mishap, and the misery

which followed it. From time to time her soft
voice shook, and her tears would not be disciplined;
while Rachel Jupp's strayed anyhow. But Issachar
listened dryly and sternly, with one great brown
hand on his forehead. Not once did he interrupt
the young lady, by gesture, look, or question.
But when she had finished, he said very quietly,

"One name, miss, as have summat to do with it,
I've not 'ear'd you sinnify; and it were the sound
o' that very name as fust raised my coorosity.
'Scuse me, miss, but I wouldn't ax, only for good
raison."

"I hardly know what right I have to mention
any other names," replied Amy, blushing and
hesitating, for she did not wish to speak of Pearl
Garnet; "there is only one other name connected
at all with the matter, and that one of no importance."

"Ah," returned Jupp, with a glance as intense
as a cat's through a dairy keyhole, "maybe the tow-
rope ain't nothin' to do with the goin' of the barge,
miss. That name didn't happen permiskious now
to be the name of Garnet, ma'am?"

"Yes, indeed it did. But how could you know
that, Mr. Jupp?"

"Pearl Garnet were the name I 'ear'd on, and
that ain't a very common name, leastways to my
experience. Now, could it 'ave 'appened by a
haxident that her good father's name were Bull
Garnet?"

Amy drew back, for Mr. Jupp, in his triumph

and excitement, had laid down his pipe, and was stretching out his unpeeled crate of a hand, as if to take her by the shoulder, and shake the whole truth out of her. It was his fashion with Rachel, and he quite forgot the difference. Mrs. Jupp cried, "Zakey, Zakey!" in a tone of strong remonstrance. But he was not abashed very seriously.

"It couldn't be now, could it, miss; it worn't in any way possible that Pearl Garnet's father was ever known by the name of Bull Garnet?"

"But indeed that is his name, Mr. Jupp. Why should you be so incredulous?"

"Oncredulous it be, miss; oncredulous, as I be a sinner. Rachey, who'd ha' thought it? How things does come about, to be sure! Now please to tell me, miss—very careful, and not passin' lightly of anything; never you mind how small it seem—every word you knows about Pearl Garnet and that there—job there; and all you knows on her father too."

"You must prove to me first, Mr. Jupp, that I have any right to do so."

Issachar now was strongly excited, a condition most unusual with him, except when his wife rebelled, and that she had, years ago, ceased to do. He put his long black face, which was working so that the high cheek-bones almost shut the little eyes, quite close to Amy's little white ear, and whispered,

"If ye dunna tell me, ye'll cry for it arl the life long, ye'll never right the innocent, and ye'll let the guilty ride over ye. I canna tell no more just now, but every word is gospel. I be no liar, miss, though I be rough enough, God knows. Supposes He made me so."

Then Amy, trembling at his words, and thinking that she had hurt his feelings, put her soft little hand, for amends, into Zakey's great black piece of hold, which looked like the bilge of a barge; and he wondered what to do with it, such a sort of chap as he was. He had never heard of kissing a hand, and even if he had it would scarcely be a timely offering, for he was having a chaw to compose himself—yet he knew that he ought not, in good manners, to let go her hand in a hurry; so what did he do but slip off a ring (one of those so-called galvanic rings, in which sailors and bargemen have wonderful faith as an antidote to rheumatics, tick dolorous, and the Caroline Morgan), and this ring he passed down two of her fingers, for all females do love trinkets so. Amy kept it carefully, and will put it on her chatelaine, if ever she institutes one.

Then, being convinced by his words and manner, she told him everything she knew about the Garnet family—their behaviour in and after the great misfortune; the strange seclusion of Pearl, and Mr. Garnet's illness. And then she recurred to some vague rumours which had preceded their settlement in the New Forest. To all this Issachar listened, without a word or a nod, but with his narrow forehead radiant with concentration, his lips screwed up in a serrate ring, after the manner of a medlar, and a series of winks so intensely sage that his barge might have turned a corner with a team of eight blind horses, and no nod wanted for one of them.

· " Ain't there no more nor that, miss ?" he asked, with some disappointment, when the little tale was ended; " can't you racollack no more ?"

" No, indeed I cannot. And if you had not some important object, I should be quite ashamed of telling you so much gossip. If I may ask you a question now, what more did you expect me to tell you ?"

" That they had know'd, miss, as Bull Garnet were Sir Cradock Nowell's brother."

" Mr. Garnet Sir Cradock's brother ! You must be mistaken, Mr. Jupp. My father has known Sir Cradock Nowell ever since he was ten years old; and he could not have failed to know it, if it had been so."

" Most like he do know it, miss. But dunna you tell him now, nor any other charp. It be true as gospel for all that, though."

" Then Robert and Pearl are Cradock's first cousins, and Mr. Garnet is his uncle !"

" Not ezackly as you counts things," answered the bargeman, looking at the fire; " but in the way as we does."

Amy felt that she must ask no more, at least upon that subject; and that she was not likely to speak of it even to her father.

"Let him go, miss," continued Issachar, referring now to Cradock; "let him go for a long sea-vohoyage, same as doctor horders un. He be better out of the way for a spell or two. The Basingstoke ain't fur enoo, whur I meant to 'ave took him. 'A mun be quite out o' the kintry till this job be over like. And niver a word as to what I thinks to coom anigh his ear, miss, if so be you vallies his raison."

"But you forget, Mr. Jupp, that you have not told me, as yet, at all what it is you do think. You said some things which frightened me, and you told me one which astonished me. Beyond that I know nothing."

"And better so, my dear young leddy, a vast deal better so. Only you have the very best hopes, and keep your spirits roaring. Zakey Jupp never take a thing in hand but what he go well through with it. Ask Rachey about that. Now this were a casooal haxident, mind you, only a casooal haxident——"

"Of course we all know that, Mr. Jupp. No one would dare to think anything else."

"Yes, yes; all right, miss. And we'll find out who did the casooal haxident—that's all, miss, that's all. Only you hold your tongue."

She was obliged to be content with this, and on the whole it greatly encouraged her. Then she returned to the Portland Hotel under convoy of all the Jupp family, and Issachar got into two or three rows by hustling every one out of her way.

Although poor Amy was frightened at this, no
doubt it increased her faith in him through some
feminine process of dialectics unknown to the ·
author of the Organon.

Though Amy could not bear to keep anything
secret from her father, having given her word
she of course observed it, and John was greatly
surprised at the spirits in which his daughter took
leave of Cradock. But there were many points in
Amy's character, as has been observed before,
which her father never understood; and he con-
cluded that this was a specimen of them, and was
delighted to see her so cheerful.

Now, being returned to Nowelhurst, he held
counsel with sister Eudoxia, who thoroughly deserved to have a vote after contributing so to the
revenue. And the result of their Lateran—for
they both were bricks—council was as follows :
That John was bound, howsoever much it went
against his proud stomach after his previous treat-
ment, to make one last appeal from the father according to the spirit to the father according to the
flesh, in favour of the unlucky son who was now
condemned to exile, so as at least to send him away
in a manner suitable to his birth. That, if this
appeal were rejected, and the appellant treated
unpleasantly—which was almost sure to follow—
he could not, consistently with his honour and his
clerical dignity, hold any longer the benefices
(paltry as they were), the gifts of a giver now
proved unkind. That thereupon Mr. Rosedew

should first provide for Cradock's voyage so far as
his humble means and small influence permitted;
and after that should settle at Oxford, where he
might get parochial duty, and where his old tuto-
rial fame and repute (now growing European
from a life of learning) would earn him plenty of
pupils——

"And a professorship at least!" Miss Eudoxia
broke in; for, much as she nagged at her brother,
she was proud as could be of his knowledge.

"Marry, ay, and a bishopric," John answered,
smiling pleasantly; "you have often menaced me,
Doxy dear, with Jemima's apron." .

So, on a bright day in January, John Rosedew
said to Jem Pottles, "Saddle me the horse, James."
And they saddled him the "horse"—not so called
by his master through any false aggrandisement
(such as maketh us talk of "the servants," when
we have only got a maid-of-all-work), but because
the parson, in pure faith, regarded him as a horse
of full equine stature and super-equine powers.

After tightening up the girths, then—for that
noble cob, at the saddling period, blew himself out
with a large sense of humour (unappreciated by
the biped who bestraddled him unwarily), an abdo-
minal sense of humour which, as one touch of nature
makes the whole world kin, induced the pigskin to
circulate after the manner of a brass dog's collar—
tush, I mean a dog's brass collar—in order to learn
what the joke was down in those festive regions;
therefore, having buckled him up six inches, till

the witty nag creaked like a tight-laced maid, away
rode the parson towards the Hall. Much liefer
would he have walked by the well-known and pleasant footpath, but he felt himself bound, as one may
say, to go in real style, sir.

The more he reflected upon the nature of his
errand, the fainter grew his hopes of success; he
even feared that his ancient friendship would not
procure him a hearing, so absorbed were all the
echoes of memory in the pique of parental jealousy,
and the cajoleries of a woman. And the consequences of failure—how bitter they must be to him
and his little household! Moreover, he dearly
loved his two little quiet parishes; and, though he
reaped more tithe from them in kindness than in
kind or by commutation, to his contented mind
they were far sweeter than the incumbency of
Libya-cum-Gades, and both Pœni for his beadles.

He thought of Amy with a bitter pang, and of
his sister with heaviness, as he laid his hand—for
he never used whip—on the fat flank of the pony
to urge him almost to a good round trot, that suspense might sooner be done with. And when the
Hall was at last before him, he rode up, not to the
little postern hard by the housekeeper's snuggery
(which had seemed of old to be made for him), but
to the grand front entrance, where the orange-
trees in tubs were, and the myrtles, and the
pilasters.

Most of the trees had been removed, with the
aid of little go-carts, before the frosts began; but

D 2

they impressed John Rosedew none the less, so far
as his placid and simple mind was open to small
impressions.

Dismounting from Coræbus, whose rusty snaffle
and mildewed reins would have been a disgrace
to any horse, as Amy said every day, he rang the
main entrance bell, and wondered whether they
would let him in.

That journey had cost him a very severe battle,
to bear himself humbly before the wrong, and to
do it in the cause of the injured.   In the true and
noble sense of pride, there could not be a prouder
man than the gentle parson.   But he ruled that
noble human pride with its grander element, left
in it by the Son of God, His incarnation's legacy,
the pride which never apes, but is itself humility.

At last the door was opened, not by the spruce
young footman (who used to look so much at Amy,
and speer about as to her expectations, because she
was only a parson's daughter), but by that ancient
and most respectable Job Hogstaff, patriarch of
butlers.   Dull and dim as his eyes were growing,
Job, who now spent most of his time in looking for
those who never came, had made out Mr. Rosedew's approach, by virtue of the pony's most un-
mistakable shamble.   Therefore he pulled down
his best coat from a jug-crook, twitched his white
hair to due stiffness, pushed the ostiary footman
back with a scorn which rankled for many a day
under a zebra waistcoat, and hobbled off at his

utmost pace to admit the visitor now so strange, though once it was strange without him.

Mr. Rosedew walked in very slowly and stiffly, then turned aside to a tufted mat, and began to wipe his shoes in the most elaborate manner, though there was not a particle of dirt upon them. Old Job's eyes blinked vaguely at him: he felt there was something wrong in that.

"Don't ye do that, sir, now; for God's sake don't do that. I can't abear it; and that's the truth."

Full well the old man remembered how different, in the happy days, had been John Rosedew's entrance; and now every scrub on the mat was a rub on his shaky hard-worn heart.

Mr. Rosedew looked mildly surprised, for his apprehension (as we know) was swifter on paper than pavement. But he held forth his firm strong hand, and the old man bowed tearfully over it.

"Any news of our boy, sir? Any news of my boy as was?"

"Yes, Job; very bad news. He has been terribly ill in London, and nobody there to care for him."

"Then I'll throw up my situation, sir. Many's the time I have threatened them, but didn't like to be too hard like. And pretty goings on there'd be, without old Job in the pantry. But I bain't bound to stand everything for the saving of them as goes on so. And that Hismallitish woman, as

find fault with my buckles, and nice things she
herself wear—I'd a given notice a week next
Monday, but that I likes Miss Oa so, and feel
myself bound, as you may say, to see out this Sir
Cradock; folk would say I were shabby to leave
him now he be gettin' elderly. Man and boy for
sixty year, and began no more than boot-cleaning;
man and boy for sixty-three year, come next
Lammas-tide. I should like it upon my tombstone, sir, with what God pleases added, if I not
make too bold, and you the master of the churchyard, if so be you should live long enough, when
my turn come, God willing."

"It will not be in my power, Job. But if ever
it is, you may trust me."

"And I wants that in I was tellin' my niece
about, 'Put Thy hand in the hollow of my thigh.'
Holy Bible, you know, sir, and none can't object
to that."

"Come, Job, my good friend, you must not
talk so sepulchrally. Leave His own good time to
God."

"To be sure, sir; I bain't in no hurry yet.
I've a sight of things to see to, and my master
must go first, he be so very particular. I'll live to
see the young master yet, as my duty is for to do.
He 'ont carry on with a Hismallitish woman ; *he*
'ont say, 'What, Hogstaff, are your wits gone
wool-gatherin'?' and his own wits all the time, sir,
fleeced, fleeced, fleeced——"

Here John Rosedew cut short the contrast be-

tween the present and the future master (which
would soon have assumed a golden tinge as of the
Fourth Eclogue), for the parson was too much a
gentleman to foster millennial views at the expense
of the head of the household.

"Job, take my card to your master; and tell
him, with my compliments, that I wish to see him
alone, if he will so far oblige me. By-the-by, I
ought to have written first, to request an interview; but it never occurred to me."

He could scarcely help sighing as he thought
of formality re-established on the ruins of familiarity.

"He'll be in the little coved room, no doubt,
long o' that Hismallitish woman. But step in here
a moment, sir."

Instead of passing the doorway, which the butler
had thrown open for him, Mr. Rosedew stood scru-
pulously on the mat, as if it marked his territory,
until the old man came back and showed him into
the black oak parlour.

The little coved room was calmly and sweetly
equal to the emergency. The moment Job's heels
were out of sight, Mrs. Corklemore, who had been
indulging in a nice little chat with Sir Cradock,
"when she ought to have been at work all the
while, plain-sewing for her little household, for
who was to keep the wolf from the door, if she
shrank from a woman's mission—though irksome
to her, she must confess, for it did hurt her poor
fingers so"—here she held up a dish-cloth rather

rougher than a coal-sack, which she had stolen
cleverly from her host's own lower regions, and
did not know from a glass-cloth; but it suited her
because it was brown, and set off her lily hands
so;—" oh, Uncle Cradock, in all this there is something sweetly sacred, because it speaks of *home!*"
She was darning it all the while with white silk,
and took good care to push it away when any servant came in. It had lasted her now for a week,
and had earned her a hundred guineas, having
made the most profound impression upon its legitimate owner. She would earn another hundred
before the week was out by knitting a pair of
rough worsted socks for her little Flore, "though
it made her heart bleed to think how that poor
child hated the feel of them."

Now she rose in haste from her chair, and
pushed the fortunate dish-cloth, with a very expressive air, into her pretty work-basket, and drew
the strings loudly over it.

"What are you going for, Georgie? You need
not leave the room, I am sure."

"Yes, uncle dear, I must. You are so clear
and so honest, I know; and most likely I take it
from you. But I could not have anything to do
with any secret dealings, uncle, even though you
wished it, which I am sure you never could. I
never could keep a secret, uncle, because I am so
shallow. Whenever secrecy is requested, I feel as
if there was something dishonest, either done or
contemplated. Very foolish of me, I know, but

my nature is so childishly open. And of course Mr. Rosedew has a perfect right, and is indeed very wise, to conceal his scheme with respect to his daughter."

"Georgie, stay in this room, if you please; he is not coming here."

"But that poor simple Amy will, if he has brought her with him. Well, I will stay here and lecture her, uncle, about her behaviour to you."

After all this the old man set forth, in some little irritation, to receive his once-loved friend. He entered the black oak parlour in a cold and stately manner, and bowed without a word to John, who had crossed the room to meet him. The parson held out his hand, as a lover and preacher of peace should do; but the offer, ay, and the honour too, not being at all appreciated, he withdrew it with a crimson blush all over his bright clear cheeks, as deep as his daughter's would have been.

Then Sir Cradock Nowell, trying to seem quite calm and collected, addressed his visitor thus:

"Sir, I am indebted to you for the honour of this visit. I apologize for receiving you in a room without a fire. Pray take a chair. I have no doubt that your intentions are kind towards me."

"I thank you," replied the parson, speaking much faster than usual, and with the frill of his shirt-front rising; "I thank you, Sir Cradock Nowell; but I will not sit down in the house of a gentleman who declines to take my hand. I am here much against my own wishes, and only because I supposed that it was my duty to come. I am here on behalf of your son, a noble but most unfortunate youth, and now in great trouble of mind."

If he had only said "in great bodily danger," it might have made a difference.

"Your interest in him is very kind; and I trust that he will be grateful, which he never was to me. He has left his home in defiance of me. I can do nothing for him until he comes back, and is penitent. But surely the question concerns me rather than you, Mr. Rosedew."

"I am sorry to find," answered John, quite calmly, "that you think me guilty of impertinent meddling. But even that I would bear, as becomes my age and my profession,"—here he gave Sir Cradock a glance, which was thoroughly understood, because they had been at school together, —"and more than that I would do, Cradock Nowell, for a man I have loved like you, sir."

That "sir" came out very oddly. John poked it in, as a retractation for having called him "Cradock Nowell," and as a salve to his own self-respect, lest he should have been too appealing. And to follow up this view of the subject, he made a bow such as no man makes to one from whom he begs anything. But Sir Cradock Nowell lost altogether the excellence of the bow. The parson had put up his knee in a way which took the old man back to Sherborne. His mind

was there playing cob-nut as fifty years since,
with John Rosedew. Once more he saw the
ruddy, and then pugnacious, John bringing his
calf up, and priming his knee, for the cob-nut to
lie upon it. This he always used to do, and not
care a flip for the whack upon it, instead of using
his blue cloth cap, as all the rest of the boys did;
because his father and mother were poor, and
could only afford him one cap in a year.

And so the grand bow was wasted, as most
formalities are; but if John had only known
when to stop, it might have been all right after
all, in spite of Georgie Corklemore. But urged
by the last infirmity (except gout) of noble minds,
our parsons never do know the proper time to
stop. Excellent men, and admirable, they make
us shrink from eternity, by proving themselves
the type of it. Mr. Rosedew spoke well and
eloquently, as he was sure to do; but it would
have been better for his cause if he had simply
described the son's distress, and left the rest to
the father's heart. At one time, indeed, poor old
Sir Cradock, who was obstinate and misguided,
rather than cold and unloving, began to relent,
and a fatherly yearning fluttered in his grey-
lashed eyes.

But at this critical moment, three little kicks
at the door were heard, and the handle rattled
briskly; then a shrill little voice came through
the keyhole:

"Oh pease let Fore tum in. Pease do, pease do, pease do. Me 'ost me ummy top. Oh you naughty bad door!"

Then another kick was administered by small but passionate toe-toes. Of course your mother did not send you, innocent bright-haired popples, and with a lie so pat and glib in that pouting pearl-set mouth. Foolish mother, if she did, though it seal Attalic bargain!

Sir Cradock went to the door, and gently ordered the child away. But the interruption had been enough—*ibi omnis effusus labor.* When he returned and faced John Rosedew the manner of his visage was altered. The child had reminded him of her mother, and that graceful, gushing, loving nature, which tried so hard not to doubt the minister. So he did what a man in the wrong generally does instinctively; he swept back the tide of war into his adversary's country.

"You take a very strong interest, sir, in one whose nearest relations have been compelled to abandon him."

"I thought that your greatest grievance with him was that he had abandoned you."

"Excuse me; I cannot split hairs. All I mean is that something has come to my knowledge—not through the proper channel, not from those who ought to have told me—something which makes your advocacy seem a little less disinterested than I might have supposed it to be."

"Have the kindness to tell me what it is."

"Oh, perhaps a mere nothing. But it seems a significant rumour."

"What rumour, if you please?"

"That my—that Cradock Nowell is attached to your daughter, who behaved so ill to me. Of course, it is not true?"

"Perfectly true, every word of it." And John Rosedew looked at Sir Cradock Nowell as proudly as ever a father looked. Amy, in his opinion, was peeress for any mortal. And perhaps he was not presumptuous.

"Ah!" was the only reply he received: an "ah" drawn out into half an ell.

"Why, I would have told you long ago, the moment that I knew it, but for your great trouble, and your bitterness towards him. You have often wished that a son of yours should marry my daughter Amy. Surely you will not blame him for desiring to do as you wished?"

"No, because he is young and foolish; but I may blame you for encouraging it, now that he is the only one."

"Do you dare to think that I am in any way influenced by interested motives?"

"I dare to think what I please. No bullying here, John, if you please. We all know how combative you are. And, now you have forced me to it, I will tell you what will be the conviction, ay, and the expression of every one in this

county, except those who are afraid of you. 'Mr.
Rosedew has entrapped the future Sir Cradock
Nowell, hushed up the crime, and made all snug
for his daughter at Nowelhurst Hall.'"

Sir Cradock did not mean half his words, any
more than the rest of us do, when hurt; and he
was bitterly sorry for them the moment they were
uttered. They put an impassable barrier between
him and John Rosedew, between him and his
own conscience, for many a day and night to
come.

Have you ever seen a pure good man, a man of
large intellect and heart, a lover of truth and
justice more than of himself, confront, without
warning, some black charge, some despicable
calumny, in a word (for I love strong English,
and nothing else will tell it), some damned lie?
If not, I hope you never may, for it makes a man's
heart burn so.

John Rosedew was not of the violent order.
Indeed, as his sister Eudoxia said, and to her own
great comfort knew, his cistern of wrathfulness
was so small, and the supply-pipe so unready—as
must be where the lower passions filter through
the intellect—that most people thought it impos-
sible "to put the parson out." And very few of
those who knew him could have borne to make
the trial.

Even now, hurt as he was to the very depth of
his heart, he was indignant more than angry.

"It would have been more manly of you, Sir Cradock Nowell, to have said this very mean thing yourself, than to have put it into the mouths of others. I grieve for you, and for myself, that so mean a man was ever my friend. Perhaps you have still some relics of gentlemanly feeling which will lead you to perform a host's duty towards his visitor. Have the kindness to order my horse."

Then John Rosedew, so punctilious, so polite to the poorest cottager, turned his broad back upon the baronet, and as he slowly walked to the door, these words came over his shoulder :—

"To-day you will receive my resignation of your two benefices. If I live a few years more, I will repay you all they have brought me above a curate's stipend. My daughter is no fortune-hunter. She never shall see your son again, unless he renounce you and yours for ever, or you come and implore us humbly as now you have spoken arrogantly, contemptibly, and meanly."

Then, fearing lest he had been too grand about a little matter—not his daughter's marriage, but the aspersion upon himself—he closed the door very carefully, so as not to make any noise, and walked away towards his home, forgetting Coræbus utterly. And, before his fine solid face began to recover its healthy and bashful pink, he was visited by sore misgivings as to his own behaviour; to wit, what claim had any man, however elate with the pride of right and the scorn of wrong, to talk about any fellow-man becoming humble to him? Nevertheless, he could not manage to retract the wrong expression in his letter of resignation; not from any false pride — oh no!— but for fear of being misunderstood. But that very night he craved pardon of Him before whom alone we need humbly bow; who alone can grant us anything.

CHAPTER IV.

WHAT is lovelier, just when Autumn throws her lace around us, and begs us not to begin to think of any spiteful winter, because she has not yet unfolded half the wealth of her bosom, and will not look over her shoulder—when we take that rich one gaily for her gifts of beauty; what among her clustered hair, freshened with the hoar-frost in imitation of the Spring (all fashions do recur so), tell us what can be more pretty, pearly, light, and elegant, more memoried of maidenhood, than a jolly spider's web?

See how the diamonds quiver and sparkle in the September morning; what jeweller could have set them so? All of graduated light and metrical proportion, every third pre-eminent, strung on soft aerial tension, as of woven hoar-frost, and every carrying thread encrusted with the breath of fairies, then crossed and latticed at just angles, with narrowing interstices, to a radiated octagon—the more we

look, the more we wonder at the perfect tracery.
Then, if we gently breathe upon it, or a leaf of the
bramble shivers, how from the open centre a whiff
of waving motion flows down every vibrant radius,
every weft accepts the waft slowly and lulling
vibration, every stay-rope jerks and quivers, and
all the fleeting subtilty expands, contracts, and
undulates.

Yet if an elegant spider glide out, exquisite,
many-dappled, pellucid like a Scotch pebble or a
calceolaria, with a dozen dimples upon his back,
and eight fierce eyes all up for business, the moment he slips from the blackberry-leaf all sense of
beauty is lost to the gazer, because he thinks of
rapacity.

And so, I fear, John Rosedew's hat described in
the air a flourish of more courtesy than cordiality,
when he saw Mrs. Corklemore gliding forth from
the bend of the road in front of him. Although
she had left the house after him, by the help of a
short cut through the gardens, where the rector
would no longer take the liberty of trespassing, she
contrived to meet him as if herself returning from
the village.

"Oh, Mr. Rosedew, I am *so* glad to see you,"
cried Georgie, as he tried to escape with his bow:
"what a fortunate accident!"

"Indeed!" said John, not meaning to be rude,
but unwittingly suggesting a modified view of the
bliss.

"Ah, I am so sorry; but you are prejudiced

against me, I fear, because my simple convictions incline me to the Low Church view."

That hit was a very clever one. No other bolt she could have shot would have brought the parson to bay so, upon his homeward road, with the important news he bore.

"I assure you, Mrs. Corklemore, I beg to assure you most distinctly, that you are quite wrong in thinking that. Most truly I hope that I have allowed no prejudice, upon such grounds, to dwell for a moment with me."

"Then you are not a ritualist? And you think, so far as I understand you, that the Low Church people are quite as good as the High Church?"

"I hope they are as good; still I doubt their being as right. But charity is greater even than faith and hope. And, for the sake of charity, I would wash all rubrics white. If the living are rebuked for lagging to bury their dead, how shall they be praised for battling over the Burial Service?"

Mrs. Corklemore, quick as she was, did not understand the allusion. Mr. Rosedew referred to a paltry dissension over a corpse in Oxfordshire, which had created strong disgust, far and near, among believers; while infidels gloried in it. It cannot be too soon forgotten and forgiven.

"Oh, Mr. Rosedew, I am so glad that your sentiments are so liberal. I had always feared that liberal sentiments proceeded from, or at least were associated with, weak faith."

"I hope not, madam. The most liberal One I
have ever read of was God as well as man. But I
cannot speak of such matters casually, as I would
talk of the weather. If your mind is uneasy, and
I can in any way help you, it is my duty to do so."

"Oh, thank you. No; I don't think I could do
that. We are such Protestants at Coo Nest.
Forgive me, I see I have hurt you."

"You misunderstand me purposely," said John
Rosedew, with that crack of perception which
comes (like a chapped lip) suddenly to folks who
are too charitable, "or else you take a strangely
intensified view of the simplest matters. All I
intended was——"

"Oh yes, oh yes, I am always misunderstanding
everybody. I am so dreadfully stupid and simple.
But you *will* relieve my mind, Mr. Rosedew?"

Here Georgie held out the most beautiful hand
that ever darned a dish-cloth, so white, and warm,
and dainty, from her glove and pink muff-lining.
Mr. Rosedew, of course, was compelled to take it,
and she left it a long time with him.

"To be sure I will, if it is in my power, and
you will only tell me how."

"It is simply this," she answered, meekly, dropping her eyes, and sighing; "I do so long to do
good works, and never can tell how to set about it.
Unhappily, I am brought so much more into con-
tact with the worldly-minded, than with those who
would improve me, and I feel the lack of something, something sadly deficient in my spiritual

state. Could you assign me a district anywhere? I am sadly ignorant, but I might do some little ministering, feeling as I do for every one. If it were only ten cottages, with an interesting sheep-stealer! Oh, that would be so charming. Can I have a sheep-stealer?"

"I fear I cannot accommodate you"—the parson was smiling in spite of himself, she looked so beautifully earnest; "we have no felons here, and scarcely even a hen-stealer. Though I must not take any credit for that. Every house in the village is Sir Cradock Nowell's, and Mr. Garnet is not long in ousting the evil-doers."

"Oh, Sir Cradock; poor Sir Cradock!" Here she came to the real object of her expedition. "Oh, Mr. Rosedew, tell me kindly, as a Christian minister; I am in so difficult a position,—have you noticed in poor Sir Cradock anything strange of late, anything odd and lamentable?"

Mr. Rosedew hated to be called a "minister,"— the Dissenters love the word so, and even the great John had his weaknesses.

"I trust I should tell you the truth, Mrs. Corklemore, whether invoked as a minister, or asked simply as a man."

"No doubt you would—of course you would. I am always making such mistakes. I am so unused to clever people. But do tell me, in any capacity which may suit you best"—it was foolish of her not to forego that little repartee—"whether you have observed of late anything odd and deplorable,

anything we who love him so——" Here she
hesitated, and wiped her eyes.

"Though Sir Cradock Nowell," replied Mr.
Rosedew, slowly, and buttoning up his coat at the
risk of spoiling his cock's-comb frill, "is no longer
my dearest friend, as he was for nearly fifty years,
it does not become me to speak about him confidentially and disparagingly to a lady whom I have
not had the honour of seeing more than four times,
including therein the celebration of Divine service,
at which a district-visitor should attend with *some*
regularity, if only for the sake of example. Mrs.
Corklemore, I have the honour of wishing you
good morning."

Although the parson had neither desire nor power
to pierce the lady's schemes, he felt, by that peculiar
instinct which truly honest men have (though they
do not always use it), that the lady was dishonest,
and dishonestly seeking something. Else had he
never uttered a speech so unlike his usual courtesy.
As for poor simple Georgie, she was rolled over too
completely to do anything but gasp. Then she
went to the gorse to recover herself; and presently
she laughed, not spitefully, but with real amusement at her own discomfiture.

Being quite a young woman still, and therefore
not *spe longa*, and feeling a want of sympathy in
waiting for dead men's shoes, Mrs. Corklemore,
who had some genius—if creative power prove it;
if *gignere*, not *gigni*, be taken as the test, though
perhaps it requires both of them,—that sweet

mother of a sweeter child (if so much of the saccharine be admitted by Chancellors of the Exchequer, themselves men of more alcohol), what did she do but devise a scheme to wear the shoes, *ipso vivo,* and put the old gentleman into the slippers.

How very desirable it was that Nowelhurst Hall, and those vast estates, should be in the possession of some one who knew how to enjoy them, and make a proper use of them! Poor Sir Cradock never could do so; it was painfully evident that he never more could discharge his duties to society, that he was listless, passive, somnolent,—somnambulant perhaps she ought to say, a man walking in a dream. She had heard of cases,—more than that, she had actually known them,—sad cases in which that pressure on the brain, which so frequently accompanies the slow reaction from sudden and terrible trials, had crushed the reason altogether, especially after a "certain age." What a pity! And it might be twenty years yet before it pleased God to remove him. He had a tough and wiry look about him. In common kindness and humanity, something surely ought to be done to relieve him, to make him happier.

Nothing rough, of course; nothing harsh or coercive. No personal restraint whatever, for the poor old dear was not dangerous; only to make him what she believed was called a "Committee in Chancery"—there she was wrong, for the guardian is the Committee—and then Mr. Corklemore, of course, and Mr. Kettledrum would act for him.

At least she should think so, unless there was some
obnoxious trustee, under his marriage-settlement.
That settlement must be got at; so much depended
upon it. Probably young Cradock would succeed
thereunder to all the settled estate upon his father's
death. If so, there was nothing for it, except to
make him incapable, by convicting him of felony.
Poor fellow! She had no wish to hang him. She
would not have done it for the world; and she had
heard he was so good-looking. But there was no
fear of his being hanged, like the son of a trades-
man or peasant.

Well, when he was transported for life, with
every facility for repentance, who would be the
next to come bothering? Why, that odious Eoa.
As for her, she would hang her to-morrow, if she
could only get the chance. Though she believed
it would never hurt her; for the child could stand
upon nothing. Impudent wretch! Only yesterday she had frightened Georgie out of her life
again. And there was no possibility of obtaining
a proper influence over her. There was hardly
any crime which that girl would hesitate at, when
excited. What a lamentable state of morality!
She might be made to choke Amy Rosedew, her
rival in Bob's affection. But no, that would never
do. Too much crime in one family. How would
society look upon them? And it would make the
house unpleasant to live in. There was a simpler
way of quenching Eoa—deny at once her legiti-
macy. The chances were ten to one against her

having been born in wedlock—such a loose, wild man as her father was. And even if she had been, why, the chances were ten to one against her being able to prove it. Whereas it would be very easy to get a few Hindoos, or Coolies, or whatever they were, to state their opinion about her mother.

Well, supposing all this nicely managed, what next? Why, let poor Sir Cradock live out his time, as he would be in her hands entirely, and would grow more and more incapable; and when it pleased God to release him, why then, "thou and Ziba divide the land," and for the sake of her dear little Flore, she would take good care that the Kettledrums did not get too much.

This programme was a far bolder one than that with which Mrs. Corklemore had first arrived at the Hall. But she was getting on so well, that of course her views and desires expanded. All she meant at first was to gain influence over her host, and irrevocably estrange him from his surviving son, by delicate insinuations upon the subject of fratricide; at the same time to make Eoa do something beyond forgiveness, and then to confide the reward of virtue to obituary gratitude.

Could anything be more innocent, perhaps we should say more laudable? What man of us has not the privilege of knowing a dozen Christian mothers, who would do things of nobler enterprise for the sake of their little darlings?

But now, upon the broader gauge which the lady had selected, there were two things to be done, ere ever the train got to the switches. One was, to scatter right and left, behind and before, and up and down, wonder, hesitancy, expectation, interrogation, commiseration, and every other sort of whisper, confidential, suggestive, cumulative, as to poor Sir Cradock's condition. The other thing was to find out the effect in the main of his marriage-settlement. And this was by far the more difficult.

Already Mrs. Corklemore had done a little business, without leaving a tongue-print behind her, in the distributory process; and if Mr. Rosedew could just have been brought, after that rude dismissal, to say that he had indeed observed sad eccentricity, growing strangeness, on the part of his ancient friend, why then he would be committed to a line of most telling evidence, and the parish half bound to approval.

But John's high sense of honour, and low dislike of Georgie, had saved him from the neat, and neatly-baited, trap.

That morning Mr. Rosedew's path was beset with beauty, though his daughter failed to meet him; inasmuch as she very naturally awaited him on the parish road. When he had left the chase, and was fetching a compass by the river, along a quiet footway, elbowed like an old oak-branch, overlapped with scraggy hawthorns, paved on either side with good intention of primroses, there, just in a nested bend where the bank overhangs the stream, and you would like to lie flat and flip in a trout fly about the end of April, over the water came lightly bounding, and on a mossy bank alighted, young Eoa Nowell.

"To and fro, that's the way I go; don't you see, Uncle John, I must; only the water is so narrow. It scarcely keeps me in practice."

"Then your standard, my dear, must be very high. I should have thought twice about that jump, in my very best days!"

" *You* indeed!" said Eoa, with the most complacent contempt; eyeing the parson's thick-set figure and anterior development.

" Nevertheless," replied John, with a laugh, " it is but seven and forty years since I won first prize at Sherborne, both for the long leap and the high leap; and proud enough I was, Eoa, of sixteen feet four inches. But I should have had no chance, that's certain, if you had entered for the stakes."

"But how could I be there, Uncle John, don't you see, thirty years before I was born?"

"My dear, I am quite prepared to admit the validity of your excuse. Tyrio cothurno! child, what have you got on?"

" Oh, I found them in an old cupboard, with tops, and whips, and whistles; and I made Mother Biddy take them in at the ancle, because I do hate needles so. And I wear them, not on account of the dirt, but because people in this country are so nasty and particular; and now they can't say a word against me. That's one comfort, at any rate."

She wore a smart pair of poor Clayton's vamp-
lets, and a dark morning-frock drawn tightly in,
with a little of the skirt tucked up, and a black
felt hat with an ostrich feather, and her masses
of hair rolled closely. As the bright colour shone
in her cheeks, and the heartlight outsparkled the
sun in her eyes, John Rosedew thought that he
had never seen such a wildly beautiful, and yet
perfectly innocent, creature.

" Well, I don't know," he answered, very gravely,
" about your gaiters proving a Palladium against
calumny. But one thing is certain, Eoa, your
face will, to all who look at you. But why don't
you ride, my dear child, if you must have such
rapid exercise ?"

" Because they won't let me get up the proper
way on a horse. Me to sit cramped up between
two horns, as if a horse was a cow ! Me, who can
stand on the back of a horse going at full gallop !
But it doesn't matter now much. Nobody seems
to like me for it."

She spoke in so wistful and sad a tone, and cast
down her eyes so bashfully, that the old man, who
loved her heartily, longed to know what the matter
was.

" Nobody likes you, Eoa ! Why, everybody
likes you. You are stealing everybody's heart.
My Amy would be quite jealous, only she likes
you so much herself."

" I am sure, I have more cause to be jealous of
her. Some people like me, I know, very much ;
but not the people I want to do it."

" Oh, then you don't want us to do it. What harm have we done, Eoa?"

" You don't understand me at all, Uncle John. And perhaps you don't want to do it. And yet I did think that you ought to know, as the clergyman of the parish. But I never seem to have right ideas of anything in this country!"

" Tell me, my dear," said Mr. Rosedew, taking her hand, and speaking softly, for he saw two great tears stealing out from the dark shadow of her lashes, and rolling down the cheeks that had been so bright but a minute ago; " tell me, as if you were my own daughter, what vexes your pure heart so. Very likely I can help you, and I will promise to tell no one."

" Oh no, Uncle John, you never can help me. Nobody in the world can help me. But do you think that you ought to know?"

" That depends upon the subject, my dear. Not if it is a family-secret, or otherwise out of my province. But if it is anything with which I have to deal, or which I understand——"

" Oh yes, oh yes! Because you manage, you manage all—all the banns of matrimony."

This last word was whispered with such a sob of despairing tantalization, that John, although he was very sorry, could scarcely keep from laughing.

" You need not laugh, Uncle John. You wouldn't if you were in my place, or could at all understand the facts of it. And as for its being a family-secret, ever so many people know it, and I don't care two pice who knows it now."

" Then let me know it, my child. Perhaps an old man can advise you."

The child of the East looked up at him, with a mist of softness moving through the brilliance of her eyes, and spake these unromantic words:—

" It is that I do like Bob so; and he doesn't care one bit for me."

She looked at the parson, as much as to say, " What do you think of that, now? I am not at all ashamed of it." And then she stooped for a primrose bud, and put it into his button-hole, and then she burst out crying.

" Upon my word," said John, " upon my word, this is too bad of you, Eoa."

" Oh yes, I know all that; and I say it to myself ever so many times. But it seems to make no difference. You can't understand, of course, Uncle John, any more than you could jump the river. But I do assure you that sometimes it makes me feel quite desperate. And yet all the time I know how excessively foolish I am. And then I try to argue, but it seems to hurt me here. And then I try not to think of it, but it will come back again, and I am even glad to have it. And then I begin to pity myself, and to be angry with every one else; and after that I get better and whistle a tune, and go jumping. Only I take care not to see him."

" There you are quite right, my dear: and I would strongly recommend you not to see him for a month."

" As if that could make any difference! And

he would go and have somebody else. And then I should kill them both."

"Well done, Oriental! Now, will you be guided by me, my dear? I have seen a great deal of the world."

"Yes, no doubt you have, Uncle John. And you are welcome to say just what you like; only don't advise me what I don't like; but tell the truth exactly."

"Then what I say is this, Eoa: keep away from him altogether—don't allow him to see you, even when he wishes it, for a month at least. Hold yourself far above him. He will begin to think of you more and more. Why, you are ten times too good for him. There is not a man in England who might not be proud of you, Eoa, when you have learned a little dignity."

Somehow or other none of the Rosedews appreciated the Garnets.

"Yes, I dare say; but don't you see, I don't want him to be proud of me. I only want him to like me. And I do hate being dignified."

"If you want him to like you, do just what I have advised."

"So I will, Uncle John. Kiss me now, to make it up. Oh, you are such a dear!—don't you think a week would do, now?"

.

CHAPTER V.

At high noon of a bright cold day in the early part of March, a labourer who had been "frithing," that is to say, cutting underwood in one of the forest copses, came out into the green track, which could scarce be called a "lane," to eat his well-earned dinner.

As it happened to be a Monday, the poor man had a better dinner than he would see or smell again until the following Sunday. For there, as throughout rural England, a working man, receiving his wages on the Saturday evening, lives upon a sliding scale throughout the dreary week. He has his bit of hot on Sunday, smacking his lips at every morsel; and who shall scold him for staying at home to see it duly boiled, and feeling his heart move with the steaming and savoury pot-lid more kindly than with the dry parson?

And he wants his old woman 'long of him; he see her so little all the week, and she be always best-tempered on Sundays. Let the young uns go to school to get larning—though he don't much see the use of it, and his father lived happy without it —'bating that matter, which is beyond him, let them go, and then hear parson, and bring home the news to the old folk. Only let 'em come home good time for dinner, or they had best look out. "Now, Molly, lift the pot-lid again. Oh, it do smell so good! Got ever another onion?"

Having held high feast on Sunday, and thanked the Lord, without knowing it (by inhaling happiness, and being good to the children—our Lord's especial favourites), off he sets on the Monday morning, to earn another eighteenpence—twopence apiece for the young uns. And he means to be jolly that day, for he has got his pinch of tobacco and two lucifers in his waistcoat pocket, and in his frail a most glorious dinner hanging from a hedge-stake.

All the dogs he meets jump up on his back; but he really cannot encourage them, with his own dog so fond of bones, and having the first right to them. Of course, his own dog is not far behind; for it is a law of nature, admitting no exception, that the poorer a man is, the more certain he is to have a dog, and the more certain that dog is to admire him.

Pretermitting the dog, important as he is, let us ask of the master's dinner. He has a great hunk of cold bacon, from the cabbage-soup of yesterday, with three short bones to keep it together, and a cross junk from the clod of beef (out of the same great pot) which he will put up a tree for Tuesday; because, if it had been left at home, mother couldn't keep it from the children; who do scarce a stroke of work yet, and only get strong victuals to console them for school upon Sundays. Then upon Wednesday our noble peasant of this merry England will have come down to the scraping of bones; on Thursday he may get bread and dripping from some rich man's house; on Friday and Saturday nothing but bread, unless there be cold potatoes. And he will not have fed in this fat rich manner unless he be a good workman, a hater of public-houses, and his wife a tidy body.

Now this labourer who came out of the copse, with a fine appetite for his Monday's dinner (for he had not been "spreeing" on Sunday), was no other than Jem—not Jem Pottles, of course, but the Jem who fell from the 'oak-branch, and must have been killed or terribly hurt but for Cradock Nowell's quickness. Everybody called him "Jem," except those who called him "father;" and his patronymic, not being important, may as well continue latent. Now why could not Jem enjoy his dinner more thoroughly in the copse itself, where the witheys were gloved with silver and gold, and the primroses and the violets bloomed, and the first of the wood-anemones began to star the dead ash-leaves? In the first place, because in the timber-track happen he might see somebody just to give "good day" to; the chances were against it in such

a lonesome place, still it might so happen ; and a
man who has been six hours at work in the deep
recesses of a wood, with only birds and rabbits
moving, is liable to a gregarious weakness, especially at feeding-time. Furthermore, this particular
copse had earned a very bad name. It was said to
be the harbourage of a white and lonesome ghost, a
ghost with no consideration for embodied feelings,
but apt to walk in the afternoon, in the glimpses
of wooded sunshine. Therefore Jem was very
uneasy at having to work alone there, and very
angry with his mate for having that day abandoned
him. And but that his dread of Mr. Garnet was
more than supernatural, he would have wiped his
billhook then and there, and gone all the way
to the public-house to fetch back that mate for
company.

Pondering thus, he followed the green track as
far as the corner of the coppice hedge, and then he
sat down on a mossy log, and began to chew more
pleasantly. He had washed his hands at a little
spring, and gathered a bit of watercress, and fixed
his square of cold bacon cleverly into a mighty
hunk of brown bread, like a whetstone in its
socket ; and truly it would have whetted any plain
man's appetite to see the way he sliced it, and the
intense appreciation.

With his mighty clasp-knife (straight, not curved
like a gardener's) he cut little streaky slips along,
and laid each on a good thickness of crust, and
patted it like a piece of butter, then fondly looked

F 2

at it for a moment, then popped it in, with the
resolution that the next should be a still better one,
supposing such excellence possible. And all the
while he rolled his tongue so, and smacked his
lips so fervently, that you saw the man knew
what he was about, dealt kindly with his hunger,
and felt a good dinner—when he got it.

"There, Scratch," he cried to his dog, after
giving him many a taste, off and on, as in fairness
should be mentioned; "hie in, and seek it there,
lad."

With that he tossed well in over the hedge—for
he was proud of his dog's abilities—the main bone
of the three (summum bonum from a canine point
of view; and, after all, perhaps they are right),
and the flat bone fell, it may be a rod or so, inside
the fence of the coppice. Scratch went through
the hedge in no time, having watched the course
of the bone in air (as a cricketer does of the ball,
or an astronomer of a comet) with his sweet little
tail on the quiver. But Scratch, in the coppice,
was all abroad, although he had measured the distance; and the reason was very simple—the bone
was high up in the fork of a bush, and there it
would stay till the wind blew. Now this apotheosis
of the bone to the terrier was not proven; his
views were low and practical; and he rushed (as
all we earth-men do) to a lowering conclusion.
The bone must have sunk into ĕra's bosom, being
very sharp at one end, and heavy at the other.
The only plan was to scratch for it, within a limited

area; and why was he called "Scratch," but for
scarifying genius?

Therefore that dog set to work, in a manner
highly praiseworthy (save, indeed, upon a flower-
bed). First he wrought well with his fore-feet,
using them at a trot only, until he had scooped out
a little hole, about the size of a rat's nest. This
he did in several places, and with sound assurance,
but a purely illusory bonus. Presently he began
in earnest, as if he had smelled a rat; he put out
his tongue and pricked his ears, and worked away
at full gallop, all four feet at once, in a fashion
known only to terriers. Jem came through the
hedge to see what it was, for the little dog gave
short barks now and then, as if he were in a rabbit-
hole, with the coney round the corner.

"Mun there, mun, lad; show whutt thee carnst
do, boy."

Thus encouraged, Scratch went on, emulative
of self-burial, throwing the soft earth high in the
air, and making a sort of laughing noise in the
rapture of his glory.

After a while he sniffed hard in the hole, and
then rested, and then again at it. The master
also was beginning to share the little dog's excitement, for he had never seen Scratch dig so hard
before, and his mind was wavering betwixt the
hope of a pot of money, and the fear of finding
the skeleton belonging to the ghost.

Scratch worked for at least a quarter of an hour,
and then ran to the ditch and lapped a little, and

came back to work again, while Jem stood by at a
prudent distance, and puffed his pipe commensu-
rately, and wished he had somebody with him.
Presently he saw something shining in the peaty
and sandy trough, about two feet from the surface,
something at which Scratch tried his teeth, but
found the subject ungenial. So Jem ran up,
making sure this time that it was the pot of money.
Alas, it was nothing of the sort, nothing at all
worth digging for. Jem was so bitterly disappointed that he laid hold of Scratch, and cuffed
him well, and the little dog went away and howled,
and looked at his bleeding claws, and stood penitent, with his tail down.

Nevertheless, the thing dug up had cost some
money in its time, for gunmakers know the way
to charge, if never another soul does. It was a
pair of gun-barrels, without any stock, or lock, or
ramrod, heavily battered and marked with fire, as
if an attempt had been made to burn the entire
implement, and then, the wood being consumed,
the iron parts had been kicked asunder, and the
hot barrels fiercely trampled on. Now Jem knew
nothing whatever of guns, except that they were
apt to go off, whether loaded or unloaded; so after
much ponderous thinking and fearing—*fiat experi-
mentum in corpore vili*—he summoned poor Scratch,
and coaxed him, and said, "Hie, boy, vetch thic
thur thin'!"

When he found that the little dog took the
barrels in his mouth without being hurt by them,

and then dragged them along the ground, inasmuch as he could not carry them, Jem plucked up courage and laid them by, to take them home that evening.

After his bit of supper that night, Jem and his wife held counsel, the result of which was that he took his prize down to Roger Sweetland's shop, at the lower end of the village. There he found the blacksmith and one apprentice working overtime, repairing a harrow, which must be ready for Farmer Blackers next morning. The worthy Vulcan received Jem kindly, for his wife was Jem's wife's second cousin; and then he blew up a sharp yellow fire, and examined the barrels attentively.

"Niver zeed no goon the likes o' thissom, though a 'ave 'eered say as they makes 'em now to shut out o' t'other end, man. Whai, her han't gat niver na brichin'! A must shut the man as shuts wi' her."

"What wull e' gie vor un, Roger? Her bain't na gude to ussen."

"Gie thee a zhillin', lad, mare nor her be worth, on'y to bate up vor harse-shoon."

After vainly attempting to get eighteen-pence, Jem was fain to accept the shilling; and this piece of beautiful workmanship, and admirable "Damascus twist," was set in the corner behind the door, to be forged into shoes for a cart-horse. So, as Sophocles well observes, all things come round with the rolling years: the best gun-barrels used to be made of the stub-nails and the horse-shoes (though the thing was a superstition); now good horse-shoes shall be made out of the best gun-barrels.

But, in despite of this law of nature, those gun-barrels never were made into horse-shoes at all, and for this simple reason:—Rufus Hutton came over from Nowelhurst to have his Polly shodden; meanwhile he would walk up to the Hall, and see how his child Eoa was. It is a most worshipful providence, and as clever as the works of a watch, that all the people who have been far abroad, whether in hot or cold climates (I mean, of course, respectively, and not that a Melville Bay har-pooner would fluke in with a Ceylon rifleman), somehow or other, when they come home, groove into, and dovetail with, one another; and not only feel a *pudor* not to contradict a brother alien, but feel bound by a *sacramentum* to back up the lies of each other. To this rule of course there are some exceptions (explosive accidents in the *Times*, for instance), but almost every one will admit that it is a rule; just as it is not to tell out of school.

As regards Rufus and Eoa, this association was limited (as all of them are now-a-days, except in their powers of swindling), strictly limited to a keen and spicily patriarchal turn. Eoa, somehow or other, with that wonderful feminine instinct (which is far in advance of the canine, but not a whit less jealous) felt that Rue Hutton had ad-mired her, though he was old enough to be her grandfather in those precocious climates. And though she would not have had him, if he had come out of Golconda mine, one stalactite of diamonds, she really never could see that Rosa had any business with him. Therefore, on no account would she go to Geopharmacy Lodge, and she regarded the baby, impending there, as an outrage and an upstart.

Dr. Hutton knew more about shoeing a horse than any of the country blacksmiths; and as Polly, in common with many fast trotters, had a trick of throwing her hind-feet inwards, and "cutting" (as it is termed in the art), she liked to have her hind-shoes turned up, and her hoofs rasped in a peculiar manner, which Sweetland alone could execute to her perfect satisfaction.

"Ha, Roger, what have you got here?" said Rufus, having returned from the Hall, and inspected Polly's new shoes, which she was very proud to show him.

"Naethin' at all, yer honour, but a bit o' a old anshent goon, as happed to coom in last avening."

"Ancient gun, man! Why, it is a new breech-loader, only terribly knocked about. I found it all out in London. But there are none in this part of the country. How on earth did you come by it? And what made you spoil it, you stupid, in your forge-fire?"

"Her han't a bin in my varge-vire. If her had, her'd nivir a coom out alaive. Her hath bin in a wood vire by the look o' the smo-uk."

Then Roger Sweetland told Rufus Hutton, as briefly as it is possible for any New Forest man to tell anything, all he knew about it; to which the inquisitive doctor listened with the keenest interest.

"And what will you take for it, Sweetland? Of course it is utterly ruined; but I might stick it up in my rubbish-hole."

"I'll tak whutt I gie vor 'un ; no mare, nor no less. Though be warth a dale mare by the looks ov 'un."

"And what did you give for it—twopence ?"

"As good a croon-pace as wor iver cooined. Putt un barck in carner, if a bain't worth thart."

Dr. Hutton was glad to get it for that, but the blacksmith looked rather blue when he saw him, carefully wielding it, turn his mare's head towards the copse where poor Jem was at work. For to lose the doctor's custom would make his lie at four shillings premium an uncommonly bad investment, and Jem was almost sure to "let out" how much he had got for the gun-barrels.

After hearing all that Jem had to say, and seeing the entire process of discovery put dramatically, and himself searching the spot most carefully without any further result, and (which was the main point of all, at least in Jem's opinion) presenting the woodman with half-a-crown, and bidding him hold his tongue, Rufus Hutton went home, and very sagely preferred Harpocrates to Hymen.

The which resolution was most ungrateful, for Hymen had lately presented him with a perfect little Cupid, according to the very best judges, including the nurse and the mother, and the fuss that was made at the Lodge about it (for to us men a baby is neuter, a heterogeneous vocable, unluckily indeclinable); really the way everybody went on, and worst of all Rufus Hutton, was enough to make a sane bachelor bless the memory of Herod. However, of that no more at present. Some one was quite awake to all the ridiculous parts of it, and perfectly ready to turn it all to profitable account, as an admirable reviewer treats the feeble birth of a novel.

Mrs. Corklemore's sympathetic powers were never displayed more brilliantly, or to better effect; and before very long she had added one, and that the primal, step to the ascending scale of the amiable monarch. For she could manage baby, and baby could manage Rosa, and Rosa could manage Rufus. Only Rufus was not king of the world, except in his own opinion.

As soon as Dr. Hutton could get away, he took the barrels to his own little room, and examined them very carefully. Scarred as they were, and battered, and discoloured by the fire, there could be no question as to their having formed part of a patent breech-loading gun; even the hinge and the bolt still remained, though the wooden continuation of the stock was, of course, consumed; moreover, there was no loop for ramrod, nor screw-thread to take the breeching. Then Rufus went to a little cupboard, and took out a very small bottle of a strong and rodent acid, and with a feather slightly touched the battered, and crusted, and rusty "bridge," in the place where a gun-maker puts his name, and for the most part engraves it wretchedly. In breech-loading guns, the bridge itself is only retained from the force of habit, and our conservatism of folly; for as the breech-end is so much thicker than the muzzle-end of the barrel, and the interior a perfect cylinder, the line of sight (if meddled with) should be raised instead of being depressed at the muzzle-end, to give us a perfect parallel. Of course we know that shot falls in its flight, and there is no pure point-blank; but surely the allowance for, and correction of, these defeasances, according to distance, &c., should be left to the marksman's eye and practice, not slurred by a crossing of planes at one particular distance.

Leaving that to wiser heads, which already are correcting it (by omitting the bridge entirely), let us see what Dr. Hutton did. As the acid began to work, it was very beautiful to watch the cloud-ing and the clearing over the noble but fiercely-abused metal. There is no time now to describe it—for which readers will be thankful—enough that the result revealed the maker's name and address, " L——, C——r-street," and the number of the gun. Dr. Hutton by this time had made the acquaintance of that eminent gunmaker, who, after improving greatly upon a French design, had introduced into this country a rapid and striking improvement; an implement of slaughter as far in advance of the muzzle-loader as a lucifer-match is of flint and tinder. And Rufus, although with a set design to work out his suspicions, would have found it a very much slower work, but for a bit of accident.

He was sauntering along one day from Charing Cross to the westward, looking in at every window (as his manner was, for he loved all information), when suddenly he espied the very "moral"—as the old women say—the exact fac-simile of the thing in his waistcoat pocket.

Instantly he entered the shop, and asked a number of questions. Though it was clear that he came to purchase nothing, he was received most courteously, for it is one of the greatest merits of men who take the lead with us, that they scale or skin the British dragon, and substitute for John Bull's jumble of surliness and serfdom, the courtesy of self-respect.

Then the brevity and simplicity of the new invention—for everything is new with us during five-and-twenty years; and it took thirty years of persistent work to make Covent Garden own rhubarb—all the great advantages, which true Britons would "consider of," were pointed out to Rufus Hutton, and he saw them in a moment, though of guns he had known but little.

And now he saw so much of import in his new

discovery, that he resolved to neglect all other
business, and start for London the very next
morning, if Rosa could be persuaded to let him,
without having heard his purpose. But, in spite
of all his eagerness, he did nothing of the sort; for
Rufus junior that very night was taken with some
infantile ailment of a serious kind, and for more
than a month the doctor could not leave home for
a day even, without breach of duty towards his
wife, and towards the unconscious heir of his
orchard-house and pyramids.

Troubles were closing round Bull Garnet, but
he knew nothing of them; and, to tell the truth,
he cared not now what the end would be, or in
what mode it would visit him. All he cared for
was to defer (if it might be so) the violence of the
outburst, the ruin of the household, until his darling son should be matured enough of judgment,
and shaped enough in character, to feel, and to
make others feel, that to answer for our own sins
is quite enough for the best of us.

Yet there was one other thing which Mr. Garnet fain would see in likely course of settlement,
ere the recoil of his own crime should sweep upon
his children. It regarded only their worldly
affairs; their prospects, when he should have none.
And being the mixture he happened to be—so
shrewd, and so sentimental—he saw how good it
was to exert the former attributive, when his
children were concerned; and the latter, and far
larger one, upon the world at large.

He had lately made some noble purchase from the Government Commissioners—who generally can be cheated, because what they sell is not their own—and he felt that he was bound by the very highest interests to be a capable grantee, till all was signed, and sealed, and safely conveyed to uses beyond attaint of felony. Therefore he was labouring hard to infuse some of his old energy into the breasts of lawyers—which attempt proves the heat of his nature more than would a world of testimony.

CHAPTER VI.

"Why should I care for life or death? The one is no good, and the other no harm. What is existence but sense of self, severance for one troubled moment from the eternal unity? We disquiet ourselves, we fume, and pant—lo, our sorrows are gone, like the smoke of a train, and our joys like the glimmer of steam. Why should I fear to be mad, any more than fear to die? What harm if the mind outrun the body upon the road of return to God? And yet we look upon madness as the darkest of human evils!

"How this gliding river makes one think of life and eternity! Not because the grand old simile lives in every language. Not because we have read and heard it, in a hundred forms and more. A savage from the Rocky Mountains feels the same idea—for ideas strongly stamped pierce into the feelings.

"Why does the mind so glide away to some calm

sea of melancholy, when we stand and gaze intently upon flowing water? And the larger the
spread of the water is, and the grander the march
of the current, the deeper and more irresistible
grows the sadness of the gazer.

"That naval captain, so well known as an ex-
plorer of the Amazon, who dined with us at
Nowelhurst one day last July, was a light-
hearted man by nature, and full of wit and
humour. And yet, in spite of wine and warmth,
he made the summer twilight creep with the sadness of his stories. Nevertheless, we hung upon
them with a strange enchantment; we drew more
real pleasure from them than from a world of
drolleries. Poor Clayton tried to run away, for he
never could bear melancholy; but all he did was
to take a chair nearer to the voyager. As for me,
I cried; in spite of myself, I cried; being carried
away by the flow of his language, so smooth, and
wide, and gliding, with the mystery of waters.

"And he was not one of those shallow men who
talk for effect at dinner-parties. Nothing more
than a modest sailor, leaving his mind to its natural
course. Only he had been so long upon that
mighty river, that he nevermore could cease from
gliding, ever gliding, with it.

"Once or twice he begged our pardon for the
sweep of hazy sadness moving (like the night on
water) through his tales and scenery. He is gone
there again of his own free choice. He must die
upon that river. He loves it more than any patriot

ever loved his country. Betwixt a man and flowing water there must be more than similitude, there must be a sort of sympathy."

" *Tap-Robin*, ahoy there! Ahoy, every son of a sea-cook of you. Heave us over a rope, you lubbers. Would yer swamp us with parson aboard of me ? "

This was Mr. Jupp, of course, churning up Crad's weak ideas, like a steam-paddle in a fishpond. Perhaps the reason why those ideas had been of such sad obscurity, and so fluxed with sorry sentiment, was that the vague concipient believed himself to be shipped off for an indefinite term of banishment, without even a message from Amy. Whereas, in truth, he was only going for a little voyage to Ceylon, in the clipper ship *Taprobane*, A 1 for all time at Lloyd's, and never allowed to carry more than twice as much as she could.

How discontented mortals are! He ought to have been jollier than a sandboy, for he had a cabin all to himself (quite large enough to turn round in), and, what of all things we Britons love best, a happy little sinecure. He was actually appointed—on the strength of his knowledge of goods earned at the Cramjam terminus, but not through any railway influence (being no chip of the board, neither any attorney's "love-child"—if there be such a heterogeny), only through John Rosedew's skill and knowledge of the world, Cradock was actually made "under-supercargo" of a vessel bound to the tropics.

The clipper had passed Greenhithe already, and

none had hailed her or said "Farewell." The
Taprobane would have no tug. She was far too
clean in the bows for that work. Her mother and
grandmother had rún unaided down the river;
even back to the fourth generation of ships, when
the Dutchmen held Ceylon, and doubtless would
have kept it, but for one great law of nature: no
Dutchman must be thin. But even a Dutchman
loses fat within ten degrees of the line. So
Nature reclaimed her square Dutchmen from the
tropics, which turned them over. Most likely
these regions are meant, in the end, for the
Yankee, who has no fat to lose, and is harder to
fry than a crocodile.

But who can stop to theorize while the *Taprobane* is dancing along under English colours, and
swings on her keel just in time to avoid running
down Mr. Rosedew and Issachar? Mr. Jupp is
combining business with pleasure, being, as you
may say, under orders to meet the *Saucy Sally*, and
steer her home from Northfleet to the Surrey
Docks. So he has taken a lift in a collier, and
met Mr. Rosedew at Gravesend, according to
agreement, and then borrowed a boat to look out
alike for *Saucy Sally* and *Taprobane*.

When words and gifts had been interchanged—
what Amy sent is no matter now; but Loo Jupp
sent a penny 'bacco-box, which beat father's
out and out (as he must be sure to tell Cradock),
and had "Am I welcome?" on it, in letters of gold
at least—when "God bless you" had been said for

the twentieth time, and love tied the tongue of gratitude, the *Taprobane* lay-to for a moment, and the sails all shivered noisily, and the water curled crisply, and hissed and bubbled, and the little boats hopped merrily to the pipe of the rising wind.

Then Mr. Rosedew came down the side, lightly of foot and cleverly; while the under-supercargo leaned upon the rail and sorrowfully watched him. Ponderously then and slowly, with his great splay feet thrust into the rope-ladder, even up to the heel, quite at his leisure descended that good bargeman, Issachar Jupp. This noble bargee had never been seen to hurry himself on his own account. He and his deeds lagged generally on the bight of a long and slack tow-rope.

The sailors, not entering into his character, thought that he was frightened, and condemned his apprehensive luminaries, in words of a quarter the compass. Then Mr. Jupp let go with both hands, stood bolt upright on the foot-rope, and shook his great fists at them. " Let him catch them ashore at Wapping, if the devil forewent his due; let him catch them, that was all!" Thereupon they gave him a round of cheers, and promised to square the account, please God.

Mr. Rosedew and the bargeman looked up from the tossing wherry, and waved their last farewell, the parson reckless of Sunday hat, and letting his white locks glance and flutter on the cold March wind. But Cradock made no reply.

" All right, gov'nor!" said Jupp, catching hold

of the parson; "no call for you to take on so. I've a been the likes o' that there mysel' in the days when I tuk' blue ruin. The rattisination of it are to fetch it out of him by travellin'. And the *Tap-Robin* are a traveller, and no mistake. D'rectly moment I comes to my fortin', I'll improve self and family travellin'."

Zakey, to assert his independence as his nature demanded, affected a rough familiarity with the man whom he revered. The parson allowed it as a matter of course. His dignity was not so hollow as to be afraid of sand-paper. The result was that Issachar Jupp, every time, felt more and more compunction at, and less and less of comfort in, the unresented liberties.

As he said "good-bye" at the landing-place—for he had seen the *Sally* coming—he put out his hand, and then drew it back with a rough bow (disinterred from long-forgotten manners), and his raspy tongue thrust far into the coal-mine of his cheek. But John Rosedew accepted his hand, and bowed, as he would have done to a nobleman. Even if a baby smiled at him, John always acknowledged the compliment. For he added Christian courtesy, and the humility of all thoughtful minds, to a certain grand and glorious gift of radiating humanity.

Cradock Nowell was loth to be sent away, and could not see the need of it; but doubtless the medical men were right in prescribing a southern voyage, a total change of scene and climate, as the

likeliest means to re-establish the shattered frame
and the tottering mind. And so he sailed for the
gorgeous tropics, where the sun looks not askance,
where the size of every climbing, swimming, fluttering, or crawling thing (save man himself) is
doubled; where life of all things bounds and
beats—until it is quickly beaten—as it never gets
warm enough to do in the pinching zones, tight-
buckled.

Meanwhile John Rosedew went to his home—a
home so loved and fleeting—and tried to comfort
himself on the road with various Elzevirs. Finding them fail, one after another, for his mind was
not in cue for them, he pulled out his little Greek
Testament, and read what a man may read every
day, and never begin to be weary; because his
heart still yearns the more towards the grand ideal,
and feels a reminiscence such as Plato the divine,
alone of heathens, won.

John Rosedew read once more the Sermon on
the Mount, and wondered how his little griefs
could vex him as they did. That sermon is grander
in English, far grander, than in the Greek; for
the genius of our language is large, and strong,
and simple—the true spirit of the noblest words
that ever on earth were spoken. How cramped
they would be in Attic Greek (like Mount Athos
chiselled); in Latin how nerveless and alien!
Ours is the language to express; and ours the race
to receive them.

What man, in later life, whose reading has led

him through vexed places—whence he had wiser
held aloof—does not, on some little touch, brighten,
and bedew himself with the freshness of the morning, thrill as does the leaping earth to see the sun
come back again, and, dashing all his night away,
open the power of his eyes to the kindness of his
Father?

John Rosedew felt his cares and fears vanish
like the dew-cloud among the quivering tree-tops ;
and bright upon him broke the noon, the heaven
wherein our God lives.   Earth and its fabrics may
pass away ; but that which came from heaven shall
not be without a home.

Meditating, comforted, strengthened on the way,
John Rosedew came to his little hearth, and was
gladdened again by little things, such as here are
given or lent us to amuse our exile life.   Most of
us, with growing knowledge and keener sense of
honesty, more strongly desire from year to year
that these playthings were distributed more equally
amongst us.   But let us not say " equably."   For
who shall impugn the power of contrast even in
heightening the zest of heaven?

Amy met him, his own sweet Amy, best and
dearest of all girls, a thoroughly English maiden,
not salient like Eoa, but warmly kind, and thoughtful, and toned with self-restraint.   But even that
last she threw to the winds when she saw her
father returning, and ran with her little feet
pattering, like sweet-gale leaves, over the gravel,
to the unpretentious gate.

"Darling father!" was all she said; and perhaps it was quite enough.

Of late she had dropped all her little self-will (which used to vex her aunt so), and her character seemed to expand and ripen in the quiet glow of her faithful love.

Thenceforth, and for nearly a fortnight, Amy Rosedew, if suddenly wanted, was sure to be found in a garret, whose gable-window faced directly towards the breadth of sea. When a call for her came through the crazy door, she would slam up with wonderful speed her own little Munich telescope, having only two slides and a cylinder, but clearer and brighter than high-powered glasses, ten stories long perhaps, and of London manufacture : and then she would confront the appellant, with such a colour to be sure, and a remark upon the weather, as sage as those of our weather-clerks, who allow the wind so much latitude that they never contrive to hit it. But which of the maids knew not, and loved her not the more for knowing, that she was a little coast-guard, looking out for her *eau de vie?* Of course she saw fifty *Taprobanes* —every one more genuine than its predecessor— and more than fifty Cradocks, some thirty miles away, leaning over hearts of oak, with a faint sweet smile, waving handkerchiefs as white as their own unsullied constancy, and crying with a heavy sigh, "My native land, good night!"

Facts, however, are stubborn things, and will not even make a bow to the sweetest of young

ladies. And the fact was that the Ceylon trader
fetched away to the southward before a jovial
north-east wind, and, not being bound to say anything to either Plymouth or Falmouth, never came
near the field of gentle Amy's telescope.

That doctor knew something of his subject—the
triple conglomerate called man—who prescribed
for Cradock Nowell, instead of noxious medicines
—*medicina a non medendo*—the bounding ease and
buoyant freedom of a ship bound southward.

Go westward, and you meet the billows, headers
all of them, staggering faith even in the Psalmist's
description (for he was never in the Bay of Biscay),
and a wind that stings patriotic tears with the everlasting brine. Go eastward, and you meet the ice,
or (in summer) shoals and soundings, and a dreary
stretch of sand-banks. Go northward, and the
chances are that you find no chance of return.
But go full-sail to the glorious south, and once
beyond the long cross-ploughings and headland of
the Gulf Stream, you slide into a quiet breast, a
confidence of waters, over which the sun more duly
does his work and knows it, and under which the
growth of beauty clothes your soul with wonder.

When shall we men leave off fighting, cease to
prove the Darwinian theory, and the legends of
Kilkenny (by leaving only our tails behind us, a
legacy for new lawsuits); and in the latter days
ask God the reason we were made for? When our
savage life is done with, and we are no longer cannibals—and at present cannibals are perhaps of

more practical mind than we, for they have an
object in homicide, and the spit justifies the
battle-field—when we do at last begin not to hate
one another; not to think the evil first, because in
nature prior; not to brand as maniacs, and marks
for paltry satire, every man who dares to think
that he was not born a weasel, and that ferocity
is cowardice—then a man of self-respect may
begin to be a patriot. At present, as our nations
are, all abusing one another, none inquiring, none
allowing, all preferring wrong to weakness, if it hit
the breed and strain; each proclaiming that it is
the favoured child of God, the only one He looks
upon (merging His all-seeing eye in its squint
ambition)—at present even we must feel that
" patriotism " is little more than selfishness in a
balloon.

Poor Cradock, wasted so and altered (when he
left black London) that nothing short of woman's
true love could run him home without check,
began to feel the change of sky, and drink new
health from the balmy air, and relish the wholesome mind-bread, leavened with the yeast of
novelty. A man who can stay in the same old
place, and work the blessed old and new year at
the same old work, dwell on and deal with the
same old faces, receive and be bound to reciprocate
the self-same old ideas, without crying out, " Oh
bother you !" without yearning for the sea-view, or
pining for the mountain—that man has either a very

great mind, or else he has none at all. For a very
great mind can create its own food, fresh as the
manna, daily, or dress in unceasing variety the
fruit of other intellects, and live thereon amid
the grand and ever-shifting scenery of a free
imagination. On the other hand, a man of no
mind gets on quite contentedly, having never
tasted thought-food; only wind him up with the
golden key every Saturday night, and oil him with
respectability at the Sunday service.

Now the under-supercargo of the *Taprobane*
was beginning to eat his meals like a man, to be
pleased with the smell of new tar, and the head-
over-heel of the porpoises, and to make acquaintance with sailors of large morality. In a word, he
was coming back, by spell and spate, to Cradock
Nowell, but as yet so merely skew-nailed to the
pillar of himself, that any change of weather caused
a gape, a gap, a chasm.

Give him bright sun and clear sky, with a gentle
breeze over the water spreading wayward laughter,
with an amaranth haze just lightly veiling the
union of heaven and ocean, and a few flying-fish,
or an albatross, for incident in the foreground—
and the young man would walk to and fro as
briskly, and talk as clearly and pleasantly, as any
one in the ship could.

But let the sky gather weight and gloom, and
the sullen sun hang back in it, and the bright flaw
of wind on the waters die out, and the sultry air,

in oppressive folds, lean on the slimy ocean—and Cradock's mind was gone away, like a bat flown into darkness.

Sometimes it went more gradually, giving him time to be conscious that his consciousness was departing; and that of all things was perhaps the most woeful and distressing. It was as if the weak mind-fountain bubbled up reproachfully, like a geyser over-gargled, and flushed the thin membrane and cellular tissue with more thought than they could dispose of. Then he felt the air grow chill, and saw two shapes of everything, and fancied he was holding something when his hands were empty. Then the mind went slowly off, retreating, ebbing, leaving shoal-ground, into long abeyance, into faintly-known bayous, feebly navigated by the nautilus of memory.

It is not pleasant, but is good, now and then to see afar these pretty little drawbacks upon our self-complacency — an article imported hourly, though in small demand for export. However, that is of little moment, for the home consumption is infinite. How noble it is to vaunt ourselves, how spirited to scorn as *faber* Him who would be father; when a floating gossamer breathed between the hemispheres of our brain makes imperial reason but the rubbish of an imperious flood. Then the cells and clever casemates, rammed home with explosive stuff to blow God out of heaven, are no mortar, but a limekiln, crusted and collapsing (after three days' fire); a

stranded cockle, dead and stale, with the door of
his shell a bubble; and so ends the philosopher.

Upon a glaring torpid sea, a degree or two south
of the line, the *Taprobane* lay so becalmed that the
toss of a quid into the water was enough to drive
her windward, or leeward, whichever you pleased
to call it. The last of the trade winds, being long
dead, was buried on the log by this time; and the
sailors were whistling by day and by night, and
piping into the keys of their lockers; but no re-
sponsive dimple appeared in the sleek cadaverous
cheek of the never-changing sea.

What else could one expect? They had passed
upon the wind's-eyes so adverse a decision—without hearing counsel on either side—that really, to
escape ophthalmia, it must close its eyelids. So
everything was heavy slumber, sleep of parboiled
weariness. Where sea and sky met one another—
if they could do it without moving—the rim of
dazzled vision whitened to a talc-like glimmer.
Within that circle all was tintless, hard as steel,
yet dull and oily, smitten flat with heat and haze.
Not a single place in sky and sea to which a man
might point his finger, and say to his mate, "Look
there!" No skir of fish, not even a shark's fin, or
a mitching dolphin, no dip of wing, no life at all,
beyond the hot rim of the ship, or rather now the
"vessel," where many a man lay frying, with
scarcely any lard left. And oh, how the tar and
the pitch did smell, running like a cankered
apricot-tree, and the steam of the bilge-water

found its way up, and reeked through the yawning deck-seams!

But if any man durst look over the side (being gifted with an Egyptian skull, for to any thin head the sunstroke is death, when taken upon the crown), that daring man would have seen in blue water, some twenty fathoms below him, a world of life, and work, and taste, complex, yet simple, more ingenious than his wisest labours. For here no rough rivers profane the sea with a flood of turbulent passion, like a foul oath vented upon the calm summer twilight; neither is there strong indraught from the tossing of distant waters, nor rolling leagues of mountain surf, as in the Indian Ocean. All is heat and sleep above, where the sheer dint of the sun lies; but down in the depth of those glassy halls they heed not the fervour of the noon-blaze, nor the dewy sparkle of starlight.

"Typhoon by-and-by," said the first mate, yawning, but too lazy to stretch, under the awning of a sail which they wetted with a hydropult, a most useful thing on shipboard, as well as in a garden.

"Not a bit of it," answered the captain, looking still more lazy, but managing to suck cold punch.

"We shall see," was all the mate said. It was a deal too hot to argue, and he was actually drinking ale, English bottled ale, hoisted up from a dip in blue water, but as hot as the pipes in a pinery.

The under-supercargo heeded not these laconic

interchanges. The oppression was too great for him. Amid that universal blaze and downright pour of stifling heat, his mind was gone wool-gathering back into the old New Forest. The pleasant stir of the stripling leaves, the shadows weaving their morrice-dance, and trooping away on the grass-tufts at the pensive steps of evening; the sound and scent of the vernal wind among the blowing gorse; the milky splash of the cuckoo-flower in swarded breaks of woodland, the bees in the belfry of cowslips, the frill of the white wind-flower, and the fleeting scent of violets—all these in their form and colour moved, or lay in their beauty before him, while he was leaning against the side-rail, and it burned his hand to touch it.

"Wants a wet swab on his nob,". said the first mate, tersely; "never come to himself sure as my name is Cracklins."

"Don't agree with you," answered the captain, who always snubbed the mate; "he's a sight better now than at Blackwall. Poor young gent, I like him."

"So do I," said the mate, pouring out more boiling beer; "but that ain't much to do with it. There's the wet swab anyhow."

About an hour before sunset, when the sky was purple, and the hot vapours piling away in slow drifts, like large haycocks walking, a gentle breeze came up and made little finger-marks on the water. First it awoke shy glances and glosses, light as the play upon richly-glazed silk, or the glimpse upon mother-of-pearl. Then it breathed on the lips of men, and they sucked at it as at spring-water. Then it came sliding, curling, ruffling, breaking the image of sky upon sea, but bringing earthly life and courage, hope, and the spirit of motion. Many a rough and gruff tar shed tears, not knowing the least about them, only from nature's good-will and power, as turpentine flows from the pine-wood.

"Hearty, my lads, and bear a hand." "Pipe my eye, and be blessed to me!" They rasped it off with their tarry knuckles, and would knock down any one of canine extraction, who dared to say wet was the white of their eyes.

The gurgling of the water sounded like the sobs of a sleeping child, as it went dapping and lipping and lapping, under the bows and along the run of the sweetly-gliding curvature. Soon you could see the quiet closure of the fluid behind her, the fibreing first (as of parted hair) convergent under the counter, the dimples circling in opposite ways on the right and left of the triangle, and then the linear ruffles meeting, and spreading away in broad white union, after a little jostling. You may see the same at the tail of a mill-stream, when the water is bright in July, and the alder-shade falls across it. For the sails were beginning to draw again now, and the sheets and tacks were tightening, and the braces creaking merrily, and every bit of man-stuff on board felt his heart go, and his lungs work. Therefore all were glad and chaffing, as the manner is of Britons, when the man in the foretop shouted down, "Land upon the port-bow."

"I have looked for it all day," said the captain; "I was right to half a league, Smith."

The skipper had run somewhat out of his course to avoid a cyclone to the westward, but he had not allowed sufficiently for the indraught of the Gulf of Guinea, and was twenty leagues more to the eastward than he had any idea of being. Nevertheless, they had plenty of sea-room, and now from the trending of the coast might prudently stand due south. They had passed Cape Lopez three days ago, of course without having sighted it, and had run by the log three hundred miles thence, despite the dead calm of that day. So they knew that they could not be very far from the mouth of the river Congo.

As they slipped along with that freshening breeze, the water lost its brightness, and soon became of a yellowish hue, as if mixed with a turbulent freshet. Then they lay to in fifteen fathoms, and sent off a boat to the island, for the intense heat of the last few days had turned their water putrid. The first and second mates were going, and the supercargo took his gun, and declared that he would stretch his legs and bring home some game for supper. What island it was they were not quite sure, for there was nothing marked on the charts just there, to agree with their reckoning and log-run. But they knew how defective charts are.

When the water-casks were lowered, and all were ready to shove off, and the mast of the yawl was stepped, and the sail beginning to flap and jerk in a most impatient manner, Cracklins, who was a good-natured fellow, hollaed out to Cradock—

"Come along of us, Newman, old fellow. You want bowsing up, I see. Bring your little dog for a run, to rout up some rabbits or monkeys for Tippler. And have a good run yourself, my boy."

Without stopping to think—for his mind that day had only been a dream to him — Cradock Nowell went down the side, with Wena on his arm, and she took advantage of the occasion to lick his face all over. Then he shuddered unconsciously at the gun which lay under the transoms.

"Look sharp, Cracklins," shouted the captain from his window; "the glass is down, I see, half an inch. I can only give you two hours."

"All right, sir," answered the mate; "but we can't fill the casks in that time, unless we have wonderful luck."

The land lay about a mile away, and with the sail beginning to tug, and four oars dipping vigorously,—for the men were refreshed by the evening breeze, and wild for a run on shore,—they reached it in about ten minutes, and nosed her in on a silvery beach strewn with shells innumerable. A few dwarf rocks rose here and there, and the line of the storms was definite, but for inland view there was nothing more than a crescent ter-

race of palm-trees. The air felt beautifully fresh
and pure, and entirely free from the crawling
miasma of the African coast. No mangrove
swamps, no festering mud, no reedy bayou of
rottenness.

But the boat-crew found no fresh water at first;
and they went in three parties to search for it.
The mate with three men struck off to the right,
the boatswain with three more made away to the
left, only Cradock and the supercargo walked directly inland. Wena found several rabbits, all of
a sandy colour, and she did enjoy most wonderfully her little chivies after them. Most of the
birds were going to rest, as the rapid twilight fell,
but the trees were full of monkeys, and here and
there a squirrel shook the light tracery of the
branches.

Tippler and Cradock wandered inland for half a
mile or more, keeping along a pleasant hollow
which they feared to leave, lest they should lose
the way back, and as yet they had seen neither
spring nor brook, although from the growth and
freshness they knew that water must be near
them. Then suddenly the supercargo fired his
gun at a flying green pigeon, whose beauty had
caught his eyes.

To his great amazement Cradock fell down,
utterly helpless, pale as a corpse, not trembling,
but in a syncope. His comrade tried to restore
him, but without any effect, then managed to drag
him part way up the slope, and set him with his

back to an ebony-tree, while he ran to fetch assistance. Suddenly then an ominous sound trembled
through the thick wood, a mysterious thrill of the
earth and air, at the coming of war between them.
It moved the wild grapes, the flowering creepers,
the sinuous caoutchouc, the yellow nuts of the
palm-oil-tree, and the pointed leaves of the ebony.

When the supercargo ran down to the boat, the
men were pushing off hastily, the water curling
and darkening, and a sullen swell increasing. A
heavy mass of cloud hung to leeward, and the tropical night fell heavily, till the ship was swallowed
up in it.

" Jump in, Tippler ! Just in time," cried the
first mate, seizing the tiller-ropes; " not a moment
to lose. We must go without water; we shall have
enough out of the sky to-night. I could not tell
what to do about you, and the signal's ' Return
immediately.' "

" But I tell you, we can't go, Cracklins. Poor
Newman is up there in a fit or something. Send
two men with me to fetch him."

" How far off is he ? "

" Nearly a mile."

" Then I daren't do it. We are risking our lives
already. The typhoon will be on us in half an
hour. Said so this morning—skipper wouldn't
listen. Jump in, man, jump in; or we're off without you. Can't you see how the sea is rising ?
Ease off the sheet, you lubber there. We must
down with the sail in two minutes, lads, soon as

ever we've got way on her. Lend a grip of your black fist, Julep, instead of yawing there like a nigger. Now will you come, or won't you?"

Tippler was à brave and kind-hearted man; but he thought of his wife and children, and leaped into the boat. Although he was not a sailor, he saw the urgency of the moment, and confessed that nine lives must not be sacrificed for the sake of one. The power of the wind was growing so fast, and the lift of the waves so menacing, that the nine men needed both skill and strength to recover their ship, ere the storm burst.

And a terrible storm it was, of the genuine Capricorn type, sudden, deluging, laced with blue lightning, whirling in the opposite direction to that which our cyclones take. At midnight the *Taprobane* was running under bare poles, shipping great seas heavily, with an electric coronet gleaming and bristling all around truck and dog-vane. And by that time she was sixty miles from her under-supercargo.

CHAPTER VII.

Dr. Hutton's baby was getting better, and
Rosa, who had been, as the nurse said, "losing
ground so sadly, poor dear," was beginning to pick
up her crumbs again. Therefore Rufus, who (in
common with Rosa and all the rest of the household) regarded that baby as the noblest and
grandest sublimation of humanity, if not as the
final cause of this little world's existence, was beginning now to make up his mind that he really
might go to London that week, without being (as
his wife declared he must be, if he even thought
about it) cruel, inhuman, unfatherly, utterly void
of all sense of duty, not to say common affection.
And she knew quite well what he wanted. All he
wanted was to go and see Mr. Rivers's peach-trees
in blossom, as if that was such a sight as her baby.
Yes, *her* baby, ma's own darling, a dove of a
dumpling dillikins ; to think that his own pa should
prefer nasty little trees without a hair on them,

and that didn't even know what bo meant, to the most elegant love of a goldylocks that ever was, was, was!

Master Goldylocks had received, from another quarter, a less classical, and less pleasing, but perhaps (from an objective point. of view) a more truthful and unprismatic description of the hair it pleased God to give him.

"Governor's carrots, and no mistake," cried Mrs. O'Gaghan the moment she saw him, which, of course, was upon his first public appearance—catch Biddy out of the way when any baby, of any father or mother she had ever heard of, was submitted even to the most privileged inspection—"knew he must have 'em, of course. You niver can conquer that, ma'am, if your own hair was like a sloe, and you tuk me black briony arl the time. Hould him dacent, will ye, nurse? Not slot his head down that fashion! He don't want more blood in his hair, child. Oh yes, I can see, ma'am! Niver knowed more nor two wi' that red-hot poker colour, colour of the red snuff they calls 'Irish blackguard' in the top of a hot shovel; and one of the two were Mr. Hutton, ma'am, saving your presence to spake of it; and the other were of Tim Brady, as were hung at the cross-roads, near Clonmel, for cutting the throat of his grandmother."

"Oh, Mary, take her away. What a horrid woman!"

Here Mrs. Gaghan was marched away, amid

universal indignation, which she could not at all
understand. But she long had borne against Rufus
Hutton the bitterest of all bitter spites (such as
only an Irishwoman can bear), for the exposure
of her own great mistake, and the miserable result
which (as she fully believed) had sprung from all
his meddling. And yet she was a " good-hearted "
woman. But a good heart is only the wad upon
powder, when a violent will is behind it.

Not to attach undue importance to Biddy's pre-
possessions, yet to give every facility for a verdict
upon the question, I am bound to state what an
old-young lady, growing every month more sati-
rical, because nobody would have her, yet quite
unconscious that the one drawback was the main
cause of the other (for all men hate sarcastic
women),—how tersely she expressed herself.

" Ridiculous likeness! Was he born with two
cheroots in his mouth ? "

But a lady, who would marry for ever because
she was so soft and nice, came to see darling baby
again, the moment she was quite assured that he
was equal to the interview, having denied herself
from day to day, although it had affected her appetite, and was telling upon her spirits. Neither
would she come alone—that would be too selfish :
she must make a gala day of it, and gratify her
relatives. So Mrs. Hutton had the rapture of
sitting behind her bedroom curtain, and seeing no
less than three carriages draw up in a thundering
manner, while Rufus was in the greatest fright

that they would not find room to turn, but must cut up his turf. Luckily the roller was in the way; or else those great coachmen, who felt themselves lowered by coming to a place of that size, would have had their revenge on the sod. The three carriages were, of course, that of Nowelhurst Hall in the van (no pun, if you please), with two noble footmen behind it, and Georgie in state inside. Then the "Kettledrum rattletrap," as the hypercritical termed it, with Mr. Kettledrum driving, and striking statuesque attitudes for the benefit of the horses, and Mrs. Kettledrum inside, entreating him not to be rash. Last of all the Coo Nest equipage, a very neat affair, with Mr. Corklemore inside, wanting to look at his wife in the distance, and wondering what she was up to.

"Oh, such shocking taste, I know," cried Georgie, directly the lower order were supposed to be out of hearing, " horribly bad taste to come in such force ; but what could we do, Dr. Hutton ? There was my sister, there was my husband, there was my own silly self, all waiting, as for a bulletin, to know when baby would receive. And so, at the very first moment, by some strange coincidence, here we are all at once. And I do hope darling Rosa will allow *some* of us to come in."

" Jonah," shouted Rufus Hutton, going away to the door very rudely (according to our ideas, but with Anglo-Indian instincts), " see that all those men have beer."

" Plaise, sir, there bain't none left. Brewer

hain't a been since you drank." As every one in the
house heard this, dear Georgie had some revenge.

However, babe Rufus received his ovation; and
the whole thing went off well, as most things do
in the counties of England, when plenty of good
wine produces itself. Lunch was ready in no time;
and, as all had long ago assented to Mrs. Corklemore's most unselfish proposition that she, as privileged of pet Rosa, should just steal up-stairs for
a minute, and then come down again—after giving
notice, of course, that dear baby should have all
his lace on—the pleasant overture of the host was
accepted with little coyness—

"Let us suppose that we have dined: because
the roads are so very bad. Let us venture upon a
light dessert. I have a few pears, even now in
April, which I am not altogether afraid to submit
to the exquisite taste of ladies,—'Madame Millet'
and 'Josephine.' May we think that we have
dined?"

As the company not only thought, but felt that
they had made an uncommonly good dinner, this
little proposal did pleasant violence to their sense
of time. It would be so charmingly novel to think
that they had dined at three o'clock! Oh, people
of brief memory! For Kettledrum Hall and Coo
Nest loved nothing better than to dine at two;
which, perhaps, is two hours too late, according to
nature *versus* fashion.

"For such an occasion as this," said Rufus,
under all the excitement of hospitality multiplied

by paternity, " we will have a wine worth talking of. Clicquot, of course, and Paxarette for the ladies, if they prefer it; which perhaps they will do because it is sweeter than port. But I do hope that some will deign to taste my 1820, President's unrefreshed."

Georgie's pretty lip came out, like the curl of an opening convolvulus; to think of offering her sweet wine, when choice port was forthcoming. There are few better judges of a good glass of port than Mrs. Nowell Corklemore.

"Port, sir, for my wife, if you please. She likes a rather dry wine, sir, but with plenty of bouquet. There is no subject, I may say, in which she has — ha, haw — a more profound capacity."

" My dear Nowell, why you are perfectly calumnious. Thank you, no champagne. It spoils the taste of—your beautiful water. How dreadfully we were alarmed in Ringwood. We all but drove over a child. What a providential escape! I have scarcely yet recovered it. It has made me feel so nervous. What, Dr. Hutton, port for a lady, at this time of day, and not ordered medically!"

Thereupon, of course Rufus prescribed it, till Georgie, being quite overcome by the colour, as the host himself decanted it, capitulated at last for "strictly half a glass."

After a little, the ladies withdrew, to see double perfections in the baby, and Mrs. Hutton, who knew quite well what they had been doing, while she was discussing arrowroot, received them at first rather stiffly. But she had no chance with Georgie, who entered beautifully into the interesting room, and exclaimed with great vivacity—

"Oh, dear Mrs. Hutton, as the little boys say, 'here we are again.' And so glad to get away, because your husband is so hospitable, and we thought of you all the time. I wanted so much to bring you a glass of that very exquisite—let me see, I think it must have been port, though I never know one wine from another—only I feared it might seem rude, if I had ventured to propose it. Of course Dr. Hutton knew best."

"Of course he didn't," said Rosa, pettishly; "he never thought about it. Not that I would have taken it; oh dear no! Ladies cannot have too little wine, I think. It seems to make them so masculine."

"Well, dear, you know best. Very likely you heard us laughing. I assure you we were quite merry. We drank his health 'three times three' —don't they call it about a baby? And I was nearly proposing yours; only a gentleman ought to do that. Oh, it was so interesting, and the wine superb—at least, so said the gentlemen; I do wish they had brought you some, dear."

"I am very glad they did not. It is so very lowering to a fine sense of the ideal. I heard you laughing, or making some noise; only I was so absorbed in these lovely poems. 'To my Babe' is

so very beautiful, so expressive, so elevating! I
feel every single word of it.   And this sonnet
about the first cropper!   And the stanzas to his
little red shoes, terminating with 'pinch his nose!'
You have had so many husbands, dear; you must
know all about it."

"My darling child, how I feel for you! But,
in all probability, he will come up when both de-
canters are empty; let him find you in a good
temper, dear."

But this (which must have grown into a row,
for Georgie had even more spirit than tact, and
Rosa was equal to anything), all this evil was
averted, and harmony restored by the popping in
of nurse, who had not taken her half-crowns yet,
but considered them desirable, and saw them now
endangered.

"Goldylocks, Goldylocks!   Oh, bring him here,
nurse.   Skillikins, dillikins! oh, such a dove!
And if nobody else cares for poor mamma, he has
got so much better taste, hasn't he?"

Goldylocks very soon proved that he had; and
Georgie, having quite recovered her temper, ad-
mired him so ecstatically, that even his mother
thought her judgment was really worth something.

"Give him to me; I can't do without him.   O
you beautiful cherub! Kicklewick, I am sure you
never saw any one like him."

"That indeed I never did, ma'am," answered
nurse Kicklewick, holding her arms out, as if she

must have him back again; "many a fine child I
have seen, and done for to my humble ability,
ma'am, since the time I were at Lord Eldergun's;
and her ladyship said to me—'Kicklewick,' says
she——"

"Oh, his love of a nosey-posey! Oh, then his
bootiful eyes, dick, dock! And then his golden
hair, you know, so lovely, chaste, and rare, you
know! Will um have a dancey-prancey?"

And Georgie, forgetting all dignity, went
through a little Polish dance, with the baby in her
arms, to his very grave amazement, and the delight
of all beholders.

Although of the genuine Hutton strain, he was
too young to crow yet, nevertheless he expressed
approval in the most emphatic water-colours.
Mrs. Hutton's heart was won for ever.

"Oh, darling, I am so obliged to you. He has
positively popped two bubbles. A thing he never
did before! How can I ever repay you?"

"By letting me come over and dance him twice
a week. Oh, that I only had a boy !—because I
do love boy-babies so."

"One would think that you must have had fifty,
at least, before you were five-and-twenty! How
on earth do you understand him so? I only know
half what he means, though I try for hours and
hours."

"Simply by sympathizing with him. I feel all
his ideas come home to me, and I put them into
shape."

"You are the loveliest creature I ever saw." And, indeed, Georgie did look very well, for it was not all mere humbug now, though perhaps it was at first. "Oh, no wonder baby loves you. Kicklewick, isn't it wonderful?"

"Indeed, then, and it would be, ma'am," replied Mrs. Kicklewick, rapturously—for now she had four half-crowns in her pocket—only for it bein' nature, ma'am. Nature it is as does it, as must be. Nothing else no good again it. And how I should like to be'long of you, ma'am, when your next time come, please God. Would you mind to accept of my card, ma'am, unpretenshome but in good families,—Sarah Kicklewick, late to Lord Eldergun, and have hopes to be again, ma'am, if any confidence in head-footman. 'Mrs. Kicklewick,' he says, and me upon the bridge, ma'am, with the wind a blowin'——"

"To be sure," said Georgie, "and the water flowing; how clearly you describe it!"

But we must cut her short, even as she cut nurse Kicklewick. Enough that she won such influence over the kind but not too clever Rosa, that Rufus Hutton's plans and acts, so far as they were known to his wife, were known also to his wife's best friend. But one thing there was which Mrs. Corklemore could not at all understand, — why should he be going to London so, and wanting to go again, in spite of domestic emergencies? She very soon satisfied herself that Rosa was really in the dark upon this point, and very indignant at

being so. This indignation must be fostered and
pointed to a practical end. Mrs. Kettledrum, of
course, had been kept in the background all this
time, and scarcely allowed to dandle the baby, for
fear of impairing her sister's triumph.

"How wonderfully kind and thoughtful of
you!" said Rosa, as Georgie came in again.
"Have you really brought me a glass of wine?
And no one else in the house to suppose that I
ought to have any nourishment! How can I
thank you, Mrs. Corklemore?"

"No more 'Mrs. Corklemore,' if you please. I
have begun to call you 'Rosa'—it is such a pretty
name—and you must call me 'Georgie,' darling.
Every one does who loves me."

"Then I am sure all the world must. Dearest
Georgie, how did you get it? I am sure I would
not touch it, only for your sake."

"Oh, I did such a shameful thing. Such a
liberty I never took before! I actually sent the
servant to say, with Mrs. Corklemore's compliments, that she felt the effect of the fright this
morning, and would like another glass of port, but
would not touch it if any of the gentlemen left the
table even for a moment. And they actually sent
me a dock-glass, in pleasantry, I suppose: but I
am very glad they did."

"I will take some, if you take half, dear."

"Not a drop. My poor weak head is upset in a
moment. But you really need it, dear; and I can

so thoroughly feel for you, because the poor Count, when my Flore was born, waited on me with such devotion, day and night, hand and foot."

"And I am sure Mr. Corklemore must do the same. No husband could help adoring you."

"Oh, he is very good, 'according to his lights,' as they say. But I have known him let me cough three times without getting up for the jujubes. And once—but perhaps I ought not to tell you: it was so very bad."

"Oh, you may safely tell me, dear. I will never repeat it to any one."

"He actually allowed me to sneeze in the carriage without saying that I must have a new fur cloak, or even asking if I had a cold."

"Oh dear, is that all? I may sneeze six times in an hour, and my husband take no notice, but run out and leave the front door open, and prune his horrid little trees. And then he shouts for his patent top-dressing. He thinks far more of dressing them than he does of dressing me."

"And don't you know the reason? Don't cry, sweet child; don't cry. I have had so much experience. I understand men so thoroughly."

"Oh yes, I know the reason. I am cross to him sometimes. And of course I can't expect a man with a mind like his——"

"You may expect any man to be as wise as Solomon, if you only know how to manage him. It is part of the law of nature."

"Then I am sure I don't know what that means: except that people must get married, and ought to love one another."

"The law of nature is this. Between a wife and a husband there never must be a secret, except when the lady keeps one. Now, your husband is, to some extent, a rather superior man——"

"Oh yes, to the very greatest extent. No one of any perception can help perceiving that."

"Then he is quite sure to attempt it; to reserve himself, upon *some* point, in an unsympathetic attitude. This is just what you must not allow. You have no idea how it grows upon them, and how soon it supplants affection, and makes a married man a bachelor."

"Oh, how dreadful! But I really do think, dear, that you must be wrong this once. My husband has never kept anything from me; anything, I mean, which I ought to know."

"Then he told you about that poor wild Polly? How very good and kind of him!"

"Polly! What Polly? You don't mean to say——"

"No, no, dear, nothing of that sort! Only the mare running away with him at night through the thickest part of the forest."

"My Polly that eats from my hand! Run away with Rufus!"

"Yes, your Polly. A perfect miracle that both of them were not killed. But, of course, he must have told you."

Then, after sundry ejaculations, Rosa learned all
about that matter, and was shocked first, and then
thankful, and then hurt.

"And now," said Mrs. Corklemore, when the
sense of wrong was paramount, " he has some
secret, I am almost sure, about our sad affair at
Nowelhurst. And I am sure, even if you were
not his wife, dear, he need not conceal any matter
of that sort from the daughter of Sir Cradock
Nowell's old friend, Mr. Ralph Mohorn."

" I will tell you another thing," answered Rosa,
shaking all her pillows with the vehemence of her
emotions, " whether he ought or not, he shall not
do it, Georgie, darling. As sure as I am his
lawful wife I will know every word of it before I
sleep one wink. If not, he must take the consequences upon both his wife and child."

" Darling, I think you are quite right. Only
don't tell me a word of it. It is such a dreadful
matter, it would make me so unhappy——"

" I will tell you every single word, just to prove
to you, Georgie, that I have found the whole of
it out."

After this laudable resolution, Rosa may be left
to have it out with Rufus. It requires greater skill
than ours to interfere between man and wife, even
without the *tertium quid* of an astounding baby.

*   *   *   *   *

The ides of March were come and gone, the
balance of day and night was struck; and Sleep,
the queen of half the world, had wheeled across

the equator her poppy-chintzed throne, or had got
the stars to do it for her, because she was too lazy.
Ha, that sentence is almost worthy of a great
stump-orator. All I mean to say is, that All Fools'
Day was over. Blessed are the All Fools who
begin the summer (which accounts for its being a
mull with us) ; and blessed be the All Saints
who begin the winter, and then hand it over to
Beelzebub.

"In April she tunes her bill." Several nightingales were at it, for the spring was early, and right
early were many nests conned, planned, and contracted for. Blessed birds, that never say, "What
are your expectations, sir?" or "How much will
you give your daughter?"—but feather their nests
without waiting for an appointment in the Trea-
sury. Nest-eggs, too, almost as sweet as those of
addled patronage, were beginning to accumulate ;
and it took up half a bird's time to settle seniority
and precedence among them, fettle them all with
their heads the right way, and throw overboard
the cracked ones. Perhaps, in this last particular,
they exercised a discretion, not only unknown to,
but undreamed of, by any British Government.

It was nearly dark by this time, and two
nightingales, across the valley, strove in Amoibæan
song till the crinkles of the opening leaves fluttered
with soft melody.

"In poplar shadows Philomel complaineth of her brood,
  Her callow nestlings plunder'd from her by the ploughman rude:
  From lonely branch all night she pours her weeping music's flow,
  Repeats her tale, and fills the world with melody and woe."
                                            Georg. iv. 511.

Mr. Garnet heeded neither crisp young leaf nor
bulbul; neither did his horse appear to be a judge
of music. Man and horse were drooping, flagging,
jaded and bespent; wanting only the two things
which, according to some philosophers, are all that
men want here below—a little food, and a deal of
sleep.

Bull Garnet was on his return from Winchester,
whither he now went every week, for some reason
known only to himself, or at least unknown to his
family. It is a long and hilly ride from the west
of Ytene to Winton, and to travel that distance
twice in a day takes the gaiety out of a horse, and
the salience out of a man. No wonder then that
Mr. Garnet slouched his heavy shoulders, and let
his great head droop; for at five-and-forty a
powerful man jades sooner than does a slight one.

Presently he began to drowse; for the stout
grey gelding knew every step of the road, and
would take uncommonly good care to avoid all
circumambience: and of late the rider had never
slept, only dozed, and dreamed, and started. Then
he muttered to himself, as he often did in sleep,
but never at home, until he had seen to the fasten-
ing of the door.

"Tried it again—tried very hard and failed.
Thought of Bob, at last moment. Bob to stand,
and see me hang—and hate me, and go to the
devil. No, I don't think he would hate me, though;
he would say, 'Father could not help it.' And
how nice that would be for me, to see Bob take
my part. To see him with his turn-down collars

standing proudly up, and saying, 'Father was a bad
man—according to your ideas—I am not going to
dispute them—but for all that I love him, and so
my children shall.' If I could be sure that Bob
would only think so, only make his mind up, his
mind up, his mind up—for there is nothing like it
—whoa, Grayling, what be looking at?—and take
poor little Pearl with him, I would go to-morrow
morning, and do it over at Lymington."

" Best do it to-night, gov'nor. No time like the
praysent, and us knows arl about it."

A tall man had leaped from behind a tree, and
seized Bull Garnet's bridle. The grey gelding
reared and struck him; but he kept his hold, till
the muzzle of a large revolver felt cold against.
his ear. Then Issachar Jupp fell back; he knew
the man he had to deal with, how stern in his fury,
how reckless, despite the better part of him. And
Issachar was not prepared to leave his Loo an
orphan.

" No man robs me," cried Mr. Garnet, in his
most tremendous voice, " except at the cost of my
life, and the risk of his. I have seven and sixpence about me; I will give it up to no man.
Neither will I shoot any man, unless he tries to
get it."

" Nubbody wants to rob you, gov'nor, only to
have a little rattysination with you. Possible you
know me now?"

Bull Garnet fell back in his saddle. He would
rather have met a dozen robbers. By the voice he

recognised a man whom he had once well known, and had good cause to know;—through his outrage upon whom, he had left the northern counties; the man whom he had stricken headlong down a coal-shaft, as the leader of rebellion, the night after Pearl was christened, nigh twenty years ago.

" Yes, I know you ; Jupp your name is. Small credit it is to know you."

" And smarler still to know you, Bull Garnet. Try your pistol thing, if you like. You must have rare stommick, I should think, to be up for another murder."

" Issachar, I am sorry for you. Do you call it a murder to keep such a fellow as you off ?"

" No, I dunna carl that a murder, because I be arl alive. But I do carl a murder what you did to young Clayton Nowell."

" Fool, what do you know of it? Let go my horse, I say. You know pretty well what *I* am."

" I know you ha'n't much patience, gov'nor, and be arlways in a hurry."

Jupp hesitated, but would not be beaten, whatever might be the end of it.

" I am in no hurry now, Jupp; I will listen to all you have to say. But not with your hand on my bridle."

" There goeth free then. Arl knows you be no liar."

" I am glad you remember that, Issachar. Hold the horse, while I get off. Now throw the bridle over that branch, and I will sit down here. Come

here into the moonlight, man; and look me in the
face. Here is the pistol for you, if you bear me
any revenge."

Scarcely knowing what he did, because he had
no time to think, Jupp obeyed Bull Garnet's orders
even to the last—for he took the pistol in his hand,
and tried to look straight at his adversary; but his
eyes would not co-operate. Then he laid the pistol
on the bank; but so that he could reach it.

" Issachar Jupp," said Mr. Garnet, looking at
him steadily, and speaking very quietly; " have
you any children ?"

" Only one — a leetle gal, but an oncommon
good un."

" How old is she ?"

" Fïve year old, plase God, come next Valen-
tine's Day."

" Now, when she grows up, and is pure and
good, would you like to have her heart broken ?"

" I'd break any cove's head as doed it."

" But supposing she were betrayed and ruined,
made a plaything, and then thrown away—what
would you do then ?"

" God Almighty knows, man. I can't abide to
think of it."

" And if the—the man who did it, was the
grandson of the man who had ruined your own
mother, lied before God in the church to her, and
then left her to go to the workhouse, with you
his outcast bastard—while he rolled in gold, and
laughed at her—what would you do then, Jupp ?"

" By the God that made me, I'd have my revenge, if I went to hell for it."

" I have said enough. Do exactly as you please.
Me you cannot help or harm. Death is all I long
for—only for my children."

Still he looked at Issachar, but now without a
thought of him; only as a man looks out upon the
sea or sky, expecting no return. And Issachar
Jupp, so dense and pig-headed—surly and burly,
and weasel-eyed—in a word, retrospectively British
—gazing at Bull Garnet then, got some inkling of
an anguish such as he who lives to feel—far better
were it for that man that he had never been
born.

i

CHAPTER VIII.

To bar the entail of crime. A bitter and abortive task; at least, in this vindictive world, where Christians dwell more on Mount Sinai than on the mount that did not quake and burn with fire.

And yet for this, and little else, still clung to fair fame and life the man who rather would have lain beneath the quick-lime of Newgate. It was not for the empty part, the reputation, the position, the respect of those who prove the etymon of the word by truly looking backward—not for these alone, nor mainly, did Bull Garnet bear the anguish now from month to month more bitter, deeper, less concealable. He strove with himself, and checked himself, and bit his tongue, and jerked back his heart, and nursed that shattered lie, his life, if so might be that Pearl and Bob should start anew in another land, with a fair career before them. Not that he cared, more than he could help, whether they might be rich or poor; only that he would like them to have the chance of choosing.

This chance had not been fair for him, forsaken as he was, and outcast; banned by all the laws of men, because his mother had been trustful, and his father treacherous. Yet against all chances, he, by his own rightful power, deeply hating and (which was worse) conscientiously despising every social prejudice, made his way among smaller men, taught himself by day and night, formed his own strong character, with the hatred of tyranny for its base, and tyranny of his own for its apex; and finally gained success in the world, and large views of Christianity. And in all of this he was sincere!

It was a vile and bitter wrong to which he owed his birth. Sir Cradock Nowell, the father of the present baronet, had fallen in love of some sort with a comely Yorkshire maiden, whose mother's farm adjoined the moors, whereon the shooting quarters were. Then, in that period of mean license, when fashionable servility was wriggling, like a cellar-slug, in the slime-track of low princes, Sir Cradock Nowell did what few of his roystering friends would have thought of — unfashionable Tarquinian, he committed a quiet bigamy. He had lived apart from Lady Nowell, even before her second confinement; because he could not get on with her. So Miss Garnet went with him to the quiet altar of a little Yorkshire church, and fancied she was Lady Nowell; only that must be a secret, "because they had not the king's consent, for he was not in a state to give it."

When she learned her niddering wrong, and the

despite to her unborn child, she cast her curse upon the race, not with loud rant, but long scorn, and went from her widowed mother, to a cold and unknown place.

So soon as Bull Garnet was old enough to know right from wrong, and to see how much more of the latter had fallen to his share, two courses lay before him. Two, I mean, were possible to a strong and upright nature; to a false and weak one fifty would have offered, and a little of each been taken. Conscious as he was of spirit, energy, and decision, he might apply them all to very ungenial purposes, to sarcasm, contemptuousness, and general misanthropy. Or else he might take a larger view, pity the poor old-fashioned prigs who despise a man for his father's fault, and generously adapt himself to the broadest Christianity.

The latter course was the one he chose; in solid earnest, too, because it suited his nature. And so perhaps we had better say that he chose no course at all, but had the wiser one forced upon him. Yet the old Adam of damnable temper too often would rush out of Paradise, and prove in strong language that he would not be put off together with his works. Exeter Hall would have owned him, in spite of all his backslidings, as a very "far-advanced Christian;" because he was so "evangelical." And yet he never dealt in cant, nor distributed idyllic tracts, Sabbatarian pastorals, where godly Thomas meets drunken John, and converts him to the diluted *vappa* of an unfermented Sunday.

And now this man, whom all who knew him either loved or hated, felt the troubles closing around him, and saw that the end was coming. He had kept his own sense of justice down, while it jerked (like a thistle on springs) in his heart; he had worn himself out with thinking for ever what would become of his children, whom he had wronged more heavily than his own bad father had wronged him—only the difference was that he loved them; and most of all he had let a poor fellow, whom he liked and esteemed most truly, bear all the brunt, all the misery, all the despair of fratricide.

Now all he asked for, all he prayed for—and, indeed, he prayed more than ever now, and with deeper feeling; though many would have feared to do it—now his utmost hope was to win six months of life. In that time all might be arranged for his children's interest; his purchase of those five hundred acres from the Crown Commissioners —all good land, near the Romsey-road, but too full of juice—would soon be so completed that he could sell again at treble the price he gave, so well had he reclaimed the land, while equitably his; and then Bob should have half, and Pearl take half (because she had been so injured), and, starting with the proceeds of all his earthly substance before it should escheat, be happy in America, and think fondly of dead father.

This was all he lived for now. It may seem a wild programme; but, practical as he was in business, and not to be wronged of a halfpenny, Bull Garnet was vague and sentimental when he " took on" about his children. Furious if they were wronged, loving them as the cow did (who, without a horn to her head, pounded dead the leopard), ready to take most liberal views of everything beyond them, yet keeping ever to his eyes that parental lens, whose focus is so very short, and therefore, by the optic laws, its magnifying power and aberration glorious.

Now three foes were closing round him; all of whom, by different process, and from different premises, had arrived at the one conclusion. The three were, as he knew too well, Rufus Hutton, Issachar Jupp, and Mr. Chope, of Southampton. Of the first he held undue contempt (not knowing all his evidence); the second he had for the time disarmed, by an appeal *ad hominem;* the third was the most to be feared, the most awful, because so crafty, keen, and deep, so utterly impenetrable.

Mr. Chope, the partner and " brains" of Cole, the coroner, was absent upon a lawyer's holiday at the time of the inquest. When he came home, and heard all about it, and saw the place, and put questions, he scarcely knew what to think. Only upon one point he was certain—the verdict had been wrong. Either Cradock Nowell had shot his brother purposely, or some one else had done so. To Chope's clear intuition, and thorough knowledge of fire-arms—for his one relaxation was shooting—it was plain as possible that there had been no accident. To the people who told him about the cartridge "balling," he expressed no opinion; but to himself he said, "Pooh! I have seen Cradock Nowell shoot. He always knew all he was doing. He never would put a *green* cartridge into his gun for a woodcock. And the others very seldom ball. And even if he had a green cartridge, look at the chances against it. I would lay my life Clayton Nowell was shot on purpose."

Then, of course, Mr. Chope set to, not only with hope of reward, but to gratify his own instinct, at the puzzle and wards of the question. If he had known the neighbourhood well, and all the local politics, he must have arrived at due conclusion long before he did. But a heavy piece of conveyancing came into the office of Cole, Chope, and Co., and, being far more lucrative than amateur speculations, robbed them of their attention. But now that stubborn piece was done with, and Mr. Chope again at leisure to pursue his quest. Twice or thrice every week he was seen, walking in his deliberate way, as if every step were paid for, through the village of Nowelhurst, and among the haunts of the woodcutters. He carried his great head downwards, as a bloodhound on the track does, but raised it, and met with a soft sweet smile all who cared to look at him. In his hand he bore a fishing-rod, and round his hat some trout-flies; and often he entered the village inn, and had bread and cheese in the taproom, though invited into the parlour. Although his boots were soaked and soiled as if he had been wading, and the landing-net, slung across his back, had evidently been dripping, he opened to none his fishing creel, neither had any trout fried, but spoke in a desponding manner of the shyness of the fish, and the brightness of the water, and vowed every time that his patience was now at last exhausted. As none could fish in that neighbourhood without asking Sir Cradock's permission, or trespassing against him, and as the old baronet was most duly tenacious of all his sporting rights, everybody wondered what Mark Stote was about to allow a mere far-comer to carry on so in Nowelhurst water. But Mark Stote knew a great deal better what was up than they did.

Four or five times now, Bull Garnet, riding on his rounds of business, had met Simon Chope, and bowed politely to him. On the first occasion, Mr. Chope, knowing very little of Garnet, and failing to comprehend him (as we fail, at first sight, with all antipodes), lost his slow sequacious art, because he over-riddled it. All very cunning men do this; even my Lord Bacon, but never our brother Shakespeare.

But Mr. Garnet read him truly, and his purpose also, by the aid of his own consciousness; and a thrill of deep, cold fear went through that hot and stormy heart. Nevertheless, he met the case in his

usual manner, and puzzled Mr. Chope on the third
or fourth encounter by inviting him to dinner.
The lawyer found some ready plea for declining
this invitation; sleuth and cold-blooded as he was,
he could not accept hospitality to sift his host for
murder. Of course Mr. Garnet had foreseen the
refusal of this overture; but it added to his general
alarm, even more than it contributed to his mo-
mentary relief. Clearly enough he knew, or felt,
that now he was running a race against time; and
if he could only win that race, and give the prize
to his children, how happily would he yield himself
to his only comfort—death. With his strong religious views—right or wrong, who shall dare to
say? for the matter is not of reason—he doubted
God's great mercy to him in another world no
more than he doubted his own great love to his own
begotten.

And sad it was, enough to move the tears of
any Stoic, to behold Bull Garnet now sitting with
his children. Instead of being shy and distant
(as for a while he had been, when the crime was
new upon him) he would watch them, word by
word, smile by smile, or tear for tear, as if he
never could have enough of the little that was left
to him. They had begun to talk again carelessly
in his presence, as the manner of the young is.
Bob had found that the vague, dark cloud, of
whose origin he knew nothing, was lifted a little,
and lightened; and Pearl, who knew all about it,
was trying to slip from beneath its shadow, with

the self-preservation of youth, and into the long-obscured but native sunlight of a daughter's love. And all the while their father, the man of force and violence, would look from one to the other of them, perceiving, with a curious smile, little traits of himself; often amused at, and blessing them for, their very sage inexperience; thinking to show how both were wrong, yet longing not to do it. And then he would begin to wonder which of them he loved more deeply. Pearl had gained upon him so, by the patience of her wrong, by coming to the hearth for shelter from the storms of outer love.

In all races against time, luck, itself the child of time, is apt to govern the result more than highest skill may. So far, most of the luck had been in Mr. Garnet's favour; the approach of unlucky Cradock that day, the distraction of his mind—the hurried and jostled aim which even misled himself; the distance of John Rosedew; the blundering and timid coroner and the soft-hearted jury; even the state of the weather; and since that time the perversion and weakness of the father's mind : all these had prevented that close inquiry which must have led to either his conviction or confession. For, of course, he would have confessed at once, come what might, if an innocent man had been appre-hended for his guilt.

Only in one important matter—so far at least as he knew yet, not having heard of Jem's discovery, and Mr. Hutton's advance upon it—had fortune been against him; that one was the crashing of his locked cupboard, and the exposure of the broken gun-case to Rufus Hutton's eyes. And now it was an adverse fate which brought Mr. Chope upon the stage, and yet it was a kindly one which kept him apart from Hutton. For Simon Chope and Rufus Hutton disliked one another heartily; as the old repulsion is between cold blood and hot blood.

As it happened, Mr. Chope was Mrs. Corkle-more's pet lawyer: he had been employed to see that she was defrauded of no adequate rights uxorial upon her second marriage. And uncommonly good care he took to secure the lion's share for her. Indeed, had it been possible for him to fall in love at all with anything but money, that foolish lapse would have been his, at the very first sight of Georgie. Sweetly innocent and good, she did so sympathize with "to wit, whereas, and notwithstanding;" she entered with such gush of heart into the bitter necessity of making many folios, and charging for every one of them, which the depravity of human nature has forced on a class whose native bias rather tends to poetry; she felt so acutely (when all was made plain to her, and Mr. Corklemore paid the bill) how very very wrong it was not to have implicit confidence—"in being cheated," under her breath, and that shaft was Cupid's to Mr. Chope—in a word, he was so smitten, that he doubled all his charges, and in-

K 2

serted an especial power of appointment, for (Mr.
Corklemore having the gout) he looked on her as
his reversion.

" "Hang it," he said, for his extreme idea of final
punishment was legal; "hang it, if I married that
woman, our son would be Lord Chancellor. I
never saw such a liar."

Now it was almost certain that, under Sir Cradock Nowell's settlement upon marriage, an entail
had been created. The lawyers, who do as they
like in such matters, and live in a cloud of their
own breath, are sure to provide for continuance,
and the bills of their grandchildren.

"Alas, how sad!" thought Georgie, as she lay
back in the Nowelhurst carriage on her way to
Cole, Chope, and Co.; "how very sad if it should
be so. Then there will be no cure for it, but to
get up the evidence, meet the dreadful publicity,
and get the poor fellow convicted. And they say
he is so good-looking! Perhaps I hate ugly people
so much, because I am so pretty. Oh, how I wish
Mr. Corklemore walked a little more like a gentleman. But as a sacred duty to my innocent
darling, I must leave no stone unturned."

Fully convinced of her pure integrity, Georgie
drove up in state and style to the office of Cole,
Chope, and Co., somewhere in Southampton. She
would make no secret of it, but go in Sir Cradock
Nowell's carriage, and then evil-minded persons
could not misinterpret her. Mr. Chope alone could
tell her, as she had said to " Uncle Cradock" (with

a faint hope that he might let slip something), what
really was the nature and effect of her own marriage-settlement. Things of that sort were so far
beyond her, so distasteful to her; sufficient for the
day was the evil thereof; she could sympathize
with almost any one, but really not with a person
who looked forward to any disposal of property,
unless it became, for the sake of the little ones, a
matter of strict duty; and even then it must cause
a heart-pang—oh, such a bitter heart-pang!

"Cole's brains" was not the man to make himself too common. He always required digging out,
like a fossil, from three or four mural *septa*. Being
disinterred at last from the innermost room, after
winks, and nods, and quiet knocks innumerable, he
came out with both hands over his eyes, because
the light was too much for him, he had been so
hard at work.

And the first thing he always expressed was surprise, even though he had made the appointment.
Mr. Simon Chope, attorney and solicitor, was now
about five-and-thirty years old, a square-built man,
just growing stout, with an enormous head, and a
frizzle of hair which made it look still larger.
There was a depth of gravity in his paper-white
countenance—slightly marked with small-pox—a
power of not laughing, such as we seldom see,
except in a man of great humour, who says odd
things, but rarely smiles till every one else is laughing. But if Chope were gifted, as he may have
been, with a racy vein of comedy, nobody ever

knew it. He was not accustomed to make a joke
gratis, neither to laugh upon similar terms at the
jokes of other people. Tremendous gravity, quiet
movements, very clear perception, most judicious
reticence—these had been his characteristics since
he started in life as an office-boy, and these would
abide with him until he got everything he wanted;
if any man ever does that.

With many a bow and smile, expressing surprise,
delight, and deference, Mr. Chope conducted to a
special room that lady in whom he felt an interest
transcending contingent remainder. Mrs. Corklemore swam to her place with that ease of movement which was one of her chief fascinations, and
fixed her large grey eyes on the lawyer with the
sweetest expression of innocence.

"I fear, Mr. Chope—oh, where is my husband?
he promised to meet me here—I fear that I must
give you, oh, so much trouble again. But you
exerted yourself so very kindly on my behalf about
eighteen months ago, that I cannot bear to consult
any other gentleman, even in the smallest matter."

"My services, such as they are, shall ever be at
the entire disposal of Madame la Comtesse."

Mr. Chope would always address her so; "a
countess once, a countess for ever," was his view of
the subject. Moreover, it ignored Mr. Corklemore,
whom he hated as his supplanter; and, best reason
of all, the lady evidently liked it.

"You are so very kind, I felt sure that you
would say so. But in this case, the business is

rather Mr. Corklemore's than my own. But he has left it entirely to me, having greater confidence, perhaps, in my apprehension."

She knew, of course, that so to disparage her husband, by implication, was not in the very best taste; but she felt that Mr. Chope would be pleased, as she quite understood his sentiments.

"And not without excellent reason," answered the lawyer, softly; "if any lady would be an ornament to our profession, it is Madame la Comtesse."

"Oh no, Mr. Chope, oh no! I am so very simple. And I never should have the heart to do the things you are compelled to do. But to return: this little matter, in which I hope for your assistance, is a trifling exchange of mixed land with Sir Cradock Nowell."

"Ah, to be sure!" said Chope, feeling slightly disappointed, for he had some idea that the question would be more lucrative; "if you will give me particulars, it shall have our best attention."

"I think I have heard," said Georgie, knowing thoroughly all about it, "that there is some mode of proceeding, under some Act of Parliament, which lightens, perhaps, to some extent, the legal difficulties—and, oh yes, the expenses."

Mrs. Corklemore knew how Mr. Chope had drawn her a very long bill—upon his imagination.

"Oh, of course," replied Mr. Chope, smitten yet more deeply with the legal knowledge, and full of the future Lord Chancellor; "there is a rough

and ready way of dealing with almost anything.
What they call a statutory proceeding, shockingly
careless and haphazard, and most ungermanely
thrust into an Enclosure Act. But we never
permit any clients of ours to imperil their interests
so, for the sake, perhaps, of half a sovereign.
There is such a deal of quackery in all those
dabblesome interferences with ancient institutions.
For security, for comfort of mind, for scientific
investigation, there is nothing like the exhaustive
process of a good common law conveyance. Look
at a proper abstract of title! A charming thing
to contemplate; and still more charming, if possible, the requisitions upon it, when prepared by
eminent counsel. But the tendency of the present age is to slur and cut short everything.
Melancholy, most melancholy!"

"Especially for the legal gentlemen, I suppose,
Mr. Chope?"

"Yes. It does hurt our feelings so to see all
the grand safeguards, invented by men of consummate ability, swept away like old rubbish. I even
heard of a case last week, where a piece of land,
sold for 900l., actually cost the purchaser only 50l.
for conveyance!"

"Oh, how disgraceful!" cried Georgie, so nicely,
that Chope detected no irony: "and now, I presume, if we proceed in the ordinary way, we must
deliver and receive what you call 'abstracts of
title.'"

"Quite so, quite so, whichever way you proceed.

It is a most indispensable step. It will be my
duty and privilege to deduce Mr. Corklemore's
title ; and Mr. Brockwood's, I presume, to show
Sir Cradock Nowell's. All may be completed in
six months' time, if both sides act with energy. If
you will favour me with the description of parcels,
I will write at once to Mr. Brockwood ; or, indeed,
I shall see him to-night. He will be at the Masons'
dinner."

For a moment Mrs. Corklemore was taken quite
aback. It is needless to say that no interchange
of land had ever been dreamed of, except by herself, as a possible method of learning " how the
land lay ;" and indeed there was no intermixed
land at all, as Mr. Chope strongly suspected.
Neither was he, for the matter of that, likely to
meet Mr. Brockwood ; but when it becomes a
professional question, a man can mostly out-lie a
woman, because he has more experience.

" Be guided by me, if you please," said Georgie,
smiling enough to misguide any one ; " we must
not be premature, lest we seem too anxious about
the bargain. And, I am sure, we have done our
very best to be perfectly fair with Sir Cradock.
Only we trust you, of course, to be sure that he
has reposing, composing—oh, how stupid I am! I
mean disposing power ; that there is no awkward
entail."

Here she looked so preternaturally simple, which
she would never have done but for her previous
flutter, that Simon Chope in a moment knew ex-

actly what her game was. Nevertheless, he answered nicely in that tantalizing way which often
makes a woman flash forth.

"We shall see, no doubt, ere long. Of course
Sir Cradock would not propose it, unless he had
full power. Is it quite certain that poor Clayton
Nowell left no legitimate offspring?"

Oh, what a horrible suggestion! Such a thing
would quite upset every scheme. Georgie had
never thought of it. And yet it might even be
so. There was something in the tone of Mr.
Chope's whisper, which convinced her that he had
heard something.

And only think; young men are so little looked
after at Oxford, that they can get married very
easily, without anything being heard of it. At
least, so thought Mrs. Corklemore. And then oh,
if poor Clayton had left a child, how his grandfather would idolize him! Sir Cradock would
slip from her hands altogether; and scarcely any
hope would remain of diverting the succession.
Even if the child was a daughter, probably she
would inherit, and could not yet have committed
felony. Oh, what a fearful blow it would be!

All this passed through that rapid mind in about
half a second, during which time, however, the
thinker could not help looking nonplussed. Mr.
Chope of course perceived it, and found himself
more and more wide-awake.

"Well, what a strange idea!" she exclaimed,
with unfeigned surprise. "There has not been

the slightest suggestion of anything of the kind. And indeed I have lately heard what surprised me very much, that he had formed an—an improper attachment in a quarter very near home."

"Indeed! Do you know to whom?" It was Mr. Chope who was trying now to appear indifferent.

"Yes. I was told. But it does not become me to repeat such stories."

"It not only becomes you in this case, but it is your absolute duty, and—and your true interest."

"Why, you quite frighten me, Mr. Chope. Your manner is so strange."

"It would grieve me deeply indeed to alarm Madame la Comtesse," answered the lawyer, trying in vain to resume his airiness; "but I cannot do justice to any one who does not fully confide in me. In a case like this, especially, such interests are concerned, the title is so—so complicated, that purely as a matter of business we must be advised about everything."

"Well, I see no reason why I should not tell you. It cannot be of any importance. Poor Clayton Nowell had fallen in love with a girl very far beneath him—the daughter, I think she was, of a Mr. Garnet."

"Oh, I think I had heard a report of that sort"—he had never heard, but suspected it—"it can, of course, signify nothing, if the matter went no further; nevertheless, I thank you for your gratifying confidence. I apologize if I alarmed you; there is nothing alarming at all in it. I was thinking of something very different." This was utterly false ; but it diverted her from the subject.

"Oh, yes, I see. Of something, you mean, which might have caused a disagreement between the unfortunate brothers. Now tell me your opinion—in the strictest confidence, of course—as to that awful occurrence. Do you think—oh, I hope not——"

"I was far away at the time, and can form no conclusion. But I know that my partner, Mr. Cole, the coroner, was too sadly convinced,—oh, I beg your pardon, I forgot for the moment that Madame la Comtesse——"

"Pray forget my relationship, or rather consider it as a reason; oh, I would rather know the sad, sad truth. It is the suspense, oh the cruel suspense. What was Mr. Cole's conclusion ?"

"That if Cradock Nowell were put on' his trial, he would not find a jury in England but must convict him."

"Oh, how inexpressibly shocking ! Excuse me, may I ask for a glass of water ? Oh, thank you, thank you. No wine, if you please. I must hurry away quite rudely. The fresh air will revive me. I cannot conclude my instructions to-day. How could I think of such little matters ? Please to do nothing until you hear from me. Yes, I hear the carriage. I told Giles to allow me ten minutes only, unless Mr. Corklemore came. You see how thoroughly well I know the value of your time.

We feel it so acutely; but I must not presume; no further, if you please!"

Having thus appraised Mr. Chope, and apprised him of his distance, from a social point of view, Georgie gave him a smile which disarmed him, at least for the moment. But he was not the lawyer, or the man, to concede her the last word.

"We lawyers never presume, madam, any more than we assume. We must have everything proved."

"Except your particulars of account, which you leave to prove themselves."

"Ha, ha! You are too clever for the whole profession. We can only prove our inferiority."

He stood, with his great bushy head uncovered, looking after the grand apparatus, and three boys sitting behind it; and then he went sadly back, and said, "Our son might have been Lord Chancellor. But I beat her this time in lying."

CHAPTER IX.

Two months of opening spring are past, and the
forest is awaking. Up, all we who love such
things; come and see more glorious doings than of
man or angel. However hearts have been winter-
bound with the nip of avarice, and the iron frost of
selfishness, however minds have checked their sap
in narrowness of ideal, let us all burst bands awhile
before the bright sun, as leaves do. Heaven's
young breath is stirring through crinkled bud and
mossy crevice, peaceful spears of pensioned reeds,
and flags all innocent of battle. Lo, where the wind
goes, while we look, playing with and defying us,
chasing the dip of a primrose-bank, and touching
sweet lips with dalliance. Lifting first the shining
tutsan, gently so, and apologizing, then after a
tender whisper to the nodding milkwort, away to
where the soft blue eyes of the periwinkle hesitate.
Last, before he dies away, the sauntering ruffler
looks and steps into a quiet tufted nook, overhung

with bank, and linteled with the twisted oak-roots. Here, as in a niche of Sabbath, dwells the nervous soft wood-sorrel, feeding upon leaf-mould, quivering with its long-stalked cloves, pale of hue, and shunning touch, delicate wood-sorrel, coral-rooted, shamrock-leafed, loved and understood of few, except good Fra Angelico.

Tut—we want stronger life than that; and here we have it overhead, with many a galling boss and buff, yet, on the whole, worth tree's exertion, and worth man's inspection. See the oak-leaves bursting out, crimped and crannied at their birth, with little nicks and serrate jags like "painted lady" chrysalids, or cowries pushing their tongues out, throwing off the hidesome tuck, and frilled with pellucid copper. See, as well, the fluted beech-leaves, started a full moon ago, offering out of fawn-skin gloves, and glossed with waterproof copal. Then the ash—but hold, I know not how the ash comes out, because it gives so little warning; or rather, it warns a long, long time, and then does it all of a sudden. Tush—what man cares now to glance at the yearly manuscript of God? Let the leaves go; they are not *inscripti nomina regum.*

Yet the brook—though time flees faster, who can grudge one glance at brooklet? Where the mock-myrtle begins to dip, where the young agrimony comes up, and the early forget-me-not pushes its claim upon our remembrance, and the water-lily floats half-way up, quivering dusk in the clearness,

like a trout upon the hover.   Look how the little
waves dance towards us, glancing and casting over,
drawing a tongue with limpid creases from the
broad pool above, then funnelling into a narrow
neck over a shelf of gravel, and bubbling and bab-
bling with petulant freaks into corners of calmer
reflection.   There an old tree leans solemnly over,
with brows bent, and arms folded, turning the
course of the brook with his feet, and shedding a
crystal darkness.

Below this, the yellow banks break away into a
scoop on either side, where a green lane of the
forest comes down and wades into the water.   Here
is a favourite crossing-place for the cattle of the
woodland, and a favourite bower for cows to rest
in, and chew the cud of soft contemplation.   And
here is a grey wooden bridge for the footpath,
adding to rather than destroying the solitude of
the scene, because it is plain that a pair of feet
once in a week would astonish it.   Yet in the
depth of loneliness, and the quiet repose of shadow,
all is hope, and reassurance, sense of thanks, and
breath of praise.   For is not the winter gone by,
and forgotten, the fury and darkness and terror,
the inclination of March to rave, and the April too
given to weeping?   Surely the time of sweet
flowers is come, and the glory of summer approaching, the freedom of revelling in the sun, the vesture
of the magnificent trees, and the singing of birds
among them.

Through the great Huntley Wood, and along

the banks of the Millaford brook, this fine morning of the May, wander our Rosalind and Celia, Amy to wit, and Eoa. It is a long way from Nowelhurst, but they have brought their lunch, and mean to make a day of it in the forest, seeking balm for wounded hearts in good green leaf and buoyant air. Coming to the old plank-bridge, they sit upon a bank to watch the rising of the trout, for the stone-fly is on the water. Eoa has a great idea that she could catch a trout with a kidney-bean stick and a fly; but now she has not the heart for it; and Amy says it would be so cruel, and they are so pretty.

"What a lovely place!" says Amy; "I could sit here all day long. How that crab-apple, clothed with scarlet, seems to rouge the water!"

"It isn't scarlet, I tell you, Amy, any more than you are. It's only a deep, deep pink. You never can tell colours."

"Well, never mind. It is very pretty. And so are you when you are good and not contradictory—'contradictionary,' as James Pottles calls Coræbus."

"Well, it does just as well. What's the good of being so particular? I am sure I am none the better for it; and I have not jumped the brook ever so long, and have thrown away my gaiters just because Uncle John said—oh, you are all alike in England."

"What did my father say, if you please, that possessed such odious sameness?"

"There, there, I am so glad to see you in a passion, dear; because I thought you never could be. Uncle John only said that no doubt somebody would like me better, if I gave up all that, and stayed in-doors all day. And I have been trying hard to do it; but he is worse than he was before. I sat on a bench in the chase last Monday, and he went by and never noticed me, though I made quite a noise with my hat on the wood until I was nearly ashamed of myself. But I need not have been alarmed, for my lord went by without even looking."

"And what do you mean to do about it?" Amy took the deepest interest in Eoa's love-affair.

"Oh, you need not smile, Amy. It is all very well for you, I dare say; but it makes me dreadfully angry. Just as if I were nobody! And after I have told Uncle Cradock of my intentions to settle."

"You premature little creature! But my father was quite right in his advice, as he always is; and not for that reason only. You belong to a well-known family, and, for their sake as well as your own, you are bound to be very nice, dear, and to do only what is nice, instead of making a tomboy of yourself."

"Tomboy, indeed! And nice! Nice things they did, didn't they—shooting one another?"

Almost before she had uttered the words, she was thoroughly ashamed of herself, for she knew about Amy and Cradock from the maiden's own confession. Amy arose without reply, and, taking her little basket, turned into the homeward path, with a little quiet sigh. Eoa thought for a moment, and then, having conquered herself, darted after the outraged friend.

"I wish to have no more to do with you. That is all," cried Amy, with Eoa's strong arms round her waist.

"But, indeed, you shall. You know what a brute I am. I can't help it; but I will try. I will bite my tongue off to be forgiven."

"I simply wish, Miss Nowell, to have nothing more to do with you."

"Then you are a great deal worse than I am; because you are unforgiving. I thought you were so wonderfully good; and now I am sorry for you, even more than for myself. I had better go back to the devil's people, if this is the way of Christians."

"Could you forgive any one in a moment who had wounded you most savagely?"

"In a moment,—if they were sorry, and asked me."

"Are you quite sure of that?"

"Sure, indeed! How could I help it?"

"Then, Eoa, you cannot help being more like a Christian than I am. I am very persistent, and steadily bitter to any one who wrongs me. You are far better than I am, Eoa; because you cannot hate any one."

"I don't know about being better, Amy; I only
know that I don't hate any one—with all my heart
I mean—except Mrs. Nowell Corklemore."

Here Amy could not help laughing at Eoa's
method of proving her rule; and the other took
advantage of it to make her sit down, and kiss her,
and beg her pardon a dozen times, because she was
such a little savage; and then to open her own
lunch-basket, and spread a white cloth, and cover
it with slices of rusk and reindeer's tongue, and
hearted lettuce, and lemonade, and a wing of cold
duck at the corner.

"I left it to Hoggy," she cried in triumph, "and
he has deserved my confidence. Beat that if you
can now, my darling."

"Oh, I can beat that out and out," said Amy,
who still was crying, just a drop now and then,
because her emotions were "persistent:" then she
smiled, because she knew so well no old butler could
touch her in catering; but I must not tell what
Amy had, for fear of making people hungry.
Only in justice it should be said that neither
basket went home full; for both the young ladies
were "hearty;" and they kissed one another in
spite of the stuffing.

"Oh, Amy, I do love you so, whenever you
don't scold me. I am sure I was meant for a
Christian. Here's that nasty sneak's lawn handkerchief. I picked her pocket this morning. I
do twice a week for practice. But I won't wipe
your pretty eyes with it, darling, because I do so

loathe her. Now, if you please, no more crying, Amy. What a queer thing you are!"

"Most truly may I return the compliment," answered Amy, smiling through the sparkle of her tears. "But you don't mean to say that you keep what you steal?"

"Oh no; it is not worth it. And I hate her too much to keep anything. Last week I lit the fire in my dressing-room, on purpose to burn her purse. You should have seen the money melting. I took good care, of course, not to leave it in the ashes, though. I am forming quite a collection of it; for I don't mind keeping it at all, when it has been through the fire. And you can't think how pretty it is, all strings and dots of white and yellow."

"Well! I never heard such a thing. Why, you might be transported, Eoa!"

"Yes, I know, if they found me out; but they are much too stupid for that. Besides, it is such fun; the only fun I have now, since I left off jumping. You know the old thing is so stingy."

"Old thing, indeed! Why, she is not five-and-twenty!"

"I don't care; she has got a child. She is as old as Methusalem in her heart, though she is so deucedly sentimental"—the old Colonel's daughter had not forgotten all her beloved papa's expressions—"I know I shall use what you call in this country 'physical force,' some day, with her. I must have done it long ago, only for picking her pocket. She would be but a baby in my hands, and she is quite aware of it. Lôok at my arm; it's no larger than yours, except above the elbow, and it is nearly as soft and delicate. Yet I could take you with one hand, Amy, and put you into the brook. If you like, I'll do it."

"Much obliged, dear; but I am quite content without the crucial test. I know your wonderful strength, which none would ever suspect, to look at you. I suppose it came to you from your mother."

"Yes, I believe. At any rate, I have heard my father say so; and I could hold both his hands most easily. But oh, she is such a screw, Amy, that sympathetic Georgie! She never gives any one sixpence; and it is so pleasant to hear her go on about her money, and handkerchiefs, and, most of all, her gloves. She is so proud of her nasty little velvet paws. She won't get her gloves except in Southampton, and three toll-gates to pay, and I steal them as fast as she gets them. She grumbles about it all dinner-time, and I offered her eighteenpence for turnpikes—out of her own purse, of course—because she was so poor, I said. But she flew into such a rage that I was forced to pick her pocket again at breakfast-time next morning. And the lies she told about the amount of money in her purse! Between eight and nine pounds, she said the last time, and there was only two pounds twelve. Uncle Cradock made it good to her, because he guessed that I had done it, though he was afraid to tell me so. But, thank God, I stole it again the next day when she went out walking; and that of course he had nothing to say to, because it did not occur in his house. Oh what a rage she was in! She begins to suspect me now, I think; but she never can catch me out."

"You consummate little thief! why, I shall be afraid to come near you."

. "Oh, I would never do it to any one but her. And I should not do it to her so much, only she thinks me a clumsy stupid. Me who was called 'Never-spot-the-dust!' But I have got another thing of hers, and she had better take care, or I'll open it."

"Something else! Take care, Eoa, or I will go and tell."

"No, you know better than that. It is nothing but a letter she wrote, and was going to post at Burley. I knew by her tricks and suspicious ways that there was something in it; and she would not let it go in the post-bag. So I resolved to have it; and of course I did. And she has been in such a fright ever since; but I have not opened it yet."

"And I hope you never will. Either confess, or post it at once, or never call me your friend any more."

"Oh, you need not be hot, Amy; you don't understand the circumstances. I know that she is playing a nasty game; and I need not have any scruples with her, after what I caught her doing. Twice she has been at my desk, my own new desk Uncle Cradock gave me, where I put all the letters and relics that were found on my dear, dear father." Here Eoa burst out crying, and Amy came near again and kissed her.

"Darling, I did not mean to be cross; if the wretch would do such a thing as that, it justifies almost anything."

"And what do you think I did?" said Eoa, half crying, and half laughing: "I set a fishhook with a spring to it, so that the moment she lifted the cover, the barb would go into her hand; and the next day she had a bad finger, and said that little Flore bit it by accident while she was feeling her tooth, which is loose. I should like to have seen her getting the barb out of her nasty little velvet paw."

"I am quite surprised," cried Amy; "and we all call you so simple—a mere child of nature! If so, nature is up to much more than we give her credit for. And pray, what is your next device?"

"Oh, nothing at all, till she does something. I am quits with her now; and I cannot scheme as she does."

Suddenly Amy put both her hands on Eoa's graceful shoulders, and poured the quick vigour of English eyes into the fathomless lustre of darkly-fringed Oriental orbs.

"You will not tell me a story, dear, if I ask you very particularly?"

"I never tell stories to any one; you might know that by this time. At any rate, not to my friends."

"No, I don't think you would. Now, do you think that Mrs. Corklemore is at the bottom of this vile thing?"

"What vile thing? The viler it is, the more likely she is to have done it."

"Oh no, she cannot have done it, though she may have had something to do with it. I mean, of course, about poor Cradock."

"What about Cradock? I love Cousin Cradock, because he is so unlucky; and because you like him, dear."

"Don't you know it? You must have seen that I was in very poor spirits. And this made me feel it so much the more, when you said what you did. We have heard that an application has been made in London, at the Home Office, or somewhere, that a warrant should be issued against Cradock Nowell, and a reward be offered for him as—— Oh, my Cradock, my Craddy!"

"Put your head in here, darling. What a brute you must have thought me! Oh, I do so love you. Don't think twice about it, dear. I will take care that it all comes right. I will go to London to-day, dearest, and defy them to dare to do it. And I'll open that letter at once. It becomes a duty now; as that nasty beast always says, when she wants to do anything wrong."

"No, no!" sobbed Amy, "you have no right to open her letter, and you shall not do it, Eoa,

unless my father says that it is right. Will you
promise me that, dear? Oh, do promise me that."

How can I promise that, when I would not have
him know, for a lac of rupees, that I had ever
stolen it? He would never perceive how right it
was; and, though I don't know much about
people, I am sure he would never forgive me. He
is such a fidget. But I will promise you one
thing, Amy—not to open it without *your* leave."

Amy was obliged at last to be contented with
this; though she said it was worse than nothing,
for it forced the decision upon her; and, scrupu-
lously honest and candid as she was, she would
feel it right to settle the point against her own
desires.

" Old Biddy knows I have got it," cried Eoa,
changing her humour: " and she patted me on the
back, and said, ' Begorra, thin, you be the cliver
one; hould on to that same, me darlint, and we'll
bate every bit of her, yit; the purtiest feet and
ancles to you, and the best back legs, more than
iver she got, and now you bate her in the stalin'.
And plase, Miss, rade yer ould Biddy every con-
sumin' word on it. Mullygaslooce, but we've
toorned her, this time, and thank Donats for it.' "

Eoa dramatised Biddy so cleverly, even to the
form of her countenance, and her peculiar manner
of standing, that Amy, with all those griefs upon
her, could not help laughing heartily.

" Come along, I can't mope any longer; when
I have jumped the brook nine times, you may say

something to me. What do you think of a bathe, Amy? I am up for it, if you are—and our table-cloths for towels. Nobody comes here once in a year; and if they did, they would run away again. What a lovely deep pool! I can swim like a duck; and you like a stone, I suppose."

Amy, of course, would not hear of it, and her lively friend, having paddled with her naked feet in the water, and found it colder—oh, ever so much—than the tributaries of the Ganges, was not so very sorry (self-willed though being) to keep upon the dry land, only she must go to Queen's Mead, and Amy must come with her, and run the entire distance, to get away from trouble.

Amy was light enough of foot, when her heart was light; but Eoa could " run round her," as the sporting phrase is, and she gave herself the rein at will that lovely afternoon; as a high-mettled filly does, when she gets out of Piccadilly. And she chatted as fast as she walked all the time, hoping so to divert her friend from this new distress.

" I should not be one bit surprised, if we saw that—Bob, here somewhere._ We are getting near one of his favourite places—not that I know any-thing about it; and he is always away now in Mark Ash Wood, or Puckpits, looking out for the arrival of honey-buzzards, or for a merlin's nest. Oh, of course we shall not see him."

" Now, you know you will," replied Amy, laugh-ing at Eoa's clumsiness; "and you have brought

me all this way for that very reason. Now, if we
meet him, just leave him to me, and stay out of
hearing. I will manage him so that he shall soon
think you the best and the prettiest girl in the
world."

" Well, I wish he would," said Eoa, blushing
beautifully; " wouldn't I torment him then ?"

" No doubt you would, and yourself as well.
Now where do you think he will be ?"

" Oh, Amy, how can I possibly guess? But if
I did guess at all, I should say there was just an
atom of a chance of his being not far from the
Queen's Mead."

" Suppose him to be there. What would bring
him there ? Not to see you, I should hope ?"

" As if he would go a yard for that ! Oh no,
he is come to look for—at least, perhaps he might,
just possibly, I mean——"

" Come to look for whom ?" Amy was very
angry, for she thought that it was herself, under
Eoa's strategy.

" A horrid little white mole."

" A white mole ! Why, I had no idea that there
was such a thing."

" Oh yes, there is: but it is very rare; and he
has set his heart upon catching this one."

" That he shan't. Oh, I see exactly what to do.
Come quickly, for fear he should catch it before
we get there. Oh, I do hate such cruelty. Ah,
there, I see him ! Now, you keep out of sight."

In a sunny break of tufted sward, embayed among long waves of wood, young Bob Garnet sat, more happy than the king of all the world of fairies. At his side lay several implements of his own devising, and on his lap a favourite book with his open watch upon it. From time to time he glanced away at a chain of little hillocks about twenty yards in front of him, and among which he had stuck seven or eight stout hazel rods, and brought them down as benders. He was trying not only to catch his mole, but also to add another to his many observations as to the periods of molar exertion. Whether nature does enforce upon those clever miners any Three Hour Act, as the popular opinion is; or whether they are free to work and rest, at their own sweet will, as seems a world more natural.

Amy walked into the midst of the benders, in her self-willed, characteristic manner, as if they were nothing at all. She made believe to see nought of Bob, who, on the other side of the path was fluttering and blushing, with a mixture of emotions. "Some very cruel person," she exclaimed, in loud self-commune, "probably a cruel boy, has been setting mole-traps here, I see. And papa says the moles do more good than harm, except perhaps in my flower-beds. Now I'll let them all off very quietly. The boy will think he has caught a dozen; and then how the moles will laugh at him. He will think it's a witch, and leave off, very likely, for all cruel boys are ignorant. My pretty little darlings; so glossy, and so clever!"

" Oh, please not to do that," cried Bob, having tried in vain to contain himself, and now leaping up in agony; "I have taken so much trouble, and they are set so beautifully."

" What, Master Robert Garnet! Oh, have you seen my companion, Miss Nowell, about here?"

" Look there, you have spoiled another! And they'll never set so well again. Oh, you can't know what they are, and the trouble I have had with them."

" Oh yes, Master Garnet, I know what they are; clumsy and cruel contrivances to catch my innocent moles."

" *Your* moles!" cried Bob, with great wrath arising, as she coolly destroyed two more traps; " why are they *your* moles, I should like to know? I don't believe you have ever even heard of them before."

" Suppose I have not?" answered Amy, screwing up her lips, as she always did when resolved to have her own way.

" Then how can they be your moles? Oh, if you haven't spoiled another!"

" Well, God's moles, if you prefer it, Master Garnet. At any rate, you have no right to catch them."

" But I only want to catch one, Amy; a white one, oh, such a beauty! I have heard of him since he was born, and had my eye on him down all the galleries; and now he must be full-grown, for he was born quite early in August."

"I hope he'll live to be a hundred. And I will thank you, Master Garnet, to speak to *me* with proper respect."

Up went another riser. There was only one left now, and that a most especial trap, which had cost a whole week's cogitation.

"I declare you are a most dreadful girl. You don't like anything I do. And I have thought so much of you."

"Then, once for all, I beg you never more to do so. I have often wished to speak with you upon that very subject."

"What—what subject, Miss Rosedew? I have no idea what you mean."

"That is altogether false. But I will tell you now. I mean the silly, ungentlemanly, and very childish manner, excusable only in such a boy, in which I have several times observed you loitering about in the forest."

Bob knew what she meant right well, although she would not more plainly express it—his tracking of her footsteps. He turned as red as meadow-sorrel, and stammered out what he could.

"I am—very—very sorry. But I did not mean it. I mean—I could not help it."

"You will be kind enough to help it now, for once and for all. Otherwise, my father, who has not heard of it yet, shall speak to yours about it. Insufferable impudence in a boy just come from school !"

Amy was obliged to turn away, for fear he should look up again, and see the laughter in her eyes. For all her wrath was feigned, inasmuch as to her Bob Garnet was far too silly a butterfly-boy to awake any real anger. But of late he had been intrusive, and it seemed high time to stop it.

"If I have done anything wrong, Miss Rose-dew, anything in any way unbecoming a gentle-man——"

"Yes, try to be a good boy again," said Amy, very graciously; at the same time giving the stroke of grace to his masterpiece of mechanism, designed to catch the white mole alive; " now take up your playthings and go, if you please; for I expect a young lady here directly; and your little tools for cockchafer-spinning would barbarize the foreground of our sketch, besides being very ugly."

"Oh !" cried Bob, with a sudden access of his father's readiness—" you spin a fellow worse than any cockchafer, and you do it in the name of humanity !"

"Then think me no more a divinity," answered Amy; because she must have the last word; and even Bob, young as he was, knew better than to paragogize the feminine termination. Utterly dis-comfited, as a boy is by a woman—and Amy's trouble

had advanced her almost to that proud claim—Bob
gathered up his traps and scuttled cleverly out of
sight. She, on the other hand (laughing all the
while at herself for her simple piece of acting, and
doubting whether she had been right in doing
even a little thing so much against her nature),
there she sat, with her sketching-block ready, and
hoped that Eoa would have the wit to come and
meet her beloved Bob, now labouring under his
fierce rebuff.

But Eoa could not do it. She had wit enough,
but too much heart. She had heard every word of
Amy's insolence, and was very indignant at it. Was
Bob to be talked to in that way? As if he knew
nothing of science! As if he really had an atom
of any sort of cruelty in him! Was Amy so very
ignorant as not to know that all Bob did was done
with the kindest consideration, and for the interest
of the species, though the pins through the backs
were unpleasant, perhaps? But that was over in a
moment, and he always carried ether; and it was
nothing to the Fakirs, or the martyrs of Christianity.

Therefore Eoa crouched away, behind a tuft of
thicket, because her maidenhood forbade her to
come out and comfort him, to take advantage of
his wrong, and let him know how she felt it.
Therefore, too, she was very sharp with Amy all
the homeward road; vindicating Bob, and snapping at all proffered softness; truth being that she
had suspected his boyish whim for Amy, and now

was sorry for him about it, and very angry with both of them.

From that little touch of woman's nature she learned more dignity, more pride, more reservation, and self-respect, than she could have won from a score of governesses, or six seasons of "society."

●

CHAPTER X.

"Not another minute to lose, and the sale again deferred! All the lots marked, and the handbills out, and the particulars and conditions ready; and then some paltry pettifogging, and another fortnight will be required to do 'justice to my interests.' Justice to my interests! How they do love round-mouthed rubbish! The only justice to me is, from a legal point of view, to string me up, and then quick-lime me; and the only justice to my interests is to rob my children, because I have robbed them already. Robbed them of their birth and name, their power to look men in the face, their chance of being allowed to do what God seems chiefly to want us for—to marry and have children, who may be worse than we are; though, thank Him, mine are not. Robbed them even of their chance to be met as Christians (though I have increased their right to it), in this wretched, money-seeking, servile, and contemptuous age. But

M 2

who am I to find fault with any, after all my wasted
life? A life which might, in its little way, have
told upon the people round me, and moved, if not
improved thêm. Which might, at least, have set
them thinking, doubting, and believing. Oh the
loss of energy, the loss of self-reliance, and the
awful load of fear and anguish—I who might have
been so different! Pearl is at the window there.
I know quite well who loves her—an honest, upright, hearty man, with a true respect for women.
But will he look at her when he knows——Oh
God, my God, forsake me, but not my children!—
Bob, what are you at with those cabbages?"

"Why, they are clubbed, don't you see, father,
beautifully clubbed already, and the leaves flag
directly the sun shines. And I want to know
whether it is the larva of a *curculio*, or *anthomyia
brassicæ*; and I can't tell without pulling the
plants up, and they can't come to any good, you
know, with all this ambury in them."

"I know nothing of the sort, Bob. I know nothing at all about it. Go into the house to your
sister. I can't bear the sight of you now."

Bob, without a single word, did as he was told.
He knew that his father loved him, though he
could not guess the depth of that love, being himself so different. And so he never took offence at
his father's odd ways to him, but thought, "Better
luck next time; the governor has got red spider
this morning, and he won't be right till dinner-
time."

Bull Garnet smiled at his son's obedience, with a mighty fount of pride in him; and then he sighed, because Bob was gone — and he never could have enough of him, for the little time remaining. He loved his son with a love surpassing that of woman, or that of man for woman. Men would call him a fool for it. But God knows how He has made us.

Thinking none of this, but fretting over fierce heart-troubles, which now began to be too many even for his power of life—as a hundred wolves kill a lion—he turned again down the espalier-walk, where the apple-trees were in blossom. Pinky shells spread to the sun, with the little close tuft in the middle; some striped, some patched, some pinched with white, some streaking as the fruit would be, and glancing every gloss of blush —no two of them were quite alike, any more than two of us are.' Yet the bees knew every one among the countless multitude, and never took the wrong one; even as the angels know which of us belongs to them, and who wants visitation.

Bull Garnet, casting to and fro, and taking heed of nothing, not even of the weeds which once could not have lived before his eyes, began again in a vague loose manner (the weakness of which would have angered him, if he had been introspective) to drone about the law's delays, and the folly of institution. He stood at last by his wicket gate, where the hedge of Irish yew was, and there carried on his grumbling.

"Lawyers indeed! And cannot manage a simple
thing of that sort! Thank God, I know nothing of
law."

"Excuse me, Mr. Garnet. It is possible that
you may want to know something of law, shortly."

"By what right, sir, dare you break in upon my
privacy like this?"

Pale as he was, and scorning himself for the
way in which his blood shrunk back, Bull Garnet
was far too strong and quick ever to be dumb-
foundered. Chope looked at him, with some
admiration breaking through the triumph of his
small comprehensive eyes.

"Excuse me, Mr. Garnet. I forgot that a
public man like you must have his private moments, even at his own gate. I am sorry to see
you so hot, my dear sir; though I have heard that
it is your character. That sort of thing leads to
evil results, and many deplorable consequences.
But I did not mean to be rude to you, or to disturb you so strangely."

"You have not disturbed me at all, sir."

"I am truly happy to hear it. All I meant, as
to knowledge of law, was to give you notice that
there is some heavy trouble brewing, and that you
must be prepared to meet some horrible accusa-
tions."

"May I trespass further upon your kindness, to
ask what their subject is?"

"Oh, nothing more than a very rash and un-
founded charge of murder."

Mr. Chope pronounced that last awful word in a deeply sepulchral manner, and riveted his little eyes into Bull Garnet's great ones. Mr. Garnet met his gaze as calmly as he would meet the sad clouded aspect of a dead rabbit, or hare, in a shop where he asked the price of them, and regarded their eyes as the test of their freshness. Chope could not tell what to make of it. The thing was beyond his experience.

But all this time Bull Garnet felt that every minute was costing him a year of his natural life, even if he ever got any chance of living it out.

" How does this concern me ?   Is it any one on our estates ?"

" Yes, and the heir to 'your estates.' Young Mr. Cradock Nowell."

Bull Garnet sighed very heavily ; then he strode away, and came back again, with indignation swelling out the volume of his breast, and filling the deep dark channels of brow, and the turgid veins of his eyeballs.

" Whoever has done this thing is a fool ; or a rogue—which means the same."

" It may be so. It may_ be otherwise. We always hope for the best. Very likely he is inno-cent. Perhaps they are shooting at the pigeon in order to hit the crow."

" Perhaps you know best what their motives are. I see no use in canvassing them. You have heard, I suppose, the rumour that Mr. Cradock Nowell has left England ?"

"I know very little about it. I have nothing to
do with the case; or it might have been managed
differently. But I heard that the civil authorities,
being called upon to act, discovered, without much
trouble, that he had sailed, under a false name, in
a ship called the *Taprobane*, bound direct for
Ceylon. And that, of course, told against him
rather heavily."

"Ah, he sailed for Ceylon, did he? A wonderful place for insects. I had an uncle who died
there."

"Yes, Ceylon, where the flying foxes are. Not
so cunning, perhaps, as our foxes of the Forest.
And yet the fox is a passionate animal. Violent,
hot, and hasty. Were you aware of that fact?"

"Excuse me; my time is valuable. I will send
for the gamekeeper, if you wish to have light
thrown upon that question; or my son will be only
too glad——"

"Ah, your son! Poor fellow!"

Those few short words, pronounced in a tone of
real feeling, with no attempt at inquiry, quite
overcame Bull Garnet. First extrinsic proof of
that which he had so long foreseen with horror—
the degradation of his son. He dropped his eyes,
which had borne, till now, and returned the lawyer's
gaze; and the sense of his own peril failed to keep
the tears from moving. Up to this time Mr. Chope
had doubted, and was even beginning to reject his
shrewd and well-founded conclusion. Now he saw
and knew everything. And even he was over-

come. Passion is infectious; and lawyers are
like the rest of us. Mr. Chope had loved his
mother.

Bull Garnet gave one quick strange glance at
the eyes of Simon Chope, which now were turned
away from him, and then he looked at the ground,
and said,

"Yes; I have wronged him bitterly."

Simon Chope drew back from him mechani-
cally, instinctively, as our skin starts from cold
iron in the arctic regions. He could not think,
much less could he speak, though his mind had
been prepared for it. To human nature it is so
abhorrent to take the life of another: to usurp the
rights of God. To stand in the presence of one
who has done it, touches our pulse with death. We
feel that he might have done it to us, or that we
might have done it to him; and our love of ourselves is at once accelerated and staggered. And
then we feel that "life for life" is such low revenge;
the vendetta of a drunkard. Very slowly we are
beginning to see the baseness of it.

Bull Garnet was the first to speak, and now he
spoke quite calmly.

"You came with several purposes. One of them
was, that I should break to Sir Cradock Nowell
these tidings of new trouble; the news of the warrant which you and others have issued against his
luckless son. I will see to it to-day, and I will try
to tell him. Good God, he does not deserve it—I
have watched him—he is no father. Oh, I wish

you had a son, Chope; then you could feel for me."

Mr. Chope had two sons, not to be freely discoursed of; whom he meant to take into the office, pseudonymously, some day; and he was rather inclined to like the poor little *nullius filii*. First, because they were his own; secondly, because they had big heads; thirdly, because they had cheated all the other boys. Nevertheless, he was in no hurry to be confidential about them. Yet without his knowing it, or at least with only despising it, this little matter shaped its measure upon his present action. The lawyer lifted his hat to Bull Garnet in a very peculiar manner, conveying to the quick apprehension, what it would not have been safe to pronounce—to wit, that Mr. Chope quite understood all that had occurred; that he would not act upon his discovery until he had well considered the matter, for, after all, he had no evidence; lastly, that he was very sorry for Mr. Garnet's position, but would rather not shake hands with him.

The steward watched him walking softly among the glad young leaves, and down the dell where the sunlight flashed on the merry leaps of the water. Long after the lawyer was out of sight, Bull Garnet stood there watching, as if the forest glades would show him the approaching destiny. Strong and firm as his nature was, he had suffered now such wearing, wearying agonies, that he almost wished the weak man's wish—to have the mastery taken from him, to have the issue settled without his own decision.

"Poor Cradock sailed in the *Taprobane!* What an odd name," he continued, with that childishness to which sometimes the overtaxed brain reverts, "tap, tap-root, tap-robin! Tush, what a fool I am! Oh God, that I could think! Oh God, that I could only learn whether my first duty is to you, or to my children. I will go in and pray."

In the passage he met his son, and kissed his forehead gently, as if to atone for the harshness with which he had sent him away.

"Father," said Bob, "shall you want me to-day? Or may I be from home till dark? I have so many things, most important things, to see to."

"Birds' nests, I suppose, and grubs, field-mice, and tadpoles. Yes, my son, you are wise. Enjoy them while you can. And take your sister also for a good run, if you can. You may carry your dinner with you: I shall do well enough."

"Oh, it's no use asking Pearl; she never will come with me. And I am sure I don't want her. She does much more harm than good; she can't kill anything properly, nor even blow an egg. But I'll ask her, as you wish it, sir; because I know that she won't come."

Mr. Garnet had not the heart to laugh at his children's fine sense of duty towards him; but he saw Bob start with all his tackle, in great hopes, and high spirits. The father looked sadly after him, wondering at his enjoyment, yet loving him the

more, perhaps, for being so unlike himself. And
as he gazed, he could not help saying to himself,
"Very likely I shall never see him thus again—
only look at him when he will not care to look on
me. Yet he must know, in the end, and she, the
poor thing, she must know how all my soul was on
them. Now God in heaven, lead me aright. Half
an hour shall settle it."

CHAPTER XI.

MEANWHILE, supposing the warrant to issue, let us see what chance there is of its ever being served. And it may be a pleasant change awhile to flit to southern latitudes from the troubles and the drizzle, and the weeping summer of England.

Poor Cradock, as we saw him last, backed up by the ebony-tree, and with Wena crouching close to him, knew nothing of his lonely plight and miserable abandonment; until the sheets of plashing rain, and long howls of his little dog, awoke him to great wonderment. Then he arose, and rubbed his eyes, and thought that his sight was gone, and felt a heavy weight upon him, and a destiny to grope about, and a vain desire to scream, such as we have in nightmare. Meanwhile, he felt something pulling at him, always in the same direction, and he did not like to put his hand down, for he had some idea that it was Beelzebub. Suddenly a great flash of lightning, triple thrice repeated, lit up the whole of the wood, like day; and he saw black Wena tugging at him, to draw him into good shelter. He saw the shelter also, ere the gush of light was gone, an enormous and hollow mowana-tree, a little higher up the hill. Then all was blackest night again; and even Wena was swallowed up in it. But with both hands stretched out, to fend the blows of hanging branch or creeper, he committed himself to the little dog's care, and she took him to the mowana-tree. Then another great flash lit up all the hollow; and Wena was frightened and dropped her tail, but still held on to her master.

Cradock neither knew, nor cared, what the name of the tree was, nor whether it possessed, as some trees do, especial attractions for lightning. "Any harbour in a storm," was all he thought, if he thought at all; and he lay down very snugly, and felt for Amy's present to him, and then, in spite of the crashing thunder and the roaring wind, snugly he went off to sleep; and at his feet lay Wena.

In the bright morning, the youth arose, and shook himself, and looked round, and felt rather jolly than otherwise. Travellers say that the baobab, or mowana-tree, is the hardest of all things to kill, and will grow along the ground, when uprooted, and not allowed to grow upright. Frenchmen have proved, to their own satisfaction, that some baobabs, now living, grew under the deluge of Noah, and not improbably had the great ark floating over

their heads.   Be that as it may, and though it is a
Cadmeian job to cut down the baobab, for every
root thereupon claims, and takes, a distinct existence; we can all of us tell the travellers of a thing
yet harder to kill—the hope in the heart of a man.
And, the better man he is, the more of hope's
spores are in him ; and the quicker they grow
again, after they have all been stamped upon.   A
mushroom in the egg likes well to have the ground
beaten overhead with a paviour's rammer, and
comes up all the bigger for it, and lifts a pave-stone
of two hundred-weight.   Shall then the pluck of
an honest man fail, while his true conscience stirs
in him, though the result be like a fleeting fungus,
supposed to be born in an hour by those who know
nothing about it, and who make it the type of an
upstart—shall not his courage work and spread,
although it be underground, as he grows less and
less defiant; and rear, perhaps in the autumn of
life, a genuine crop, and a good one?

Cradock Nowell found his island not at all a
bad one.   There was plenty to eat at any rate,
which is half the battle of life.   Plenty to drink is
the other half, in the judgment of many philosophers.   But I think that plenty to look at it ought
to be at least a third of it.   The pride of the
eyes, if not exercised on that vanishing point, one-
self, is a pride legitimate, and condemned by no
apostle.   And here there was noble food for it ;
and it is a pride which, when duly fed, slumbers
off into humility.

Oh the glory of everything, the promise, and the brightness; the large leading views of sky and sea, and the crystal avenues onward. The manner in which a fellow expands, when he looks at such things — if he be capable of expanding, which surely all of us are—the way in which he wonders, and never dreams about wondering, and the feeling of grandeur growing within him, and how it repents him of littleness, and all his foes are forgiven; and then he sees that he has something himself to do with all the beauty of it—upon my word, I am a great fool, to attempt to tell of it.

Cradock saw his lovely island, and was well content with it. It was not more than four miles long, and perhaps three miles across; but it was gifted with three grand things—beauty, health, and nourishment. It might have been ages, for all he saw then, since man had sworn or forsworn in it; perhaps none since the voyagers of Necho, whose grand truth was so incredible. There were no high hills, and no very deep holes; but a pleasant undulating place, ever full of leaves and breezes. And as for wild beasts, he had no fear; he knew that they would require more square miles than he owned. As for snakes, he was not so sure; and indeed there were some nasty ones, as we shall see by-and-by.

Then he went to the shore, and looked far away, even after the *Taprobane.* The sea was yet heaving heavily, and tumbling back into itself with a roar, and some fishing eagles were very busy,

stooping along the foam of it; but no ship was to
be seen anywhere, and far away in the south and
south-east the selvage of black clouds, lopping over
the mist of the horizon, showed that still the
typhoon was there, and no one could tell how bad
it was.

Cradock found a turtle, at which Wena looked
first in mute wonder, with her eyes taking jumps
from their orbits, and then, like all females, she
found tongue, and ran away, and barked furiously.
Presently she came back, sniffing along, and drawing her nose on the sand, yet determined to stick
by her master, even if the turtle should eat him.
But, to her immense satisfaction, the result was
quite the converse : she and her master ate the
turtle; beginning, *ab ovo*, that morning.

For, although Crad could not quite eat the
eggs raw (by-the-by, they are not so bad that way),
and although he 'could not quite strike a light by
twirling one stick in the back of another, he had
long ago found reason *for*, and he rapidly found
that excellent goddess *in*, the roasting of eggs.
And for that, he had to thank Amy. Only see
how thoughtful women are ! — yes, a mark of
astonishment.

But the astonishment will subside, perhaps, when
we come to know all about it; for then all the
misogynes may declare that the thought was born
of vanity. Let them do so. Facts are facts,
I say.

Amy had sent him a photograph of her faithful

self, beautifully done by Mr. Silvy, of Bayswater, and framed in a patent lover's box, I forget the proper name for it—something French, of course —so ingeniously contrived, that when a spring at the back was pressed, a little wax match would present itself, from a lining of asbestos, together with a groove to draw it in. Thus by night, as well as by day, the smile of the loved one might illumine the lonely heart of the lover.

Now this device stood him in good stead—as doubtless it was intended to do by the practical mind of the giver—for it served to light the fire wherewith man roasteth roast, and is satisfied. And a fire once lit in the hollow heart of that vast mowana-tree (where twenty men might sit and smoke, when the rainy season came), if you only supplied some fuel daily, and cleared away the ashes weekly, there need be no fear of philanthropy making a trespasser of Prometheûs. Cradock soon resolved to keep his head-quarters there, for the tree stood upon a little hill, overlooking land and sea, for many a league of solitude. And it was not long before he found that the soft bark of the baobab might easily be cut so as to make a winding staircase up it ; and the work would be an amusement to him, as well as a great advantage.

Master and dog having made a most admirable breakfast upon turtles' eggs, "roasted very knowingly"—as Homer well expresses it—with a large pineapple to follow, started, before the heat of the day, in search of water, the indispensable. Shad-

docks, and limes, and mangosteens, bananas—with
their long leaves quilling—pineapples, mawas, and
mamoshoes, cocoa-nuts, plantains, mangoes, palms,
and palmyras, custard-apples, and gourds without
end — besides fifty other ground-fruits, ay, and
tree-fruits for that matter, quite unknown to Cradock, there was no fear of dying from drought;
and yet the first thing to seek was pure water.   If
Cradock had thought much about the thing, very
likely it would have struck him that some of the
fruits which he saw are proof not so much of
human cultivation, as of human presence, at some
time.

But he never thought about that; and indeed
his mind was too full for thinking.   So he cut
himself a most tremendous bludgeon of camel-
thorn, as heavy and almost as hard as iron, and off
he went whistling, with Wena wondering whether
the stick would beat her.

He certainly took things easily; more so than is
quite in accord with human nature and reason.
But the state of his mind was to blame for it; and
the freshness of the island air, after the storm of
the night.

Even a rejected lover, or a disconsolate husband,
gives a jerk to his knee-joints, and carries his
elbows more briskly, when the bright spring morning shortens his shadow at every step.   Cradock,
moreover, felt quite sure that he would not be left
too long there ; that his friends on board the
Taprobane would come aside from their track to

find him, on their return-voyage from Ceylon;
and so no doubt they would have done, if it had
been in their power. But the *Taprobane*, as we
shall see, never made her escape, in spite of wea-
therly helm and good seamanship, from the power
of that typhoon. She was lost on the shoals of
Benguela Bay, thirty miles south of Quicombo;
and not a man ever reached the shore to tell the
name of the ship. But a Portuguese half-caste,
trading there, found the name on a piece of the
taffrail, and a boat which was driven ashore.

After all, we see then that Cradock was wonderfully lucky—at least, if it be luck to live—in having
been left behind, that evening, on an uninhabited
island. "Desolate" nobody could call it, for the
gifts of life lay around in abundance, and he soon
had proof that the feet of men, ay, of white men,
trod it sometimes. Following the shore, a little
further than the sailors had gone, he came on a
pure narrow thread of crystal, a current of bright
water dimpling and twinkling down the sand.
Wena at once lay down and rolled, and wetted
every bit of herself; and then began to lap the
water wherein her own very active and industrious
friends were drowning. That Wena was such a
ladylike dog; she washed herself before drinking,
and she never would wash in salt water. It made
her hair so unbecoming.

Cradock followed up that stream, and found
quite a tidy little brook, when he got above the
sand-ridge, full of fish, and fringed with trees, and

edged with many a quaint bright bird, scissor-bills and avosets, demoiselles and flamingoes. Wena plunged in and went hunting blue-rats, and birds, and fishes, while her master stooped down, and drank, and thanked God for this discovery.

A little way up the brook he found a rude shanty, a sort of wigwam, thatched with leaves and .water-proof, backed by a low rock, but quite open in front and at both ends. Under the shelter were blocks of ebony, billets of bar-wood piled up to the roof, a dozen tusks of ivory, bales of dried bark, and piles of rough cylinders full of caoutchouc, and many other things which Cradock could not wait to examine. But he felt quite certain that this must be some trader's depôt for shipping : the only thing that surprised him was that the goods were left unprotected. For he knew that the West Africans are the biggest thieves in the world, while he did not understand the virtue of the hideous great 'Fetich, hanging there.

It was made of a long dried codfish, with glass eyes, ground in the iris, and polished again in the· pupil, and a glaring stripe of red over them, and the neck of a bottle fixed as for a tongue, and the body skewered open and painted bright blue, ribbed with white, like a skeleton, and the tail prolonged with two spinal columns, which rattled as it went round. The effect of the whole was greatly increased by the tattered cage of crinoline in which it was suspended, and which went creaking round, now and then, in the opposite direction.

No nigger would dare to steal anything from
such a noble idol. At least so thought the Yankee
trader who knew a thing or two about them. He
had left his things here in perfect faith, while he
was travelling towards the Gaboon, to complete
his cargo.

Cradock was greatly astounded. He thought
that it must be a white man's work; and soon he
became quite certain, for he saw near a cask the
clear mark of a boot, of civilized make, unquestion-
ably. Then he prized out the head of the cask,
after a deal of trouble, and found a store of ship-
biscuit, a little the worse for weevil, but in very
fair condition. He gave Wena one, but she would
not touch it, for she set much store by her teeth,
and had eaten a noble breakfast.

Having made a rough examination of the deserted
shed, and found no sort of clothing—which did not
vex him much, except that he wanted shoes—he
resolved to continue the circuit of his new
dominions, and look out perhaps for another hut.
He might meet a man at any time; so he carried
his big stick ready, though none but cannibals
could have any good reason to hurt him. As he
went on, and struck inland to cut off the northern
promontory, the lie of the land and the look of the
woods brought to his mind more clearly and brightly
his own beloved New Forest. He saw no quad-
ruped larger than a beautiful little deer, lighter
than a gazelle, and of a species quite unknown to
him. They stood and looked at him prettily, with-

out either fear or defiance, and Wena wanted to hunt them. But he did not allow her to indulge that evil inclination. He had made up his mind to destroy nothing, even for his own subsistence, except the cold-blooded creatures which seem to feel less of the death-pang. But he saw a foul snake, with a flat heavy head, which hissed at and frightened the doggie, and he felt sure that it was venomous: monkeys also of three varieties met him in his pilgrimage, and seemed disposed to be sociable; while birds of every tint and plumage fluttered, and flashed, and flitted. Then Wena ran up to him howling, and limping, and begging for help; and he found her clutched by the seed-vessels of the terrible uncaria. He could scarcely manage to get them off, for they seemed to be crawling upon her.

When he had made nearly half his circuit, without any other discovery—except that the grapes were worthless—the heat of the noonday sun grew so strong, although it was autumn there—so far as they have any autumn—that Cradock lay down in the shade of a plantain; and, in a few seconds afterwards, was fast asleep and dreaming. Wena sat up on guard and snapped at the nasty poisonous flies, which came to annoy her master.

How heavenly tropical life would be, in a beautiful country like that, but for those infernal insects! The mosquito, for instance,—and he is an angel, compared to some of those Beelzebubs,—must have made Adam swear at Eve, even before the fall.

And then those awful spiders, whose hair tickles a
man to madness, even if he survives the horror of
seeing such devils.   And then the tampan—but
let us drop the subject, please, for fear of not sleeping to-night.   Cradock awoke in furious pain, and
spasms most unphilosophical.   He had dreamed
that he was playing football upon Cowley Green,
and had kicked out nobly with his right foot into a
marching line of red ants.   Immediately they
swarmed upon him, up him, over him, into him,
biting with wild virulence, and twisting their heads
and nippers round in every wound to exasperate it.
Wena was rolling and yelling, for they attacked
her too.   Cradock thought they would kill him;
although he did not know that even the python
succumbs to them.   He was as red all over, inside
his clothes and outside, as if you had winnowed
over him a bushel of fine rouge.   Dancing, and
stamping, and recalling, with heartfelt satisfaction,
some strong words learned at Oxford, he caught up
Wena, and away they went, two solid lumps of
ants, headlong into the sea.   Luckily he had not
far to go; he lay down and rolled himself, clothes
and all, and rolled poor Wena too in the waves,
until he had the intense delight of knowing that he
had drowned a million of them.   Ah ! and just
now he had made up his mind to respect every
form of life so.

Oh, but I defy any fellow, even the sage Arch-
bishop who reads novels to stop other people, to

have lectured us under the circumstances, or to have kept his oaths in, with those twenty thousand holes in him. The salt water went into Cradock's holes, and made him feel like a Cayenne pepper-castor; and the little dog sat in the froth of the sea, and thought that even dogs are allowed a hell.

After that there was nothing to do, except to go home mournfully—if a tree may be called a home, as no doubt it deserves to be—and then to dry the clothes, and wish that the wearer knew something of botany. Cradock had · no doubt at all that around him grew whole stacks of leaves which would salve and soothe his desperate pain; but he had not the least idea which were balm and which were poison. How he wished that, instead of reading so hard for the scholarship of Dean Ireland, he had kept his eyes open in the New Forest, and learned just Nature's rudiments! Of course he would have other leaves to deal with; but certain main laws and principles hold good all the world over. Bob Garnet would have been quite at home, though he had never seen one of those plants before.

We cannot follow him, day-by day. It is too late in the tale for that, even if we wished it. Enough that he found no other trace of man upon the island, except the trader's hut, or store, with the hideous scarecrow hanging, and signs of human labour, in the growth of some few trees—about which he knew nothing—and in a rough piece of ground

near the shanty, cleared for a kitchen-garden.
Cassavas, and yams, and kiobos, and pea-nuts, and
some other things, grew there; which, as he made
nothing of them, we must treat likewise. There
had even been some cotton sown, but the soil seemed
not to suit it. It was meant, perhaps, by the keen
American, who thought himself lord of the island,
for a little random experiment.

When would he come back? That was the
question Cradock asked, both of himself and
Wena, twenty times a day. Of course poor
Cradock knew not whether his lord of the manor
were a Yankee or a Britisher, a Portuguese or a
Dutchman; "Thebis nutritus an Argis." Only he
supposed and hoped that a white man came to that
island sometimes, and brought other white men
with him.

By this time, he had cut a winding staircase up
the walls of his castle, and added a great many
rough devices to his rugged interior. Twice every
day he clomb his tree, to seek all round the
horizon; and at one time he saw a sail in the
distance, making perhaps for Loanda. But that
ship was even outside the expansive margin of
hope. And now he divided his time between his
grand mowana citadel and the storehouse, with
whose contents he did not like to meddle much,
because they were not his property.

There he placed the ship's hydropult, which he
had found lying on the beach; for the mate had

brought it to meet the chance of finding shallow water, where the casks could not be stooped or the water bailed without fouling it; and the boat's crew, in their rush and flurry, had managed to leave it behind them. Cradock left it in the store-house, because it was useless to him where he had no water, and it amused him sometimes to syringe Wena from the brook which flowed hard by. Moreover, he thought that if anything happened to prevent him from explaining things, the owner of the place, whoever he might be, would find in that implement more than the value of the biscuits which Cradock was eating, and getting on nicely with them, because they corrected the richness of turtle.

Truly, his diet was glorious, both in quality and variety; and he very soon became quite a poma-rian Apicius. Of all fruits, perhaps the mango-steen (*Garcinia mangostana*) is the most delicious, when you get the right sort of it—which I don't think they have in Brazil—neither is the lee chee a gift to be despised, nor the chirimoya, and several others of the Anona race; some of the Granadillas, too, and the sweet lime, and the plantains, and many another fount of beauty and delight—all of which, by skill and care, might be raised in this country, where we seem to rest con-tent with our meagre hothouse catalogue.

I do not say that all these fruits were natives of "Pomona Island," as Cradock, appreciating its desserts, took the liberty of naming it; but most of them were discoverable in one part or another of it; some born from the breast of nature, others borne by man or tide. And almost all of them still would be greatly improved by cultivation.

So the head gardener of the island, who left the sun to garden for him, enjoyed their exquisite coolness, and wondered how they could be so cool in the torrid sunshine; and though he did not know the name of one in fifty of them, he found out wonderfully soon which of them were the nicest. And soon he discovered another means of varying his diet, for he remembered having read that often, in such lonely waters, the swarming fish will leap on board of a boat floating down the river. Thereupon he made himself a broad flat tray of bark, with a shallow ledge around it, and holding a tow-rope, made also of bark, launched it upon the brook. Immediately a vast commotion arose among the finny ones; they hustled, and huddled, and darted about, and then paddled gravely and stared at it. Then, whether from confusion of mind, or the reproaches of their comrades, or the desire of novelty, half a dozen fine fellows made a rush, and carried the ship by boarding. Whereupon Cradock, laughing heartily, drew his barge ashore, and soon Wena and himself were deep in a discussion ichthyological.

As may well be supposed, the pure sea breezes and wholesome diet, the peace and plenty, and

motherly influence of nature, the due exercise of
the body, without undue stagnation of mind, the
pleasure of finding knowledge expand every day,
stomachically, while body and mind were girded
alike, and the heart impressed with the diamond-
studded belt of hope—all this, we may well suppose, was beginning to try severely the nasal joints
of incessant woe.

CHAPTER XII.

But Pomona Island, now and then, had its own little cares and anxieties. How much longer was Cradock Nowell to live upon fruit, and fish, and turtle, with ship-biscuit for dessert? When would the trader come for his goods, or had he quite forgotten them? What would Amy and Uncle John think, if the *Taprobane* went home without him? And the snakes, the snakes, that cared not a rap for the enmity of man, since the rainy season set in, but came almost up to be roasted! And worst of all and most terrible thing, Crad was obliged to go about barefooted, while the thorns were of nature's invention, and went every way all at once, like a hedgehog upon a frying-pan.

For that last evil he found a cure before he had hopped many hundred yards. He discovered a pumpkin about a foot long, pointed, and with a horny rind, and contracted towards the middle. He sliced this lengthwise, and took out the seeds, and planted his naked foot there. The coolness was most delicious, and a few strips of baobab bark made a first-rate shoe of it. He wore out one pair every day, and two when he went exploring; but what did that matter, unless the supply failed? and he kept some hung up for emergency.

As to the snakes, though he did not find out the snake-wood, or the snake-stone, or the fungoid substance, like a morel, which pumices up the venom; he invented something much better, as prevention is better than cure. He discovered a species of aspalathus, perfectly smooth near the root, and not very hard to pull up, yet so barbed, and toothed, and fanged upon all except the seed-leaves, that even a python—whereof he had none—could scarcely have got through it. Of this he strewed a ring all round his great mowana-tree, and then a fenced path down the valley toward his bathing-place, and then he defied the whole of that genus so closely akin to the devil.

But Wena had saved his life ere this from one of those slimy demons. Of course we know how hateful it is to hate anything at all, except sin and crime in the abstract; but I do hope a fellow may be forgiven for hating snakes and scorpions. At any rate, if he cannot be, he ought to be able to help it. While Cradock was making his fence aspalathine, and before he had finished the ring yet, a little snake about two feet long, semi-transparent, and jellified, of a dirty bottle-green colour, like the caterpillar known as

the pear-leech (*Selandria Æthiops*), only some
hundreds of sizes bigger, that loathsome reptile
sneaked in through and crouched in a corner,
while Cradock thought that he smelled something
very nasty, as he smoked a pipe of the trader's
tobacco, before turning into his locker.

He had cut himself a good broad coving from
the inside of the mowana-tree, about three feet
from the ground, fitted up with a flap and a pillow-
place, and strewn with fresh plantain-leaves. Across
the niche he had fastened a new mosquito net,
borrowed from his friend the trader, whose goods
he began to look upon now as placed under his
trusteeship. And in that rude couch he slept as
snugly, after a hard day's work, as the pupa does
of the goat moth, or of the giant sirex. Under
his feet was Wena's hole, wherein she crouched
like a rabbit, and pricked her ears every now and
then, and barked if ever the wind moaned. *For-
tunatos nimium ;* there was nobody to rogue them.

And yet no sooner was Craddy asleep, upon the
night I am telling of, than that dirty bottle-green
snake, flat-headed, and with a year's supply of
venom in its tooth-bag, came wriggling on its
dappled belly around the hollow ring, while the
dying embers of the fire—for the night was rather
chilly and wet, and Cradock had cooked some fish
—showed the mean sneak, poking its head up,
feeling the temper of the time, ready to wriggle
to anything. Then it came to the bedposts of
Cradock's couch, which he had cut, in a dry sort of

humour, from the soft baobab wood. It lifted its
head, and heard him snoring, and tapped its tail,
and listened again. Very likely it was warm up
there, and the snake was a little chilly, in this
depth of the winter. So without any evil fore-
thought—for I must be just, even to a snake—
though ready to bite, at a move or a turn, of the
animal known as " man," up went that little ser-
pent, cleverly and elegantly, as on a Bohemian
vase. Cradock would have died in two hours after
that snake had bitten him. But before that lissom
coil of death had got all its tail off the ground,
fangs as keen as its own, though not poisonous, had
it by the nape of the neck. Wena knew a snake
by this time, and could treat them aright. She
gave the devilish miscreant not a chance to twist
upon her, but tore him from his belly-hold, and
walked pleasantly to the fire, and with a spit of
execration threw him into it, and ran back, and
then ran to again, and barked at the noise he made
in fizzing. Therewith Cradock awoke, and got
out of bed, and saw the past danger, and coaxed
the little dog, and kissed her, and talked to her
about Amy, whose name she knew quite as well as
her own.

After all his works were finished, and when he
hardly knew what great public improvement he
should next attempt, Cradock received visitors, unex-
pected and unfashionable. In fact, they were all stark
naked ; although that proves very little. Climbing
his tree, one beautiful morning, he saw four or five

little marks on the sea, as of so many housemaids'
thumbs, when the cheek of the grate has been
polished.   Staring thereat with all his eyes—as we
loosely express it—he found that the thumb-marks
got bigger and bigger, until they became long
canoes, paddling, like good ones, towards him.

This was not not by any means the sort of
thing he had bargained for ; and he became, to state
the matter mildly, most decidedly nervous.   He
saw that there were invading him five great
double canoes, each containing ten or twelve men ;
and he had no gun, nor a pinch of powder.   Very
likely they were cannibals, and would roast him
slowly, to brown him nicely, and then serve up
Wena for garnish.   He shook so up there among
the rough branches—for he did not so very much
mind being killed, but he could not bear to be
eaten—that Wena began to howl down below, and
he was obliged to come down to quiet her.

Then he tied up black Wena, and muzzled her,
to her immense indignation, with a capistrum of
mowana bark, which quite foreclosed her own, and
then he crept warily through the woods to observe
his black brethren's proceedings.   They were very
near the shore by this time, and making straight
for the trader's hut, of which they had doubtless
received some account.   Cradock felt his courage
rising, and therewith some indignation, for he
knew that the goods could not be theirs, and by
this time he considered himself in commission as
supercargo.   So he resolved to save the store from

pillage, if it were possible, even at the risk of his life.

For this purpose he lay down in a hollow place by the water-side, where he could just see over the tide-bank without much fear of discovery, at least, till the robbers had passed the shed, which, of course, was their principal object. It was evidently a king of men who stood at the prow of the foremost canoe, with a javelin in his great black hand, poised and ready for casting. His apparel consisted of two great ear-drops, two rings upon his right wrist, and one below either knee; also a chain of teeth was dangling down his brawny bosom. He was painted red, and polished highly, which had to be done every morning; and he looked as dignified and more powerful than a don or dean. One man in each boat was painted and polished—doubtless the sign of high rank and great birth.

When the bottom of the double canoe grated upon the beach, the negro king flung back his strong arm, and cast at the shed his javelin. It passed through the roof and buried itself in the body of the fetich, which swung horribly to and fro, while the crinoline moved round it. Hereupon a yell arose from the invading flotilla, and every man trembled, waiting to see what would come of such an impiety. Finding that nothing at all ensued, for Cradock had not the presence of mind to advance at the moment, they gave another yell and landed, washing a great deal of red from their legs. But the king was brought ashore, dry and bright, sitting on some officers' shoulders. Then they came up the bank, without any order, but each with his javelin ready, and his eyes intent on the idol. How Cradock longed for a piece of packthread, to have set the dried codfish dancing!

At last they came quite up to the shed, and held a consultation, in which it seemed the better counsel to allow the god, who looked ever so much more awful now they were near him, a certain time to vindicate himself, if he possessed the power to do so. Cradock was watching them closely, through a tussock of long sea-grass, and, in spite of their powerful frames and elastic carriage, he began to despise them in the wholesale Britannic manner. They should not steal *his* property, that he was quite resolved upon, although there were fifty of them. They were so near to him now that he could see their great white teeth, and hear them snapping as they talked.

When the time allowed, which their Agamemnon was telling upon his fingers, had quite expired, and Olympian Jove had sent as yet no lightnings, the king, who was clearly in front of his age, cast another javelin through the frame of crinoline, and leaped boldly, like Patroclus, following his dart. Suddenly he fell back, howling and yelling, cured for ever of scepticism, and with both his great eyes quite slewed up, and all his virtue in his heels. Away went every nigger, drowning the royal screams with their own, pell-mell down the beach, anyhow, only caring to cut hawser. Words like these came back to Cradock, as they rolled over one another—

" Mbongo, pongo; warakai, urelwäi ;" which mean, as interpreted afterwards by the Yankee trader,

" He is a God, a great God; he maketh rain, yea, very great rain !"

Headlong they tumbled into their boats, not stopping to carry the king even, for which he kicked them heartily, as soon as he got on board, and every son of a woman of them plied his knotted arms at the paddle, as if grim Death was behind him.

Cradock laughed so heartily, that he rolled over with the hydropult on him, and threw his heels up in the air, and if they had not yelled so, they would have been sure to hear him. Very skilfully he had brought the nose of that noble engine to bear full upon the royal countenance, and the jet of water from the little stream passed through the ribs of the fetich. That god had asserted himself to such purpose, that henceforth you might hang him with beads, and give him a wig of tobacco, and no black man would dare to look at them.

Cradock Nowell felt almost too proud of his mighty volunteer movement, and began to think more than ever that the whole of the island was his. These things show, more than anything else can, his return to human reason; for of the rational human being—as discovered ordinarily—the very

first instinct and ambition is the ownership of a
peculium. What man cannot sympathize with that
feeling who has got three fields and six children?
Therefore when a beautiful schooner, of the true
American rig, which made such lagging neddies of
our yachts a few years since, came into view one
afternoon, and fetched up, with the sails all shaking
in the wind, abreast of the shed, ere sun-down, Cradock felt like the owner of a house who sees a man
at his gate. Then he came down quietly with
Wena, and sat upon a barrel, with a pipe of
Cavendish in his mouth, and Wena crouched, like
a chrysalis, between his pumpkin'd feet.

Even the Yankee, who had not been surprised at
any incident of life since his nurse dropped him
down an oil-well, when he was two years old,
even he experienced some sensation, when he saw
a white man sitting and smoking upon his barrel of
knowingest notions, with a black dog at his feet.
But Recklesome Young was not the man to be
long taken aback.

"Darn me, but yoo are a cool hand. Britisher,
for ten dollars. Never see none like 'em, I
don't."

"You are right," answered Cradock, "I am
an Englishman. Very much at your service.
What is your business upon my island?"

"Waal," said the Yankee, turning round to the
four men who had rowed him ashore; "Zebedee,
this is just what I likes, and no mistark about it.
One of them old islanders come to dispute pos-

session. And perhaps a cannon up the hill, and a
company of sojers. Ain't it good, Zeb, ain't it?
Lor, how I do love them!"

" Now, don't be too premature," said Cradock,
" it is the fault of your nation, as the opposite is
ours."

" Darned well said, young Britisher, give us
your hand upon it; for, arter all, I likes yoo."

Cradock shook hands with him heartily, for
there was something in the man's face and manner,
when you let his chaff drift by, which an Englishman recognises, as kindly, strong, and sincere, although now and then contemptuous. The contempt alone is not genuine, but assumed to meet
ours or anybody's. The active, for fear of the
passive voice.

" You are welcome to all the island," said Cradock, " and all my improvements, if you will only
take me home again. The whole of it belongs to
me, no doubt; but I will make it all over to you,
for a passage to Southampton."

" Can't take you that way, young Boss, and
don't want your legal writings. How come you
here, to begin with?"

Cradock told him all his story, while the men
were busy; and the keen American saw at once
that every word was true.

" Strikes me," he said, with a serious drawl,
which the fun in his eyes contradicted, "that yoo,
after the way of the British, have made a trifle
free, young man, with some of my goods and

chattels he-ar; and even yoor encro-aching country can't prove tittle to them."

"Yes," replied Cradock; "and I will pay you, if I have not done so already. I will give you the thing which has saved the whole from plunder, and perhaps fire afterwards."

Then he fetched the little machine, which the Yankee recognised at once as an American invention, and he laughed till his yellow cheeks were reeking at the description of the "darned naygurs'" retreat.

"Rip me up, young man," he said, "but yoo'd be a credit to us a'most. Darn'd if I thought as any Britisher wud ever be up to so cute a dodge. Shake hands agin, young chap, I likes yoo. And yoo've airned your ticket anywhor, and a hunderd dollars to back of it. We'll take yoo to the centre of the univarsal world, and make yoo open your eyes a bit. Ship aboard of us for Noo Yerk, and if that don't make a man of yoo, call me small pumpkins arterwards."

"But I want to get to England," said Cradock, looking very black; "and I have no money for passage from New York to Southampton."

"Thur now, yoo be all over a Britisher agin, and reck-wirin enlight'ment. Yoo allays spies out fifty raisons agin a thin' smarter than one in it's favior. Harken, now, I'll have yoo sot down in the docks of Suthanton, free, and with fifty dollars to trade upon, sure as my name is Recklesome

Young. Thur, now! Bet, I don't, will yoo, and pay me out o' my spisshy?"

Not to dwell too long upon these little side-paths, it is enough to record that Captain Recklesome Young, of New York, and the schooner, *Don't you wish you may catch me,* made sail two days afterwards, with half of his best cabin allotted to Cradock and to Wena. And, keen as he was to the shave of a girl's lip, in striking a contract or cutting it, upon a large scale, he came down as nobly as the angels on Jacob's ladder. No English duke or prince of the blood could or would have behaved to Cradock more grandly than Recklesome Young did, when once he understood him. In such things the Yankees are far ahead of us. Keen as they are, and for that same reason, they have far more trust than we have, in large and good human nature. Of the best of them I have heard many a true tale, such as I never could hope to hear of our noblest London merchants. Proofs of grand faith, and Godlike confidence in a man once approved, which enlarge the heart of him who hears them, and makes him hate small satire.

CHAPTER XIII.

Bob Garnet, with his trowel, and box, and net, and many other impediments, was going along very merrily, in a quiet path of the Forest, thinking sometimes of Amy and her fundamental errors, and sometimes of Eoa, and the way she could catch a butterfly, but for the most part busy with the display of life around him, and the prospects of a great boring family, which he had found in a willow-tree. Suddenly, near the stag-headed oak, he chanced upon Miss Nowell, tripping along the footpath lightly, smiling and blushing rosily, and oh! so surprised to see him! She darted aside, like a trout at a shadow, then, finding it too late for that game, she tried to pass him rapidly, with her long eyelashes drooping.

"Oh, please to stop a minute, if you can spare the time," said Bob; "what have I done to offend you?"

She stopped in a moment at his voice, and lifted
her radiant eyes to him, and shyly tried to cloud
away the sparkling night of hair, through which
her white and slender throat gleamed like the
Milky Way. The sprays of the wood and the
winds of May had romped with her glorious
tresses; and now she had been lectured so, that
she doubted her right to exhibit her hair.

"Miss Nowell," said Bob, as she had not answered, but only been thinking about him, "only
please to stop and tell me what I have done to
offend you; and you do love beetles so—and you
never saw such beauties — what have I done to
offend you?"

An English maiden would have said, "Oh,
nothing at all, Mr. Garnet;" and then swept on,
with her crinoline embracing a thousand brambles.

But Eoa stood just where she was, with her
bright lips pouting slightly, and her gaze absorbed
by a tuft of moss.

"Only because you are not at all good-natured
to me, Bob. But it doesn't make much difference."

Then she turned away from him, and began to
sing a little song, and then called, "Amy, Amy!"

"Don't call Amy. I don't want her."

"Oh, I beg your pardon, I'm sure I rather
thought you did."

"Eoa," said Bob; and she looked at him, and
the tears were in her eyes. And then she whispered, "Yes, Bob."

"You have got on the very prettiest dress I ever saw in all my life."

Here Bob was alarmed at his own audacity, and durst not watch the effect of his speech.

"Oh, is that all?" she answered. "But I am very glad indeed that you like—my frock, Bob." Here she looked down at it, with much interest.

"And, to tell you the truth," continued he, "I think, if you will please not to be offended, that you look very well in it."

"Oh yes, I am very well. I wish I was ill, · sometimes."

"Now, I don't mean that. What I mean is, very nice."

"Well, I always try to be nice. But how can I, out butterfly-hunting?"

"Now, you won't understand me. You are as bad as a weevil that won't take chloroform. What I mean is, very pretty."

"I don't know anything about that," said Eoa, drawing back; "and I don't see that you have any right even to talk about it. Oh, there goes a lovely butterfly!"

"Where, where? What eyes you have got! I do wish I was married to you. What a collection we would have! And you would never let my traps off. I am sure that you are a great deal better and prettier than Amy. And I like you more than anybody I have ever seen."

"Do you, Bob? Are you sure of that?"

She fixed her large eyes upon his; and in one

moment her beauty went to the bottom of his heart. It changed him from a boy to a man, from play to passion, from dreams to thought. And happy for him that it was so, with the trouble impending over him.

She saw the change; herself too young, too pure (in spite of all the evil that ever had drifted by her) to know or ask what it meant. She only felt that Bob liked her now better than he liked Amy. She had no idea of the deep anticipation of her eyes.

"Eoa, won't you answer me?" He had been talking some nonsense. "Why are you crying so dreadfully? Do you hate me so much as all that?"

"Oh no, no, Bob. I am sure I don't hate you at all. I only wish I did. No, I don't, Bob. I am so glad that I don't. I don't care a quarter so much, Bob, for all the rest of the world put together."

"Then only look up at me, Eoa. I can't tell what I am saying. Only look up. You are so nice. And you have got such eyes."

"Have I?" said Eoa, throwing all their splendour on him; "oh, I am so glad you like them."

"Do you think that you could give me just a sort of a kiss, Eoa? People always do, you know. And, indeed, I feel that you ought."

"I scarcely know what is right, Bob, after all the things they have told me. But now, you know, you must guide me."

"Then, I'll tell you what. Just let me give you one. The leaves are coming out so."

"Well, that's a different thing," said Eoa. "Amy can't see us, can she?"

Sir Cradock Nowell was very angry when his niece came home, and told him, with an air of triumph, all that Bob had said to her.

"That butterfly-hunting boy, Eoa! To think of his presuming so! A mere boy! A boy like that!"

"That's the very thing, uncle. Perhaps if he had been a girl, you know, I should not have liked him half so much. And as for his hunting butterflies, I like him all the better for that. And we'll hunt them all day long."

"Oh!" exclaimed Uncle Cradock, smiling at the young girl's earnestness in spite of all his wrath; "that is your idea of married life then, is it? But I never will allow it, Eoa: he is not your equal."

"Of course not, uncle. He is my superior in every possible way."

"Scarcely so, in the matter of birth; nor yet, my child, I fear, in a pecuniary sense."

"For both of those I don't care two pice. You know it is all very nice, Uncle Cradock, to live in large rooms, where you can put three chairs together, and jump over them all without knocking your head, and to have beautiful books, and prawns for breakfast, and flowers all the year round; and to be able to scold people without their daring to answer. But I could do without all that very well, but I never could do without Bob."

"I fear you must, indeed, my dear. As other people have had to do."

"Well, I don't see why, unless God takes him; and then He should take me too. And, indeed, I had better tell you once for all, Uncle Cradock, that I do not mean to try. It would be so shabby of me, after what I told him just now, and after his saving my life; and you yourself said yesterday that no Nowell had ever been shabby. You have been very kind to me and good, and I love you very much, I am sure. But in spite of all that, I wish you clearly to understand, Uncle Cradock, that if you try any nonsense with me, I shall get my darling father's money, and go and live away from you."

"My dear," said the old man, smiling at the manner and tone of her menace, which she delivered as if her departure must at least annihilate him, "you are laying your plans too rapidly. You are not seventeen until next July; and you cannot touch your poor father's money until you are twenty-one."

"I don't care," she replied; "he is sure to have been right about it. But I will tell you another thing. Everybody says that I could earn ten thousand a year as an opera-dancer in London. And I should like it very much,—that is to say, if Bob did. And I would not think of changing

my name, as I have heard that most of them do.
I should be 'Miss Eoa Nowell, the celebrated
dancer.' "

"God forbid!" said Sir Cradock. "My only
brother's only child! I will not trouble you about
him, dear. Only I beg you to consider."

"To be sure I will, Uncle Cradock, I have been
considering ever since how long it must be till I
marry him. Now give me a kiss, dear, and I won't
dance, except for your amusement. And I don't
think I can dance for a long time, after what I
have been told about poor Cousin Cradock. I am
sure he was very nice, uncle, from what everybody
says of him, and I am almost certain that you behaved very badly to him."

"My dear, you are allowed to say what you like,
because nobody can stop you. But your own good
feeling should make you spare me the pain of that
sad subject."

"Not if you deserve the pain for having been
hard-hearted. And much you cared for my pain,
when you spoke of Bob so. Besides, you are quite
sure to hear of it; and it had better come from
me, dear uncle, who am so considerate."

"Something new? What is it, my child? I
can bear almost anything now."

"It is that some vile wretches are trying to get
what they call a warrant against him, and so to
put him in jail."

"Put him in jail? My unfortunate son! What
more has he been doing?"

"Nothing at all. And I don't believe that he ever did any harm. But what the brutes say is that he did that terrible thing on purpose. Oh, uncle, don't look at me like that. How I wish I had never told you!"

Poor Sir Cradock's mind was not so clear and strong as it had been, although the rumours scattered by Georgie were shameful exaggerations. The habit of brooding over his grief, whenever he was alone—a habit more and more indulged, as it became a morbid pleasure—the loss moreover of his accustomed exercise, for he never would go out riding now, having no son to ride with him; these, and the ever-present dread of some inevitable inquiry, began to disturb, though not destroy, the delicate fibres of reason, which had not too much room in his brain.

He fell into the depths of an easy-chair, and wondered what it was he had heard. The lids of his mind's eye had taken a blink, as will happen sometimes to old people, and to young ones too for that matter; neither was it the first time this thing had befallen him.

Then Eoa told him again what it was, because he made her tell it; and again it shocked him dreadfully; but that time he remembered it.

"And I have no doubt," continued his niece, with bright tears on her cheeks, "that Mrs. Corklemore herself is at the bottom of it."

"Georgie! What, my niece Georgie!"

"She is not your niece, Uncle Cradock. I am

your niece, and nobody else; and you had better
not think of wronging me. If you call her your
niece any more, I know I will never call you my
uncle. Nasty limy slimy thing! If you would only
give me leave to choke her!"

"My darling child," cried her uncle, who loved
her the more (though he knew it not) for siding
with his son so, "you are so very hot and hasty.
I am sure Mrs. Corklemore speaks of you with the
warmest pity and affection."

"Shall I tell you why she does, Uncle Crad?
Shall I tell you in plain English? Most likely you
will be shocked, you know."

"My dear, I am so used to you, that I am never
shocked now at anything."

"Then it is because she is *such a jolly liar.*"

"Eoa, I really must send you to a 'nice institution for young ladies.' You get worse and
worse."

"If you do, I'll jump over the wall the first
night, and Bob shall come to catch me. But now
without any nonsense, uncle, for you do talk a
good deal of nonsense, will you promise me one
thing?"

"A dozen, if you like, my darling. Anything
in reason. You did look so like your poor father
then."

"Oh, I am so glad of that. But it is not a
thing of reason, uncle; it is simply a thing of
justice. Now will you promise solemnly to send
away Mrs. Corklemore, and never speak to her

again, if she vows that she knows nothing of this, and if I prove from her own handwriting that it is her plot altogether, and also another plot against us, every bit as bad, if not worse?"

"Of course, Eoa, I will promise you that, as solemnly as you please. What a deluded child you are!"

"Am I? Now let her come in, and deny it. That's the first part of the business."

Without waiting for an answer, she ran to fetch Mrs. Corklemore, whom she well knew where to find, that time of the afternoon. Dear Georgie had just had her cup of tea with the darling Flore, in her private audience-chamber — "oratory" she called it, though all her few prayers were public; and now she was meditating what dress she should wear at dinner. Those dinners were so dreadfully dull, unless she could put Eoa into a vehement passion—which was not very hard to do—and so exhibit her in a pleasant light before the serving-men. Yet, strange to say, although the young lady observed little moderation, when she was baited thus, and sunk irony in invective, the sympathies of the audience were far more often on her side than on that of the soft tormentor.

"Come, now, Sugar-plums," said Eoa, who often addressed her so, "we want you down-stairs, if you please, for a minute."

"Tum, pease, Oh Ah," cried little Flore, running up; "pease tum, and tell Fore a tory."

"Can't now, you good little child. And your

mamma tells stories so cleverly, oh, so very cleverly, it quite takes away one's breath."

"I'll have my change out of you at dinner-time," said Georgie to herself most viciously, as she followed down the passage.

Eoa led her along at a pace which made her breath quite short, for she was not wont to hurry so, and she dropped right gladly into the chair which Sir Cradock politely set for her. Then, as he himself sat down, facing her with a heavy sigh, Georgie felt rather uncomfortable. She was not quite ready for the crisis, but feared that it was coming. And she saw at a glimpse that her hated foe, "Never-spot-the-dust," was quite ready, burning indeed to begin, only wanting to make the most of it. Thereupon Mrs. Corklemore, knowing the value of the weather-gage, and being unable to bear a slow silence, was the first to speak.

"Something has occurred, I see, to one of you two dear ones. Oh, Uncle Cradock, what can I do to prove the depth of my regard for you? Or——"

"To be sure, *the depth* of your regard," Eoa interrupted.

"Or is it for you, you poor wild thing? We all make such allowance for you, because of your great disadvantages. If you have done anything very wrong indeed, poor darling, anything which hard people would call not only thoughtless but unprincipled, I can feel for you so truly, because of your hot temperament and most unhappy circumstances."

"You had better not go too far!" cried Eoa, grinding her little teeth.

"Thank Heaven! I see, dear, it is nothing so very disgraceful after all, because it has nothing to do with you, or you would not smile so prettily. You take it so lightly, it must be something about dear Uncle Cradock. Oh, Uncle Cradock, tell me all about it; my whole heart will be with you."

"Black-spangled hen has broken her eggs. Nothing more," said Eoa. "De-ar, oh we do love you so!" She made two syllables of that word, as Mrs. Corklemore used to do, in her many gushing moments. Georgie looked at Eoa with wonder. She had stupidly thought her a stupid.

Then Sir Cradock Nowell rose, in a stately manner, to put an end to all this little nonsense.

"My niece, Eoa, declares, Mrs. Corklemore, that you, in some underhand manner, have promoted a horrible charge against my poor son Cradock, a charge which no person in any way connected with our family should ever dare to utter, even if he or she believed its justice, far less dare to promulgate, and even force into the courts of law. Is this so, or is it not?"

"Oh, Uncle Cradock, how can you speak so? What charge should I ever dream of?"

"See how her hands are trembling, and how white her lips are; not with telling black lies, Uncle Cradock, but with being found out."

"Eoa, have the kindness not to interrupt again."

"Very well, Uncle Cradock; I won't, unless you make me."

"Then, as I understand, madam, you deny entirely the truth of this accusation?"

"Of course I do, most emphatically. What can you all be dreaming about?"

"Now, Eoa, it is your turn to establish what you have said."

"I can't establish anything, though I know it, Uncle Cradock."

"*Know* it indeed, you poor wild nautch-girl! *Dreamed* it you mean, I suppose."

"I mean," continued Eoa, not even looking at her, but bending her fingers in a manner which Georgie quite understood, "that I cannot prove anything, Uncle Cradock, without your permission. But here I have a letter, with the seal unbroken, and which I promised some one not to open without her leave, and now she has given me leave to open it with your consent and in the presence of the writer. Why, how pale you are, Mrs. Corklemore!"

"My Heavens! And this is England! Stealing letters, and forging them——"

"Which of the two do you mean, madam?" asked Sir Cradock, looking at her in his old magisterial manner, after examining the envelope; "either involves a heavy charge against a member of my family. Is this letter yours, or not?"

"Yes, it is," replied Georgie, after a moment's debate, for if she called it a forgery, it must of

course be opened; "have the kindness to give me
my property. I thought there was among well-
bred people a delicacy as to scrutinizing even the
directions of one another's letters."

" So there is, madam; you are quite right—except, indeed, under circumstances altogether excep-
tional, and of which this is one. Now for your
own exculpation, and to prove that my niece
deserves heavy punishment (which I will take
care to inflict), allow me to open this letter. I see
it is merely a business letter, or I would not ask
even that; although you have so often assured me
that you have no secret in the world from me.
You can have nothing confidential to say to
' Simon Chope, Esq.;' and if you had, it should
remain sacred and secure with me, unless it in-
volved the life and honour of my son. Shall I
open this letter?"

" Certainly not, Sir Cradock Nowell. How dare
you to think of such a thing, so mean, so low, so
prying?"

" After those words, madam, you cannot continue to be a guest of mine; or be ever received
in this house again, unless you prove that I have
wronged you, by allowing me to send for your
husband, and to place this letter in his hands,
before you have in any way communicated with
him."

" Give me my letter, Sir Cradock Nowell,
unless your niece inherits the thieving art from
you. As for you, wretched little Dacoit," here

she bent upon Eoa flashing eyes quite pale from wrath, for sweet Georgie had her temper, "bitterly you shall rue the day when you presumed to match yourself with me. You would like to do a little murder, I see. No doubt it runs in the family; and the Thugs and Dacoits are first cousins, of course."

Never had Eoa fought so desperate a battle with herself, as now to keep her hands off Georgie. Without looking at her again, she very wisely ran away, for it was the only chance of abstaining. Mrs. Corklemore laughed aloud; then she took the letter, which the old man had placed upon the table, and said to him, with a kind look of pity:

"What a fuss you have made about nothing! It is only a question upon the meaning of a clause in my marriage-settlement; but I do not choose to have my business affairs exposed, even to my husband. Now do you believe me, Uncle Cradock?"

"No, I cannot say that I do, madam. And it does not matter whether I do or not. You have used language about my family which I can never forget. A carriage will be at your service at any moment you please."

"Thanks for your hospitable hint. You will soon find your mistake, I think, in having made me your enemy; though your rudeness is partly excused, no doubt, by your growing hallucinations. Farewell for the present, poor dear Uncle Cradock."

With these words, Mrs. Corklemore made him an elegant curtsey, and swept away from the room, without even the glisten of a tear to mar her gallant bearing, although she had been so outraged. But when she got little Flore's head on her lap, she cried over it very vehemently, and felt the depth of her injury.

When she had closed the door behind her (not with any vulgar bang, but firmly and significantly), the master of the house walked over to a panelled mirror, and inspected himself uncomfortably. It was a piece of ancient glass, purchased from an Italian chapel by some former Cradock Nowell, and bearing a mystic name and fame among the maids who dusted it. By them it was supposed to have a weird prophetic power, partly, no doubt, from its deep dark lustre, and partly because it was circular, and ever so slightly, and quite imperceptibly, concave. As upon so broad a surface no concavity could be, in the early ages of mechanism, made absolutely true—and for that matter it cannot be done ad *unguem*, even now—there were, of course, many founts of error in this Italian mirror. Nevertheless, all young ladies who ever beheld it were charmed with it, so sweetly deeply beautiful, like Galatea watching herself and finding Polypheme over her shoulder, in the glass of the blue Sicilian sea.

To this glass Sir Cradock Nowell went to examine his faded eyes, time-worn, trouble-worn, stranded by the ebbing of the brain. He knew too well what Mrs. Corklemore meant by her last thrust; and the word "hallucination" happened, through a great lawsuit then in progress, to be invested with an especial prominence and significance. While he was sadly gazing into the convergence of grey light, and feebly reassuring himself, yet like his image wavering, a heavy step was heard behind him, and beside his flowing silvery locks appeared the close-cropped massive brow and the gloomy eyes of Bull Garnet.

CHAPTER XIV.

As the brothers confronted one another, the legitimate and the base-born, the man of tact and the man of force, the luxurious and the labourer, strangely unlike in many respects, more strangely alike in others; each felt kindly and tenderly, yet timidly, for the other.

The old man thought of the lying wrong inflicted upon the stronger one by their common father; the other felt the worse wrong—if possible —done by himself to his brother. The measure of such things is not for us. God knows, and visits, and forgives them.

Even by the failing light—for the sun was westering, and a cloud flowed over him—each could see that the other's face was not as it should be, that the flight of weeks was drawing age on, more than the lapse of years should.

" Garnet, you do a great deal too much. I shall recall my urgent request, if you look so

harassed and haggard. Take a holiday now for a
month, before the midsummer rents fall due. I
will try to do without you; though I may want
you any day."

"I will do nothing of the sort; work is needful
for me—without it I should die. But you also
look very unwell. You must not attempt to pre-
scribe for me."

"I have not been happy lately. By-and-by
things will be better. What is your impression of
Mrs. Nowell Corklemore ?"

"That she is an arrant hypocrite, unscrupulous,
foul, and deadly."

"Well, that is plain speaking ; by no means
complimentary. Poor Georgie, I hope you mis-
judge her, as she says bad people do. But for the
present she is gone. There has been a great fight,
all along, between her and Eoa; they could not
bear one another. And now my niece has discovered a thing which brings me to her side in the
matter, for she at least is genuine."

"That she is indeed, and genuinely passionate ;
you may trust her with anything. She has been
very rude indeed to me ; and yet I like her wonderfully. What has she discovered ?"

"That Mrs. Corklemore is at the bottom of this
horrible application for a warrant against my
son."

"I can well believe it. It struck me in a moment; though I cannot see her object. I never
understand plotting."

"Neither do I, Garnet; I only know she has made me insult the dearest friend I had on earth."

"Yes, Mr. Rosedew; I heard of it, and wondered at your weakness. But it did not become me to interfere."

" Certainly not : most certainly not. You could not expect me to bear it. And the Rosedews never liked you."

"That has nothing to do with it. Very probably they are right; for I do not like myself. And you will not dislike, but hate me, when you know what I have to say."

Bull Garnet's mind was now made up. For months he had been thinking, forecasting, doubting, wavering—a condition of mind so strange to him, so adrift from all his landmarks, that this alone, without sense of guilt, must have kept him in wretchedness.

Sir Cradock Nowell only said, "Keep it for another time. I cannot bear any more excitement; I have had so much to-day."

Bull Garnet looked at him sorrowfully. He could not bear to see his brother beaten so by trouble, and to feel his own hard hand in it.

"Don't you know what they say of me ? Oh, you know what they say of me ; and nothing of the kind in the family!" The old man seemed to prove that there was, by the vague flashing of his eyes: "Garnet, you are my brother ; after all, you are my brother. And they say I am going mad ;

and I know they will try to shut me up, without a
horse, or a book, or a boy to brush my trousers. Oh,
Garnet, you have been bitterly wronged, shamefully wronged, detestably; but you will not let
your own brother—brother, who has no sons now
to protect him,—be shut up, and made nothing of?
Bull Garnet, promise me this, although we have so
wronged you."

Garnet knew not what to do. Even he was
taken aback, shocked by this sudden outburst,
which partly proved what it denied. And this
altogether changed the form of the confession he
was come to make — and changed it for the
better.

"My brother"—it was the first time he had ever
so addressed him; not from diffidence, but from
pride—"my brother, let us look at things, if possible, as God made them. I have been injured no
doubt, and so my mother was; blasted, both of us,
for life, according to the little ideas of this creeping
world. In many cases, the thief is the rogue; in
even more, the robbed one is the only villain. Now
can you take the large view of things which is
forced upon us outsiders when we dare to think at
all?"

"I cannot think now of such abstract things.
My mind is astray with trouble. Did I ever tell
you your mother's words, when she came here ten
or twelve years ago, and demanded a share of the
property? Not for her own sake, but for yours, to
get you into some business."

"No, I never heard of it. How it must have hurt her!" Bull Garnet was astonished; because it had long been understood that his mother should not be spoken of.

"And me as well. I gave her a cheque for a liberal sum, as I thought. She tore it, and threw it at me. What more could I do? Did I deserve her curse, Garnet? Is all this trouble come upon me because I did not obey her?"

"I believe that you meant to do exactly what was right."

"I hope — I believe, I did. And see how wrong she was in one part of her prediction. She said that I and my father also should be punished through you, through you, her only son. What a mistake that has proved! You, who are my right arm and brain; my only hope and comfort!"

The old man came up, and looked with the deepest trust and admiration at his unacknowledged brother. A few months ago, Bull Garnet would have taken such a look as his truest and best revenge for the cruel wrong to his mother. But now he fell away from it, and muttered something, in a manner quite unlike his own. His mind was made up, he was come to tell all; but how could he do it now, and wrench the old man's latest hope away?

Then suddenly he remembered, or knew from his own feelings, that an old man's last hope in earthly matters should rest upon no friend or

brother, not even upon a wife, but upon his own
begotten, his successors in the world.   And what
he had to say, while tearing all reliance from himself, would replace it where it should be.

Meanwhile Sir Cradock Nowell, thinking that
Garnet was too grateful for a few kind words, followed him, and placed his slender tremulous and
pure-bred hand in the useful cross-bred palm which
had sent Mr. Jupp down the coal-shaft.

" Bull, you are my very best friend.   After all,
we are brothers.   Promise to defend me."

But Garnet only withdrew his hand, and sighed,
and could not look at him.

" Oh, then, even you believe it; I see you do !
It must be true.   God have mercy upon me !"

" Cradock, it is a cursed lie ; you must not dwell
upon it.   Such thoughts are spawn of madness;
turn to another subject.   Just tell me what is the
greatest thing one man can do to another ?"

" To love him, I suppose, Garnet.   But I don't
care much for that sort of thing, since I lost my
children."

" Yes, it is a grand thing to love ; but far
grander to forgive."

" Is it ?   I am glad to hear it.   I always could
forgive."

" Little things, you mean, no doubt.   Slights
and slurs—and so forth ? "

" Yes, and great things also.   But I am not
what I was, Bull.   You know what I have been
through."

" Can you forgive as deep a wrong as one man ever did to another?"

" Yes, I dare say. I am sure I don't know. What makes you look at me like that?"

" Because I shot your son Clayton ; and because I did it on purpose."

" Viley! my boy Viley! Oh, I had forgotten. What a stupid thing of me! I thought he was dead somehow. Now, I will open the door for him, because his hands are full. And let him put his game on the table — never mind the papers —he always likes me to see it. Oh, Viley, how long you have been away! What a bag you must have made! Come in, my boy; come in."

Bull Garnet's heart cleaved to his side, as the old man opened the door, and looked, with the leaping joy of a father's love, for his pet, his beloved, his treasured one. But nothing except cold air came in.

" The passage is empty. Perhaps he is waiting, because his boots are dirty. Tell him not to think twice about that. I am fidgety sometimes, I know; and I scolded him last Friday. But now he may come anyhow, if he will only come to me. I am so dull without him."

" You will never see him more"—Bull Garnet whispered through a flood of tears, like grass waving out of water—"until it pleases God to take you home, where son and father go alike; sometimes one first, sometimes other, as His holy

will is. He came to an unholy end. I tell you
again—I shot him."

" Excuse me; I don't quite understand. There
was a grey hare, with a nick in her ear, who came
to the breakfast-room window all through the hard
weather last winter, and he promised me not to
shoot her; and I am sure that he cannot have done
it, because he is so soft-hearted, and that is why I
love him so.   Talk of Cradock—talk of Cradock !
Perhaps he is cleverer than Viley—though I never
will believe it—but is he half so soft and sweet?
Will the pigeons sit on his shoulder so, and the
dogs nuzzle under his coat-lap?   Tell me that—
tell me that—Bull Garnet."   .

He leaned on the strong arm of his steward, and
looked eagerly for his answer ; then trembled with
an exceeding great fear, to see that he was weeping.   That such a man should weep !   But Garnet
forced himself to speak.

" You cannot listen to me now; I will come
again, and talk to you.   God knows the agony to
me ; and worst of all that it is for nothing.   Yet
all of it not a thousandth part of the anguish I
have caused.   Perhaps it is wisest so.   Perhaps it
is for my children's sake that I, who have killed
your pet child, cannot make you know it.   Yet it
adds to my despair, that I have killed the father
too."

Scarcely knowing voice from silence, dazed himself, and blurred, and giddy—so strong is contagion
of the mind—Bull Garnet went to the stables,

saddled a horse without calling groom, and rode
off at full gallop to Dr. Buller. By the time he
got there his business habits and wonted fashion
of thought had returned, and he put what he came
for in lucid form, tersely, crisply, dryly, as if in the
world there were no such thing as ill-regulated
emotion—except on the part of other people.

" Not a bit of it," said Dr. Buller; " his mind is
as sound as yours or mine, and his constitution excellent. He has been troubled a good deal; but
bless me—I know a man who lost his three children
in a month, and could scarcely pay for their coffins,
sir. And his wife only six weeks afterwards. That
is what I call trouble, sir!"

Bull Garnet knew, from his glistening eyes, and
the quivering of his grey locks, that the man he
spoke of was himself. Reassured about Sir Cradock, yet fearing to try him further at present,
Mr. Garnet went heavily homewards, after begging
Dr. Buller to call, as if by chance, at the Hall, observe, and attend to the master.

Heavily and wearily Bull Garnet went to the
home which once had been so sweet to him, and
was now beloved so painfully. The storms of
earth were closing round him, only the stars of
heaven were bright. Myriad as the forest leaves,
and darkly moving in like manner, fears, and
doubts, and miseries sprang and trembled through
him.

No young maid at his door to meet him lovingly
and gaily. None to say, " Oh, darling father, how
Q 2

hungry you must be, dear!" Only Pearl, so wan and cold, and scared of soft affection. And as she timidly approached, then dropped her eyes before his gaze, and took his hat submissively, as if she had no lips to kiss, no hand to lay on his shoulder, he saw with one quick glance that still some new grief had befallen her, that still another trouble was come to make its home with her.

"What is it, Pearl?" he asked her, sadly; "come in here and tell me." He never called her his Pearly now, his little native, or pretty pet, as he used to do in the old days. They had dropped those little endearments.

"You will be sorry to hear it—sorry, I mean, that it happened; but I could not have done otherwise."

"I never hear anything, now, Pearl, but what I am sorry to hear. This will make little difference."

"So I suppose," she answered. "Mr. Pell has been here to-day, and—and—oh, father, you know what."

"Indeed I have not been informed of anything. What do I know of Mr. Pell?"

"More than he does of you, sir. He asked me to be his wife."

"He is a good man. But of course you said 'No.'"

"Of course I did. Of course, of course. What else can I ever say?"

She leaned her white cheek on the high oak mantel, and a little deep sob came from her heart.

"Would you have liked to say 'Yes,' Pearl?" her father asked very softly, going to put his arm round her waist, and then afraid to do it.

"Oh no! oh no! At least, not yet, though I respect him very highly. But I told him that I never could, and never could tell him the reason. And oh, I was so sorry for him—he looked so hurt and disappointed."

"You shall tell him the reason very soon, or rather the newspapers shall."

"Father, don't say that; dear father, you are bound for our sake. I don't care for him one atom, father, compared with — compared with you, I mean. Only I thought I must tell you, because— oh, you know what I mean. And even if I did like him, what would it matter about me? Oh, father, I often think that I have been too hard upon you, and all of it through me, and my vile concealment!"

"My daughter, I am not worthy of you. Would God that you could forgive me!"

"I have done it long ago, father. Do you think a child of yours could help it, after all your sorrow?"

"My child, look kindly at me; try to look as if you loved me."

She turned to him with such a look as a man only gets once in his life, and then she fell upon

his neck, and forgot the world and all it held,
except her own dear father. Wrong he might have
done, wrong (no doubt) he had done; but who was
she, his little child, to remember it against him?
She lay for a moment in his arms, overcome with
passion, leaning back, as she had done there, when
a weanling infant. For him it was the grandest
moment of his passionate life—a father's powerful
love, ennobled by the presence of his God. Such
a moment teaches us the grandeur of our race, the
traces of a higher world stamped on us indelibly.
Then we feel, and try to own, that in spite of
satire, cynicism, and the exquisite refinements of
the purest selfishness, there is, in even the sharpest
and the shallowest of us, something kind and solid,
some abiding element of the all-pervading goodness.

"Now I will go through with it"—Bull Garnet
was recovering—"my own child; go and fetch
your brother, if it will not be too much for you.
If you think it will, only send him."

"Father, I will fetch him. I may be able to
help you both. And now I am so much better."

Presently she returned with Bob, who looked
rather plagued and uncomfortable, with a great
slice of cork in one hand and a bottle of gum in
the other, and a regular housewife of needles in the
lappet of his coat. He was going to mount a specimen of a variety of "devil's coach-horse," which
he had never seen before, and whose tail was forked
like a trident.

"Never can let me alone," said Bob; "just ready to begin I was; and I am sure to spoil his thorax. He is getting stiff every moment."

Bull Garnet looked at him brightly and gladly, even at such a time. Little as he knew or cared about the things that crawl and hop—as he ignorantly put it—skilled no more in natural history than our early painters were, yet from his own strong sense he perceived that his son had a special gift; and a special gift is genius, and may (with good luck) climb eminence. Then he thought of what he had to tell him, and the power of his heart was gone.

It was the terror of this moment which had dwelt with him night and day, more than the fear of public shame, of the gallows, or of hell. To be loathed and scorned by his only son! Oh that Pearl had not been so true; oh that Bob suspected something, or had even found it out for himself! Then the father felt that now came part of his expiation.

Bob looked at him quite innocently with wonder and some fear. To him "the governor" long had been the strangest of all puzzles, sometimes so soft and loving, sometimes so hard and terrible. Perhaps poor Bob would catch it now for his doings with Eoa.

"Sit down there, my son. Not there, but further from me. Don't be at all afraid, my boy. I have no fault to find with you. I am far luckier in my son, than you are in your father. You must

try to bear terrible news, Bob.   Your sister long
has borne it."

Pearl, who was ghastly pale and trembling, stole
a glance at each of them from the dark end of the
room,   then   came up bravely into the lamplight,
took Bob's hand and kissed him, and sat close by
to comfort him.

Bull Garnet sighed from the depths of his heart.
His children seemed to be driven from him, and to
crouch together in fear of him.

"It serves me right.   I know that, of course.
That only makes it the worse to bear."

"Father, what is it ?" cried Bob, leaping up, and
dropping his cork-slice and gum-bottle ; " whatever
the matter is, father, tell me, that I may stand by
you."

" You cannot stand by me in this.   When you
know what it is, you will fly from me."

" Will I, indeed !   A likely thing.   Oh, father,
you think I am such a soft, because I am fond of
little things."

" Would you stand by your father, Bob, if you
knew that he was a murderer ?"

" Oh come," said Bob, " you are drawing it a
little too strong, dad.   You never could be that,
you know."

" I not only can be, but am, my son."

Father and son looked at one another.   The
governor standing square and broad, with his
shoulders thrown well back, and no trace of emotion in form or face, except that his quick wide
nostrils quivered, and his lips were white.   The

stripling gazing up at him, seeking for some sign of jest, seeking for a ray of laughter in his father's eyes ; too young to comprehend the power and fury of large passion.

Ere either spoke another word—for the father was hurt at the son's delay, and the son felt all abroad in his head—between them glided Pearl, the daughter, the sister, the gentle woman—the one most wronged of all, and yet the quickest to forgive it.

·" Darling, he did it for my sake," she whispered to her brother, though it cut through her heart to say it. "Father, oh father, Bob is so slow; don't be angry with him. Come to me a moment, father. Oh, how I love and honour you!"

Those last few words to the passionate man were like heaven poured into hell. That a child of his should still honour him! He kissed her with tenfold the love young man has for maiden ; then he turned away and wept, as if the earth was water.

Very little more was said. Pearl went away to Bob, and whispered how the fatal grief befell ; and Bob wept great tears for the sake of all, and most of all for his father's sake. Then, as the father lay cramped up upon the little sofa, wrestling with the power of life and the promise of death, Bob came up, and kissed him dearly on his rugged forehead.

" Is that you, my own dear son? God is far too good to me."

CHAPTER XV.

THAT night the man of violence enjoyed the
first sweet dreamless sleep that had spread its
velvet shield between him and his guilt and sorrow.
Pearl, who had sat up late with Bob, comforting
and crying with him, listened at her father's door,
and heard his quiet breathing. Through many
months of trouble, now, she had watched him
kindly, tenderly, fearing ever some wild outbreak
upon others or himself, hiding in her empty heart
all its desolation.

The very next day, Bull Garnet resolved to
have it out with his son; not to surprise him by
emotion to a hasty issue, but now to learn what
he thought and felt, after taking his time about it.
All this we need not try to tell, only so much as
bears upon the staple of the story.

"Father, I know that you had—you had good
reason for doing it."

" There could be no good reason. There might

be, and were, many bad ones. Of this I will not speak to you. I did it in violence and fury, and under a false impression. When I saw him, with his arm cast round my pure and darling Pearl, Satan's rage is but a smile compared to the fury of my heart. He had his gun, and I had mine; I had taken it to shoot a squirrel which meddled with our firework nonsense. I tore her from him before I could speak, thrust her aside, stepped back two paces, gave him 'one, two, three,' and fired. He had time to fire in self-defence, and his muzzle was at my head, and his finger on the trigger; but there it crooked, and he could not pull. Want of nerve, I suppose. I saw his finger shaking, and then I saw him fall. Now, my son, you know everything."

" Why, father, after all then, it was nothing worse than a duel. He had just the same chance of killing you, and would have done it, only you were too quick for him."

" Even to retain your love, I will have no lie in the matter, Bob, although a duel, in my opinion, is only murder made game of. But this was no duel, no manslaughter even, but an act of down-right murder. No English jury could help con-victing me, and I will never plead insanity. It was the inevitable result of inborn violence and self-will, growing and growing from year to year, and strengthened by wrongs of which you know nothing. God knows that I have fought against it; but my weapon was pride, not humility. Now let this miserable subject never be recurred to by us, at least in words, till the end comes. As soon as I hear that poor innocent Cradock is apprehended, and brought to England, I shall surrender myself and confess. But for your sake and poor Pearly's, I should have done so at the very outset. Now it is very likely that I may not have the option. Two persons know that I did it, although they have no evidence, so far as I am aware; a third person more than suspects it, and is seeking about for the evidence. Moreover, Sir Cradock Nowell, to whom, as I told you, I owned my deed, although he could not then understand me, may have done so since, or may hereafter do so, at any lucid interval."

"Oh, father, father, he never would be so mean——"

"He is bound by his duty to do it—and for his living son's sake he must. I only tell you these things, my son, to spare you a part of the shock. One month now is all I crave, to do my best for you two darlings. I will not ruin the chance by going again to Sir Cradock. God saved me from my own rash words, doubtless for your pure sake. Now, knowing all, and reflecting upon it, can you call me still your father, Bob?"

This was one of the times that tell whether a father has through life thought more of himself or of his children. If of himself, they fall away, like Southern ivies in a storm, parasites which cannot cling, but glide on the marble surface. But if he has made his future of them, closer they cling, and clasp more firmly, like our British ivy engrailed into the house wall.

So the Garnet family clung together, although no longer blossoming, but flagging sorely with blight and canker, and daily fear of the woodman. Bob, of course, avoided Eoa, to her great indignation, though he could not quite make up his mind to tell her that all was over, without showing reason for it. In the forcing temperature of trouble, he was suddenly become a man, growing daily more like his father, in all except the violence. He roamed no more through the wilds of the forest, but let the birds nest comfortably, the butterflies hover in happiness, and the wireworm cast his shard unchallenged. He would care for all those things again, if he ever recovered his comfort.

Now Eoa, as everybody knew, did not by any means embody the spirit of toleration. She would hardly allow any will but her own in anything that concerned her. In a word, she was a child, a very warm-hearted and lovely one, but therefore all the more requiring a strong will founded on common sense to lead her into the life-brunt. And so, · if she must have Bob some day, she had better have him consolidated, though reduced to three per cent.

Not discerning her own interests, she would have been wild as a hare ought to be at the vernal equinox, but for one little fact. There was nobody to

be jealous of. Darling Amy, whom she loved as
all young ladies love one another—until they see
cause to the contrary—sweet thing, she was gone
to Oxford with her dear, good father. They had
slipped off without any fuss at all (except from
Biddy O'Gaghan, who came and threw an old shoe
at them), because Mr. Rosedew, in the first place,
felt that he could not bear it, and thought, in the
second place, that it would be an uncourteous act
towards Sir Cradock Nowell to allow any demon-
stration. And yet it was notorious that even Job
Hogstaff had arranged to totter down on Mark
Stote's arm, followed by a dozen tenants (all of
whom had leases), and the rank and file of Nowelhurst, who had paid their house-rent; and then
there would be a marshalling outside the parsonage-
gate; and upon the appearance of the fly, Job
with his crutch would testify, whereupon a shout
would arise pronouncing everlasting divorce between Church and State in Nowelhurst, undying
gratitude to the former, and defiance to the latter
power.

Yet all this programme was nullified by the departure of John and his household gods at five
o'clock one May morning. Already he had received assurance from some of his ancient co-
mates at Oriel (most cohesive of colleges) that they
would gladly welcome him, and find him plenty
of work to do. In less than six weeks' time, of
course, the long vacation would begin. What of
that? Let him come at once, and with his wide-

spread reputation he must have the pick of all the
men who would stay up to read for honours. For
now the fruit of a lifetime lore was ripening over
his honoured head, not (like that of Tantalus)
wafted into the cloud-land, not even waiting to be
plucked at, but falling unawares into his broad
and simple bosom, where it might lie uncared for,
except for the sake of Amy. So large a mind had
long outlived the little itch for fame, quite untruly
called "the last infirmity of noble minds." Their
first it is, beyond all doubt; and wisely nature
orders it. Their last is far more apt to be—at
least in this generation—contempt of fame, and
man, and God, except for practical purposes.

Mr. Rosedew's careful treatises upon the Sabel-
lian and Sabello-Oscan elements had stirred up
pleasant controversy in the narrow world of scho-
lars; and now at the trito-megistic blow of the
Roseo-rorine hammer, ringing upon no less a
theme than the tables of Iguvium, the wise men
who sit round the board of classical education,
even Jupiter Grabovius (the original of John
Bull), had clapped their hands and cried, "Hear,
hear! He knows what he is talking of; and he is
one of us."

That, after all, is the essence of it—to know
what one is talking of. And the grand advantage
of the ancient universities is, not the tone of manners, not the knowledge of life—rather a hat-box
thing with them—not even the high ideal, the
manliness, and the chivalry, which the better class

of men win ; but the curt knowledge, whether or
not they are talking of what they know. *Scire
quod nescias* is taught, if they teach us nothing
else.   And though we are all still apt to talk,
especially among ladies, of things beyond our acquaintance—else haply we talk but little—we do
so with a qualm, and quasi, and fluttering sense
that effrontery is not—but leads to—" pluck."

Nevertheless, who am I to talk, proving myself,
by every word, false to Alma Mater, having ventured all along to talk of things beyond me ?

As they rose the hill towards Carfax, Amy
(tired as she was) trembled with excitement.   Her
father had won a cure in St. Oles—derived no
doubt from *oleo*—and all were to lodge in Pembroke Lane, pending mature arrangements. Though
they might have turned off near the jail, and saved
a little cab fare, John would go by the broader way,
as his fashion always was ; except in a little post-
humous matter, wherein perhaps we have over-
defined with brimstone the direction-posts.

Be that as it may,—not to press the *scire quod
nescias* (potential in such a case, I hope, rather
than conjunctive) —there they must be left, all
three, with Jenny and Jemima outside, and Jem
Pottles on the pavement, amazed at the cheek of
everything.   Only let one thing be said.   Though
prettier girl than Amy Rosedew had never stepped
on the stones of Oxford since the time of Amy
Robsart, if even then,—never once was she in-
sulted.

Lowest of all low calumnies. There are black-guards among university men, as everybody knows, and as there must be among all men. But even those blackguards can see the difference between a lady, or rather between a pure girl and—another. And even those blackguards have an intensified reverence for the one;—but let the matter pass; for now we hide in gold these subjects, and sham not to see their flaunting.

Be it, however, confessed that Amy (whose father soon had rooms in college, not to live, but to lecture in), being a very shy young maiden, never could be brought to come and call him to his tea,—oh no. So many young men in gorgeous trappings, charms, and dangles, and hooks of gold, and eye-glasses very knowing — not to mention volunteer stuff, and knickerbockers demonstrant of calf—oddly enough they *would* happen to feel so interested in the architecture of the porter's lodge whenever Amy came by, never gazing too warmly at her, but contriving to convey their regret at the suppression of their sentiments, and their yearning to be the stones she trod on, and their despair at the possibility of her not caring if they were so—really all this was so trying, that Amy would never go into college without Aunt Doxy before her, gazing four-gunned cupolas even at scouts and manciples. And this was very pro-voking of her, not only to the hearts that beat under waistcoats ordered for her sake, but also to the domestic kettle a-boil in Pembroke Lane.

For, over and over again, Uncle John, great as
he was in chronology and every kind of "mar-
mora," and able to detect a flaw upon Potamo-
geiton's tombstone, lost all sense of time and place,
me and *te*, and *hocce* and Doxy, and calmly went
home some two hours late, and complacently received Doxology.

But alas, we must abandon Amy to the insidious
designs of Hebdomadal Board, the velvet ap-
proaches of Proctor and Pro, and the brass of the
gentlemen Bedels, while we regard more rugged
scenes, from which she was happily absent.

Rufus Hutton had found the missing link, and
at the same time the strongest staple, of the de-
sired evidence. The battered gun-barrels had
been identified, and even the number deciphered,
by the foreman of Messrs. L—— and Co. And
the entry in their books of the sale of that very
gun (number, gauge, and other particulars beyond
all doubt corresponding) was—"to Bull Garnet,
&c., Nowelhurst Dell Cottage," whom also they
could identify from his " strongly-marked physiog-
nomy," and his quick, decisive manner. And the
cartridge-case, which had lain so long in Dr.
Hutton's pocket, of course they could not depose
to its sale, together with the gun; but this they
could show, that it fitted the gauge, was not at all
of a common gauge, but two sizes larger—No. 10,
in fact—and must have been sold during the
month in which they sold the gun, because it was
one of a sample which they had taken upon

approval, and soon discarded for a case of better manufacture.

Then as to motive, Rufus Hutton himself could depose to that, or the probability of it, from what he had seen, but not understood, at the fixing of the fireworks; neither had he forgotten the furious mood of Bull Garnet, both then and in his garden.

While he was doubting how to act—for, clearly as he knew his power to hang the man who had outraged him, the very fact of his injury made him loth to use that power; for he was not at all a vindictive man, now the heat of the thing was past, and he saw that the sudden attack had been made in self-defence—while he was hesitating between his sense of duty and pity for Cradock on one hand, and his ideas of magnanimity and horror of hanging a man on the other, he was thrown, without any choice or chance, across the track of Simon Chope.

Perhaps there is no more vulgar error, no stronger proof of ignorance and slavery to catch-words, than to abuse or think ill of any particular class of men, solely on account of their profession —although, perhaps, we might justly throw the *onus probandi* their merit upon hangmen, body-snatchers, informers, and a few others—yet may I think (deprecating most humbly the omen of this conjunction) that solicitors, tailors, and Metho-dist parsons fight at some disadvantage both in fact and in fiction? Yet can they hold their

R 2

own ; and sympathy, if owing, is sure to have to
pay them—notwithstanding, goose, and amen.

Away with all feeble flippancy! Heavy tidings
came to Nowelhurst Hall, Dell Cottage, and
Geopharmacy Lodge, simultaneously, as might
be, on the 20th of June. The *Taprobane* had
been lost, with every soul on board; and this is
the record of it, enshrined in many journals :—

" By recent advices from Capetown, per the
screw-steamer *Sutler*, we sincerely regret to learn
that the magnificent clipper-built ship *Taprobana*,
of 2200 tons (new system), A 1 at Lloyd's for
15 years, and bound from the Thames to Colombo,
with a cargo valued by competent judges at
120,000*l.*, took the shore in Benguela Bay during
a typhoon of unprecedented destructiveness. It is
our melancholy duty to add that the entirety of
the valuable cargo was entirely lost, although very
amply assured in unexceptionable quarters, and
that every soul on board was consigned to a watery
grave. A Portuguese gentleman of good family
and large fortune, who happened to be in the
neighbourhood, was an eye-witness to the catastrophe, and made superhuman exertions to rescue
the unfortunate mariners, but, alas! in vain.
Senhor José de Calcavello has arrived at the
conclusion that some of her copper may be saved.
The ill-fated bark broke up so rapidly, from the
powerful action of the billows, that her identity
could only be established from a portion of her

sternpost, which was discovered half buried in
sand three nautical miles to the southward. We
have been informed, upon good authority, although
we are not at liberty to mention our source of
information, that Her Britannic Majesty's steam-
corvette *Mumbo Jumbo*, pierced for twenty-eight
guns, and carrying two, is under orders to depart,
as soon as ever she can be coaled, for the scene
of the recent catastrophe. Meanwhile, the tug
Growler has arrived with all the memorials of
the calamity, after affording the rites of sepulture
to the poor shipwrecked mariners cast up by the
treacherous billows. The set of the current being
so adverse, we have reason to fear that the rest of
the bodies must have fallen a prey to the monsters
of the deep. There are said to be some hopes of
recovering a portion of the specie."

Mrs. Corklemore happened to be calling at
Geopharmacy Lodge, when the London papers
arrived in the early afternoon. Rufus begged
pardon, and broke the cover, to see something in
which he was interested. Presently he cried,
" Good God ! " and let the paper fall ; and,
seasoned as he was, and shallowed by the shifting
of his life, it was not in his power to keep two
little tears from twinkling.

" Too late all my work," he said ; " Heaven has
settled it without me."

" How very sad ! " cried Mrs. Corklemore,
dashing aside an unbidden tear, when she came

to the end of the story; to think of all those brave men lost! And perhaps you knew some of them, Dr. Hutton? Oh, I am so sorry!"

" Why, surely you know that the *Taprobane* was the ship in which poor Cradock Nowell sailed, under Mr. Rosedew's auspices."

" Oh, I hope not. Please not to say so. It would be so very horrible! That he should go without repenting——"

" You must have forgotten, Mrs. Corklemore ; for I heard Rosa tell you the name of the ship, and her destination."

" Oh, very likely. Ah, now I remember. For the moment it quite escaped me. How truly, truly grieved— it has quite overcome me. Oh, please not to notice me—please not. I am so stupidly soft-hearted. Oh—ea, isha, ea !"

No woman in the world could cry more beautifully than poor Georgie. And now she cried her very best. It would have gone to the heart of the driest and bitterest sceptic that ever doubted all men and women because they would doubt him. But Rufus, whose form of self-assertion was not universal negation, in what manner then do you suppose that Rufus Hutton was liquefied? A simple sort of fellow he was (notwithstanding all his shrewdness), although, or perhaps I should say because, he thought himself so knowing; and his observation was more the result of experience than the cause of it. So away he ran to fetch Rosa, and

Rosa wiped dear, sensitive Georgie's eyes, and coaxed her very pleasantly, and admired her more than ever.

Bull Garnet rode home at twelve o'clock from a long morning's work. He never could eat any breakfast now, and his manner was to leave home at six (except when he went to Winchester), gallop fiercely from work to work, or sometimes walk his horse and think, often with glistening eyes (when any little thing touched him), and return to his cottage and rest there during the workmen's dinner-time. Then he had some sort of a meal himself, which Pearl began to call "dinner," and away with a fresh horse in half an hour, spending his body if only so he might earn rest of mind. All this was telling upon him fearfully; even his muscular force was going, and his quickness of eye and hand failing him. He knew it, and was glad.

Only none should ever say, though every crime was heaped upon him, that he had neglected his master's interests.

He tore the paper open in his sudden turbulent fashion, as if all paper was rags, and no more; and with one glance at each column knew all that was in the 'tween-ways. Suddenly he came to a place at the corner of a page which made him cease from eating. He glanced at Pearl, but she was busy, peeling new potatoes for him. Bob was not come in yet.

"Darling, I must go to London. If possible I shall return to-night, if I catch the one o'clock up express."

Then he opened the window, and ordered a horse, his loud voice ringing and echoing round every corner of the cottage, and in five minutes he was off at full gallop, for the express would not stop at Brockenhurst.

At 3.15 he was in London, and at 3.40 in the counting-house of Messrs. Brown and Smithson, owners, or at any rate charterers, of the *Taprobane*, Striped-ball Chambers, Fenchurch Street. There he would learn, if he could, what their private advices were.

The clerks received him very politely, and told him that they had little doubt of the truth of the evil tidings. Of course the fatality might have been considerably exaggerated, &c. &c., but as to the loss of the ship, they had taken measures to replace her. Would he mind waiting only ten minutes, though they saw that he was in a hurry? The Cape mail-ship had been telegraphed from Falmouth; they had sent to the office already, and expected to get the reply within a quarter of an hour. Every information in their power, &c.—we all know the form, though we don't always get the civility.

Bull Garnet waited heavily with his great back against a stout brass rail, having declined the chair they offered him; and in less than five minutes he received authentic detail of everything. He listened

to nothing except one statement, "every soul on
board was lost, sir."

Then he went out, in a lumpish manner, from
the noble room, and was glad to get hold of the iron
rail in the bend of the dark stone staircase.

So now he was a double murderer. Finding it
not enough to have killed one brother in his fury,
he had slain the other twin through his cowardly
concealment. Floating about in tropical slime,
without a shark to eat him, leaving behind him the
fair repute of a money-grabbing fratricide. And
he, the man who had done it all, who had loved the
boy and ruined him, miserably plotting for his own
far inferior children. No, no! Not that at any
rate,—good and noble children : and how they had
borne his villainy! God in mercy only make him,
try to make him, over again, and how different his
life would be. All his better part brought out; all
his lower kicked away to the devil, the responsible
father of it. "Good God, how my heart goes!
Death is upon me, well I know, but let me die with
my children by—unless I turn hymn-writer——"

Quick as he was in his turns of thought—all of
them subjective—he was scarcely a match for the
situation, when Mr. Chope and Bailey Kettledrum
brushed by the sleeves of his light overcoat, and
entered the doors with "push—pull" on them, but,
being both of the pushing order rather than the
pulling, employed indiscriminate propulsion, and
were out of sight in a moment. Still, retaining
some little of his circumspective powers, Bull Gar-

net knew them both from a corner flash of his sad
tear-laden eyes. There was no mistaking that great
legal head, like the breech-end of a cannon. Mr.
Kettledrum might have been overlooked, for little
men of a fussy nature are common enough in
London, or for that matter everywhere else. But
Garnet's attention being drawn, he knew them both
of course, and the errand they were come upon, and
how soon they were likely to return, and what they
would think of his being there, if they should
happen to see him. Nevertheless, he would not
budge. Nothing could matter much now. He
must think out his thoughts.

When this puff of air was past which many
breathe almost long enough to learn that it was
"life," some so long as to weary of it, none so long
as to understand all its littleness and greatness—
when that should be gone from him, and absorbed
into a boundless region even more unknown, would
not the wrong go with it, if unexpiated here, and
abide there evermore? And not to think of himself alone—what an example now to leave to his
innocent injured children! The fury hidden by
treachery, the cowardice sheathed in penitence!
D——n it all, he would have no more of it. His
cursed mind was made up. A man can die in the
flesh but once. His spirit had been dying daily,
going to the devil daily, every day for months; and
he found no place for repentance. As for his
children, they must abide it. No man of any
mind would blame them for their father's crime.

If it was more than they could bear, let them bolt to America. Anywhither, anywhere, so long as they came home in heaven—if he could only get there—to the father who had injured, ruined, bullied, cursed, and loved them so.

After burning out this hell of thought in his miserable brain, he betook himself to nature's remedy,—instant, headlong action. He rushed down the stairs, forgetting all about Chope and Bailey Kettledrum, shouted to the driver of a hansom cab so that he sawed his horse's mouth raw, leaped in, and gave him half a sovereign through the pigeon-hole, to get to D——'s bank before the closing time. But at Temple Bar, of course, there was a regular Chubb's lock, after a minor Bramah one at the bottom of Ludgate Hill. Cabby was forced to cut it, and slash up Chancery Lane, and across by King's College Hospital, and back into the Strand by Wych Street. It is easy to imagine Bull Garnet's state of mind; yet the imagination would be that, and nothing more. He sat quite calmly, without a word, knowing that man and horse were doing their utmost of skill and speed, and having dealt enough with both to know that to worry them then is waste.

The Bank had been closed, the day-porter said, as he girded himself for his walk to Brixton, exactly—let him see—yes, exactly one minute and thirty-five seconds ago. Most of the gentlemen were still inside, of course, and if the gentleman's business was of a confidential—— Here he intimated, not by words, that there were considerations——

"Bow Street police-office," Mr. Garnet cried to the driver, not even glancing again at the disappointed doorkeeper. In five minutes he was there. Man and horse seemed strung and nerved with his own excitement.

A stolid policeman stood at the door, as Bull Garnet leaped out anyhow, with his high colour gone away as in death, and his wiry legs cramped with vehemence. Then Bobby saw that he had met his master, the perception being a mental feat far beyond the average leap of police agility. Accordingly he touched his hat, and crinkled his eyes in a manner discovered by policemen, in consequence of the suggestion afforded by the pegging of their hats.

"Mr. Bennings gone?" asked Bull Garnet, pushing towards the entrance.

"His wusship is gone arf an hour, sir; or may be at most fifty minutes. Can we do anything for you, sir? His wusship always go according to the business as is on."

"Thank you," replied Mr. Garnet; "that is quite enough. What time do they leave at Marlborough Street?"

"According to the business, sir, but gone afore us a'most always. We sits as long as anybody, and gets through twice the business. But any message you like to leave, or anything to be entered, I can take the responsibility."

"No. It does not matter. I will only leave

my card. Mr. Bennings knows me. Be kind
enough to give him this, when he comes to-morrow
morning. Perhaps I may call to-morrow. At present I cannot say."

The policeman lifted his hat again, like a cup
taken up from a saucer, and Bull Garnet sat heavily
down in the cab, and banged the door-shutters
before him. " Strand," he called out to the driver;
" D—— and C——'s, the watchmakers." There
he bought a beautiful watch and gold chain for
his daughter Pearl, giving a cheque for nearly all
his balance at the banker's. The cheque was so
large that in common prudence the foreman declined to cash it without some confirmation; but
Mr. Garnet gave him a reference, which in ten
minutes was established, and in ten more he was off
again with his very handsome trinkets, and a large
sum in bank-notes and gold, the balance of his
draft.

" Where now, sir?" shouted the driver, delighted with his fare, and foreseeing another half-
sovereign.

" I will tell you in thirty seconds."

" Well, if he ain't a rum 'un," Cabby muttered
to himself, while amid volleys of strong language
. he kept his horse gyrating, like a twin-screw ship
trying circles; "but rum customers is our wind-
falls. Should have thought it a reward case, only
for the Bobby. Keep a look-out, anyhow; unless
he orders me back to Bedlam."

" Not Bedlam. Waterloo Station, main line ! "
said Bull Garnet, standing up in front, and looking

at him over the roof.   "Five minutes is all I give
you, mind."

"What a blessed fool I am," said the cabman
below his breath, but lashing his horse explosively
—"to throw away half a sovereign sooner than
hold my tongue!   He must be the devil himself
to have heard me—and as for eyes—good Lord,
I shouldn't like to drive him much."

"You are wrong," replied Mr. Garnet through
the pigeon-hole, handing him twopence for the
tollman ; "I am not the devil, sir ; as you may
some day know.   Have no fear of ever driving
me again.   You shall have your half-sovereign
when I have got my ticket.   Follow me in, and
you shall know for what place I take it."

The cabman was too dumb-foundered to do anything but resolve that he would go straight home
when he got his money, and tell his old woman
about it.   Then he applied himself to the whip in
earnest, for he could not too soon be rid of this
job; and so Bull Garnet won his train, and gave
the driver the other half-sovereign, with a peculiar
nod, having noticed that he feared to approach
while the ticket was applied for.

Bull Garnet took a second-class ticket.   His
extravagance towards the cabman was the last he .
would ever exhibit.   He felt a call upon him now
to save for his family every farthing.   All was lost
to them but money, and alas, too much of that.
Now if he cut his throat in the train, could he be
attainted of felony ?   And would God be any the

harder on him? No, he did not think He would.
It might be some sort of atonement even. But
then the shock to Pearl and Bob, to see him brought
home with his head hanging back, and hopeless
red stitches under it. It would make the poor girl
a maniac, after all the shocks and anguish he had
benumbed her with already. What a fool he had
been not to buy strychnine, prussic acid, or lauda-
num! And yet—and yet—and yet——— He
would like to see them just once more—blessed
hearts—once more.

He sat in the last compartment of the last carriage in the train, which had been added, in a hurry,
immediately behind the break van, and the swing-
ing and the jerking very soon became tremendous.
He knew not, neither cared to know, that Simon
Chope and Bailey Kettledrum were in a first-class
carriage near the centre of the train. Presently
the violent motion began to tell upon him, and he
felt a heavy dulness creeping over his excited mind;
and all the senses, which had been during several
hours of tension as prompt and acute as ever they
were in his prime of power, began to flag, and
daze, and wane, and he fell into a waking dream,
a "second person" of sorrow. But first—whether
for suicide, or for self-defence, he had tried both
doors and found them locked; and he was far
too large a man to force his way through the
window.

He dreamed, with a loose sense of identity,
about the innocent childhood, the boyhood's aspi-

ration, the young man's sense of ability endorsing
the right to aspire.   Even his bodily power and
vigour revived in the dream before him, and he
knitted his muscles, and clenched his fists, and was
ready to fight fools and liars.   Who had fought
more hard and hotly against the hard cold ways of
the age, the despite done to the poor and lowly, the
sarcasm bred by self-conscious serfdom in clever
men of the world, the preference of gold to love,
and of position to happiness?   All the weak gregarious tricks, shifts of coat, and pupa-ism, whereby
we noble Christians reduce our social history to
a passage in entomology, and quench the faith of
thinking men in Him whose name we take in vain
—the great Originator—all these feminine contra-
dictions, and fond things foully invented, fables
Atellan (if they be not actually Fescennine) had
roused the combatism of young Bull, ere he learned
his own disgrace.

     And when he learned it, such as it was—a proof
by its false incidence how infantile our civilization
is—all his mother's bitter wrong, her lifelong sense
of shame and crushing (because she had trusted a
liar, and the hollow elder-stick "institution" was
held up against her, and none would take her part
without money, even if she had wished it), then he
had chosen his mother's course, inheriting her strong
nature, let the shame lie where it fell by right and
not by rule, and carried all his energies into Neo-
Christian largeness.

     All that time of angry trial now had passed

before him, and the five years of his married life (which had not been very happy, for his wife never understood him, but met his quick moodiness with soft sulks); and then in his dream-review he smiled, as his children began to toddle about, and sit on his knees, and look at him.

Once he awoke, and gazed about him. The train had stopped at Winchester. He was all alone in the carriage still, and all his cash was safe. He had stowed it away very carefully in a hidden pocket. To his languid surprise, he fell back on the seat. How unlike himself, to be sure; and with so much yet to do! He strove to arise and rouse himself. He felt for the little flask of wine, which Pearl had thrust into his pocket, but he could not pull it out and drink; such a languor lay upon him. He had felt it before, but never before been so overcome by it. Once or twice, an hour or so before the sun came back again, this strange cold deadness (like a mammoth nightmare frozen) had lain on him, in his lonely bed, and then he knew what death was, and only came back to life again through cold sweat and long fainting.

He had never consulted any doctor about the meaning of this. With his bold way of thinking, and judging only by his own experience and feeling, he had long ago decided that all medical men were quacks. What one disorder could they cure? All they had learned, and that by a fluke, was a way to anticipate *one :* and even that way seemed worn out now.

Now he fell away, and feared, and tried to squeeze his breast, and tried to pray to God; but no words came, nor any thoughts, only sense of dying, and horror at having prayed for it. A coldness fell upon his heart, and on his brain an ignorance; he was falling into a great blank depth, and nothing belonged to him any more—only utter, utter loss, and not a dream of God.

Happy and religious folk, who have only died in theory, contemplating distant death, knowing him only as opportune among kinsfolk owning Consols, these may hope for a Prayer-book end, sacrament administered, weeping friends, the heavenward soul glad to fly through the golden door, *animula, vagula, blandula*, yet assured of its reception with a heavenly smile of foretaste—this may be; no doubt it may be, after the life of a Christian Bayard; though it need not always be, even then. All we who from our age know death, and have taken little trips into him, through fits, paralysis, or such-like, are quite aware that he has at first call as much variety as life has. But the death of the violent man is not likely to be placid, unless it come unawares, or has been graduated through years of remorse, and weakness, weariness, and repentance.

Then he tried to rise, and fought once more, with agony inconceivable, against the heavy yet hollow numbness in the hold of his deep, wide chest, against the dark, cold stealth of death, and the black, narrow depth of the grave.

The train ran lightly and merrily into Brockenhurst Station, while the midsummer twilight floated
like universal gossamer. In the yard stood the
Kettledrum " rattletrap," and the owner was right
glad to see it. In his eyes it was worth a dozen
of the lord mayor's coach.

" None of the children come, dear?" asked
Bailey, having kissed his wife, as behoves a man
from London.

" No, darling, not one. That——" here she
used an adjective which sounded too much like
" odious" for me to trust my senses—" Georgie
would not allow them. Now, darling, did you do
exactly what I told you?"

" Yes, darling Anna, I did the best I could. I
had a basin of mulligatawny at Waterloo going
up, and one of mock-turtle coming back, and at
Basingstoke ham-sandwiches, a glass of cold cognac
and water, and some lemon-chips. Since that, nothing at all, because there has been no time."

" You are a dear," said Mrs. Kettledrum, " to
do exactly as I told you. Now come round the
corner a moment, and take two glasses of sherry;
I can see quite well to pour it out. I am so glad
of her new crinoline. She won't get out. Don't
be afraid, dear."

Oh, Georgie, Georgie! To think that her
own sister should be so low, so unfeeling, and
treacherous! Mr. Kettledrum smacked his lips,
for the sake of euphony, after the second glass of
sherry; but his wife would not give him any more,

for fear of spoiling his supper. Then they came back, and both got in, and squeezed themselves up together in the front seat of the old carriage, for Mrs. Corklemore occupied the whole of the seat of honour.

"You are very polite, to keep me so long. Innocent turtles; sweet childish anxiety! The last survivor of a wrecked train! So you took advantage, Anna dear, of my not being dressed quite so vulgarly as you are, to discuss this little matter with him, keeping me in ignorance."

The carriage was off by this time, and open as it was, they had no fear of old coachey hearing, for it took a loud hail to reach him.

"Take the honour of a Kettledrum," cried Bailey, smiting his bosom, "that the subject has not even been broached between my wiser part and myself. Ladies, in this pure aerial—no, I mean ethereal—air, with the shades of night around us, and the breezes wafting, would an exceedingly choice and delicately aromatic cigar——"

"Oh, I should so like it, Bailey; and perhaps we shall have the nightingales."

"I fear we must not think of it," interposed Mrs. Corklemore, gently; "my dress is of a fabric quite newly introduced, very beautiful, but (like myself) too retentive of impressions. If Mr. Kettledrum smokes, I shall have to throw it away."

"There goes the cigar instead," cried Bailey;

"the paramount rights of ladies ever have been, and ever shall be, sacred with Bailey Kettle-drum."

But Mrs. Kettledrum was so vexed that she jumped up, as if to watch the cigar spinning into the darkness, and contrived with sisterly accuracy to throw all her weight upon a certain portion of a certain lovely foot, whereupon there ensued the neatest little passes, into which we need not enter. Enough that Mrs. Corklemore, having higher intellectual gifts, "won," in the language of the ring, "both events"—first tear, and first hysterical symptom.

"Come," cried Mr. Kettledrum, at the very first opportunity, to wit, when both were crying; "we all know what sisters are : how they mingle the—the sweetness of their affection with a certain—ah, yes—a piquancy of expression, most pleasant, most improving, because so highly conducive to self-examination!" Here he stood up, having made a hit, worthy of the House of Commons. "All these little breezes, ladies, may be called the trade-winds of affection. They blow from pole to pole."

"The trade-winds never do that," said Georgie.

"They pass us by as the idle wind, when the clouds are like a whale, ladies, having overcome us for a moment, like a summer dream. Hark to that thrush, sitting perhaps on his eggs"—"Oh, Oh!" from the gallery of nature—"can there be,

I pause for a reply, anything but harmony, where the voices of the night pervade, and the music of the spheres?"

"You — you do speak so splendidly, dear," sobbed Mrs. Kettledrum from the corner; "but it is a nasty, wicked, cruel story, about dear papa saying that of me, and he in his grave, poor dear, quite unable to vindicate himself. I have always thought it so unchristian to malign the dead!"

"What's that?" cried Georgie, starting up, in fear and hot earnest; "you are chattering so, you hear nothing."

A horse dashed by them at full gallop, with his rider on his neck, shouting and yelling, and clinging and lashing.

"Missed the wheel by an inch," cried Kettledrum, drawing his head in faster than he had thrust it out; "a fire, man, or a French invasion?" But the man was out of hearing, while the Kettledrum horses, scared, and jumping as from an equine thunderbolt, tried the strength of leather and the courage of ladies.

Meanwhile at the station behind them there was a sad ado. A man was lifted out of the train, being found in the last compartment by the guard who knew his destination—a big man, and a heavy one; and they bore him to the wretched shed which served there as a waiting-room.

"Dead, I believe," said the guard, having sent a boy for brandy, "dead as a door-nail, whoever he be."

"Not thee knaw who *he* be?" cried a forester, coming in.   "Whoy, marn, there be no mistaking *he*.   He be our Muster Garnet."

"Whew!"   And the train whistled on, as it must do, whether we live or die, or when Cyclops has made mince of us.

CHAPTER XVI.

THAT night there had been great excitement in
the village of Nowelhurst. A rumour had reached
it that Cradock Nowell, loved in every cottage
there, partly as their own production, partly as
their future owner, partly for his own sake, and
most of all for his misfortunes, was thrown into
prison to stand his trial for the murder of his
brother. Another rumour was that, to prevent any
scandal to the nobility, he had been sent to sea
alone in a seventy-four gun ship, with corks in her
bottom tied with wire arranged so as to fly all at
once, same as if it was ginger-beer bottles, on the
seventh day, when the salt-water had turned the
wires rusty.

It is hard to say of these two reports which
roused the greater indignation; perhaps on the
whole the former did, because the latter was supposed to be according to institution. Anyhow, all

the village was out in the street that night; and
the folding of arms, and the self-importance, the
confidential winks, and the power to say more (but
for hyper-Nestorean prudence) were at their acme
in a knot of gaffers gathered around Rufus Hutton,
and affording him good sport.

Nothing now could be done in Nowelhurst without Rufus Hutton. He had that especial knack
(mistaken sometimes in a statesman for really high
qualities) which becomes in a woman true capacity
for gossip. By virtue thereof Rufus Hutton was
now prime-minister of Nowelhurst; and Sir Cradock, the king, being nothing more now than the
shadow of a name, his deputy's power was absolute.
He knew the history by this time of every cottage,
and pigsty, and tombstone in the churchyard; how
much every man got every week, and how much
he gave his wife out of it, what he had for dinner
on Sundays, and how long he made his waistcoat
last. Suddenly the double-barrelled noise which
foreruns a horse at full gallop came from the
bridge, and old folk hobbled, and young got ready
to run.

" Hooraw—hooraw!" cried a dozen and a half
of boys, "here be Hempror o' Roosia coming."

Boys will believe almost anything, when they
get excited (having taken the trick from their
fathers), but even the women were disappointed,
when the galloping horse stopped short in the
crowd, and from his withers shot forward, and fell
with both hands full of mane, a personage not

more august than the porter at Brockenhurst
Station.

"Catch the horse, you fool!" cried Rufus.

"Cuss the horse," said the porter, trying to
draw breath; "better been under a train I had.
Don't stand gaping, chawbacons. Is ever a sawbones, surgeon, doctor, or what the devil you call
them in these outlandish parts, to be got for love
or money?"

"I am a sawbones," said Rufus Hutton, coming
forward with his utmost dignity; "and it's a mercy
I don't saw yours, young man, if that's all you
know of riding."

The porter touched his hair instead of his hat
(which was gone long ago), while the "chawbacons" rallied, and laughed at him, and one
offered him a "zide-zaddle," and all the women of
the village felt that Dr. Hutton had quenched the
porter, and vindicated Nowelhurst.

"When you have recovered your breath, young
man," continued Rufus, pushing, as he always did,
his advantage; "and thanked God for your escape
from the first horse you ever mounted, perhaps you
will tell us your errand, and we chawbacons will
consider it."

A gruff haw-haw and some treble he-he's added
to the porter's discomfiture, for he could not come
to time yet, being now in the second tense of
exhaustion, which is even worse than the first,
being rather of the heart than lungs.

"Station — Mr. Garnet — dead!" was all the

man could utter, and that only in spasms, and with great chest-heavings.

Rufus Hutton leaped on the horse in a moment, caught up old Channing's stick, and was out of sight in the summer dusk ere any one else in the crowd had done more than gape, and say, "Oh Lor!" By dint of skill he sped the old horse nearly as quickly to the station as the fury of Jehu had brought him thence, and landed him at the door with far less sign of exhaustion. Then walking into the little room, in the manner of a man who thoroughly knows his work, he saw a sight which never in this world will leave him.

Upon a hard sofa, shored up with an ash-log where the mahogany was sprung, and poked up into a corner as if to get a bearing there, with blankets piled upon him heavily and tucked round the collar of his coat, and his great head hanging over the rise where the beading of the brass ends, lay the ill-fated Bull Garnet,—a man from birth to death a subject for pity more than terror. Fifty years old — more than fifty years — and scarce a twelvemonth of happiness since the shakings of the world began, and childhood's dream was over. Toiling ever for the future, toiling for his children, ever since he had them, labouring to make peace with God, if only he might have his own, where passion is not, but love abides. The room smelled strongly of bad brandy, some of which was oozing now down his broad square chin, and dripping from the great blue jaw. Of course

he could not swallow it; and now one of the
women (for three had rushed in) was performing
that duty for him.

"Turn out that drunken hag!" cried Dr. Hutton, feeling he had no idea how. "Up with the
window. Bring the sofa here; and take all but
one of those blankets off."

"But, master," objected another woman, "he'll
take his death of cold."

"Turn out that woman also!" He was instantly obeyed. "Now roll up one of those
blankets, and put it under his head here—this side,
can't you see? Good God, what a set of fellows
you are to let a man's head hang down like that!
Hot water and a sponge this instant. Nearly
boiling, mind you. Plenty of it, and a foot-tub.
Now don't stare at me."

With a quick light hand he released the blue
and turgid throat from the narrow necktie, then
laid his forefinger upon the heart and watched the
eyelids intently.

"Appleplexy, no doubt, master," said the most
intelligent of the men; "I have 'eared that if you
can bleed them——"

"Hold your tongue, or I'll phlebotomise you."
That big word inspired universal confidence, because no one understood it. "Now, support him
in that position, while I pull his boots off. One
of you run to the inn for a bottle of French
cognac—not this filthy stuff, mind—and a cork-
screw and a teaspoon. Now the hot water here!

In with his feet, and bathe his legs, while I sponge his face and chest—as hot as you can bear your hands in it. His heart is all but stopped, and his skin as cold as ice. That's it; quicker yet! Don't be afraid of scalding him. There, he begins to feel it."

The dying man's great heavy eyelids slowly and feebly quivered, and a long deep sigh arose, but there was not strength to fetch it. Dr. Hutton took advantage of the faint impulse of life to give him a little brandy, and then a little more again, and by that time he could sigh.

"Bo," he whispered very softly, and trying to lift his hand for something, and Rufus Hutton knew somehow (perhaps by means of his own child) that he was trying to say, "Bob."

"Bob will be here directly. Cheer up, cheer up, till he comes, my friend."

He called him his friend, and the very next day he would have denounced him as murderer to the magistrates at Lymington. Now his only thought was of saving the poor man's life.

The father's dull eyes gleamed again when he heard those words, and a little smile came flickering over the stern lines of his face. They gave him more brandy on the strength of it, while he kept on looking at the door.

"Rub, rub, rub, men; very lightly, but very quickly. Keep your thumbs up, don't you see? Mustn't get cold again for the world. There now, he'll keep his heart up until his dear son arrives.

And then his children shall nurse him, much better than any one else could; and how glad they will be, John Thomas, to see him looking so well and so strong again!"

All this time, Rue Hutton himself, with a woman's skill and tenderness, was encouraging, by gentle friction over the stagnant heart, each feeble impulse yet to live, each little bubble faintly rising from the well of hope, every clinging of the soul to the things so hard to leave behind. "While there is life, there is hope." True and genial saying! And we hope there is hope beyond it.

Poor Bull Garnet was taken home, even that very night. For Dr. Hutton saw how much he was longing for his children, who (until he was carried in) knew nothing of his danger. "Please God," said Rufus to himself, as he crouched in the fly by the narrow mattress, even foregoing his loved cheroot, and keeping his hand on his patient's pulse; "please God, the poor fellow shall breathe his last with a child at either side of him."

Meanwhile, an urgent message from Sir Cradock Nowell was awaiting the sick man at his cottage. Eoa herself had brought word to Pearl (of whom she longed to make a friend) that her uncle was walking about the house, perpetually walking, calling aloud in every room for Mr. Garnet and John Rosedew. He had heard of no disaster, any more than she had, for he seldom read the papers now; but Mr. Brockwood had been with him a very long time that morning, and Dr.

Buller came in accidentally; and Eoa could almost vow that there was some infamous scheme on foot, and she knew whose doing it was; and oh that Uncle John would come back! But now they wanted Mr. Garnet, and he must hurry up to the Hall the moment he came home.

Mr. Garnet, of course, they could not have: his strength was wrecked, his heart benumbed, his mind incapable of effort, except to know his children, if that could ever be one. And in this paralytic state, never sleeping, never waking, never wholly conscious, he lay for weeks; and time for him had neither night nor morning.

But Mr. Rosedew could be brought to help his ancient friend, if only it was in his power to overlook the injury. He did not overlook it. For that he was too great a man. He utterly forgot it. To his mind it was thenceforth a thing that had never happened:

> " To-morrow either with black cloud
>   Let the Father fill the heaven,
>   Or with sun full-blazing:
>   Yet shall He not erase the past,
>   Nor beat abroad, and make undone,
>   What once the fleeting hour hath borne."

Truly so our Horace saith. And yet that Father gives, sometimes, to the noblest of his children, power to revoke the evil, or at least annul it,—grandeur to undo the wrong done by others to them. Not with any sense of greatness, neither hope of self-reward, simply from the lovingkindness of the deep humanity.

In truth it was a noble thing, such as not even
the driest man, sapped and carked with care and
evil, worn with undeserved rebuff, and dwelling
ever underground, in the undermining of his faith,
could behold and not be glad with a joy unbidden,
could turn away from without wet eyes, and a
glimpse of the God who loves us,—and yet the
simplest, mildest scene that a child could describe
to its mother. So will I tell it, if may be, casting
all long words away, leaning on an old man's staff,
looking over the stile of the world.

It was the height of the summer-time, and the
quiet mood of the setting sun touched with calm
and happy sadness all he was forsaking. Men
were going home from work; wives were looking
for them; maidens by the gate or paling longed
for some protection; children must be put to bed,
and what a shame, so early! Puce and purple
pillows lay, holding golden locks of sun, piled and
lifted by light breezes, the painted eider-down of
sunset. In the air a feeling was — those who
breathe it cannot tell—only this, that it does them
good; God knows how, and why, and whence—
but it makes them love their brethren.

The poor old man, more tried and troubled than
a lucky labourer, wretched in his wealth, worse
hampered by his rank and placement, sat upon a
high oak chair—for now he feared to lean his head
back—and prayed for some one to help him. Oh,
for any one who loved him; oh, for any sight of

God, whom in his pride he had forgotten! Eoa
was a darling, his only comfort now; but what
could such a girl do? Who was she to meet the
world? And the son he had used so shamefully.
Good God, his only son! And now he knew, with
some strange knowledge, loose, and wide, and wandering, that his son was innocent after all, and
lost to him for ever, through his own vile cruelty.
And now they meant to prove him mad—what use
to disguise it?—him who once had the clearest
head, chairman of the Quarter Sessions——

Here he broke down, and lay back, with his
white hair poured against the carved black oak of
the chair, and his wasted hands flung downward,
only praying God to help him, anyhow to help
him.

Then John Rosedew came in softly, half
ashamed of himself, half nervous lest he were
presuming, overdrawing the chords of youth, the
bond of the days when they went about with arm
round the neck of each other. In his heart was
pity, very deep and holy; and yet, of all that filled
his eyes, the very last to show itself.

Over against the ancient friend, the loved one of
his boyhood, he stopped and sadly gazed a moment,
and then drew back with a shock and sorrow, as of
death brought nearer. At the sound, Sir Cradock
Nowell lifted his weary eyes and sighed; and
then he looked intently; and then he knew the
honest face, the smile, the gentle forehead. Quietly

he arose, with colour flowing over his pallid cheeks, and in his eyes strong welcome, and ready with his lips to speak, yet in his heart unable. Thereupon he held the chair, and bowed with the deepest reverence, such as king or queen receives not till a life has earned it. Even the hand which he was raising he let fall again, drawn back by a bitter memory, and a nervous shame.

But his friend of olden time would not have him so disgraced, wanted no repentance. With years of kindness in his eyes and the history of friendship, he came, without a bow, and took the hand that now was shy of him.

" Cradock, oh, I am so glad."

" John, thank God for this, John !"

Then they turned to other subjects, with a sort of nervousness—the one for fear of presuming on pardon, the other for fear of offering it. Only both knew, once for all, that nothing more could come between them till the hour of death.

The rector accepted once again his well-beloved home and cares, for the vacancy had not been filled, only Mr. Pell had lived a short time at the Rectory. The joy of all the parish equalled, if not transcended, that of parson and of patron.

And, over and above the ease of conscience, and the sense of comfort, it was a truly happy thing for poor Sir Cradock Nowell, when the loss of the *Taprobane* could no longer be concealed from him, that now he had the proven friend to fall back upon once more. He had spent whole days in writing letters—humble, loving, imploring letters to the son in unknown latitudes—directing them as fancy took him to the Cape, to Port Natal, Mozambique, or even Bombay (in case of stress of weather), Point de Galle, Colombo, &c. &c., in all cases to be called for, and invariably marked "urgent." Then from this labour of love he awoke to a vague form of conviction that his letters ought to have been addressed to the bottom of the sea.

CHAPTER XVII.

AUTUMN in the Forest now, once again the
autumn. All things turning to their rest, bird,
and beast, and vegetable. Solemn and most
noble season, speaking to the soul of man, as
spring speaks to his body. The harvest of the
ample woods spreading every tint of ripeness,
waiting for the Maker's sickle, when His breath
is frost. Trees beyond trees, in depth and
height, roundings and massive juttings, some admitting flaws of light to enhance their mellowness,
some very bright of their own accord, when the
sun thought well of them, others scarcely bronzed
with age, and meaning to abide the spring. It
was the same in Epping Forest, Richmond Park,
and the woods round London, only on a smaller
scale, and with less variety. And so upon his
northern road, every coppice, near or far, even

" Knockholt Beeches " (which reminded him of the
" beechen hats "), every little winding wood of
Sussex or of Surrey brought before Cradock
Nowell's eyes the prospect of his boyhood. He
had begged to be put ashore at Newhaven, from
the American trader, which had rescued him from
Pomona Island, and his lonely but healthful so-
journ, and then borne him to New York. Now,
with his little store of dollars, earned from the
noble Yankee skipper by the service he had ren-
dered him, freely given and freely taken, as
behoves two gentlemen, and with his great store
of health recovered, and recovered mind, he must
walk all the way to London, forty miles or more;
so great a desire entered into him of his native
land, that stable versatility, those free and ever-
changing skies, which all her sons abuse and love.

Cradock looked, I do assure you, as well, and
strong, and stout, and lusty, as may consist with
elegance at the age of two-and-twenty. And his
dress, though smacking of Broadway, " could not
conceal," as our best writers say, " his symmetrical
proportions." His pantaloons were of a fine bright
tan colour, with pockets fit for a thousand dollars,
and his boots full of eyelets, like big lampreys, and
his coat was a thing to be proud of, and a pleasing
surprise for Regent-street. His hat, moreover, was
umbratile, as of the Pilgrim Fathers, with a measure of liquid capacity (betwixt the cone and the
turned-up rim) superior to that of the ordinary
cisterns of the London water-companies. Never-

theless he had not acquired the delightful hydro-
pultic art, distinctive of the mighty nation which
had been so kind to him. And, in spite of little
external stuff (only worthy of two glances—one to
note, and the other to smile at it), the youth was
improved in every point worth a man's observation.
Three months in New York had done him an
enormous deal of good; not that the place is by
any means heavenly (perhaps there are few more
hellish), only that he fell in with men of extraordinary energy and of marvellous decision, the
very two hinges of life whereupon he (being rather
too "philosophical") had several screws loose, and
some rust in the joints.

As for Wena, she (the beauty) had cocked her
tail with great arrogance at smelling English
ground again. To her straight came several dogs,
who had never travelled far (except when they
were tail-piped), and one and all cried, "Hail, my
dear! Have you seen any dogs to compare with
us? Set of mongrel parley-woos, can't bark or
bite like a Christian. Just look round the corner,
pretty, while we kill that poodle."

To whom Wena—*leniter atterens caudam*—" Cor-
dially I thank you. So much now I have seen of
the world that my faith is gone in tail-wags. If
you wish to benefit by my society, bring me a bit
from the hock of bacon, or a very young marrow-
bone. Then will I tell you something." They
could not comply with her requisitions, because
they had eaten all that themselves. And so she

trotted along the beach, like the dog of Polyphe-
mus, or the terrier of Hercules, who tinged his
nose with murex.

'Tis a very easy thing to talk of walking fifty
miles, but quite another pair of shoes to do it;
especially with pack on back, and feet that have
lost habitual sense of Macadam's tender mercies.
Moreover, the day had been very warm for the
beginning of October—the dying glance of Summer, in the year 1860, at her hitherto foregone and
forgotten England. The highest temperature of
the year had been 72° (in the month of May); in
June and July, 66° and 68° were the maxima, and
in August things were no better. Persistent rain,
perpetual chill, and ever-present sense of icebergs,
and longing for logs of dry wood. But towards
the end of September some glorious weather set in;
and people left off fires at the time when they
generally begin them. Therefore, Cradock Nowell
was hot, footsore, and slightly jaded, as he came to
the foot of Sydenham Hill, on the second day of
his journey. The Crystal Palace, which long had
been his landmark through country cross-roads,
shone with blue and airy light, as the sun was
sinking. Cradock admired more and more, as
the shadows sloped along it, the fleeting gleams,
the pellucid depth, the brightness of reflection
framed by the softness of refraction.

He had always loved that building, and now, at
the top of the hill, he resolved (weary as he was)
to enter and take his food there. Accordingly

Wena was left to sup and rest at the stables; he paid the shilling that turns the wheel, and went first to the refreshment court. After doing his duty there, he felt a great deal better; then buttoned his coat like a Briton, and sauntered into the transept. It had been a high and mighty day, for the Ancient Order of Mountaineers (who had never seen a mountain) were come to look for one at Penge, with sweethearts, wives, contingencies, and continuations. It boots not now to tell their games; enough that they had been very happy, and were gathering back in nave and transept for a last parade. To Cradock, so long accustomed to sadness, solitude, and bad luck, the scene, instead of being ludicrous (as a youth of fashion would have found it), was interesting and impressive, and even took a solemn aspect as the red rays of the sun retired, and the mellow shades were deepening. He leaned against the iron rail in front of the grand orchestra, and seeing many pretty faces, thought about his Amy, and wondered what she now was like, and whether she were true to him. From Pomona Island he could not write; from New York he had never written ; not knowing the loss of the *Taprobane*, and fearing lest he should seem once more to be trying the depth of John Rosedew's purse. But now he was come to England, with letters from Captain Recklesome Young, to his London correspondents, which ensured him a good situation, and the power to earn his own bread, and perhaps in a little while Amy's.

As he leaned and watched the crowd go by, like a dream of faces, the events of the bygone year passed also in dark parade before him. Sad, mysterious, undeserved—at least so far as he knew—how had they told upon him? Had they left him in better, or had they left him in bitter, case with his God and his fellow-man? That question might be solved at once, to any but himself, by the glistening of his eyes, the gentleness of his gaze around, the smile with which he drew back his foot when a knickerbocked child trod on it. He loved his fellow-creatures still; and love is law and gospel.

While he thought these heavy things, feeling weary of the road, of his life half weary, shrinking from the bustling world again to be encountered, suddenly a grand vibration thrilled his heart, and mind, and soul. From the great concave above him, melody was spreading wide, with shadowy resistless power, like the wings of angels. The noble organ was pealing forth, rolling to every nook of the building, sweeping over the heads of the people and into their hearts (with one soft passport), "Home, sweet home!" The men who had come because tired of home, the wives to give them a change of it, the maidens perhaps to get homes of their own, the children to cry to go home again;—all with one accord stood still, all listened very quietly, and said nothing at all about it. Only they were the better for it, with many a kind old memory rising, at least among the elder ones,

and many a large unselfish hope making the young
people look, with trust, at one another.

And what did Cradock Nowell feel? His home
was not a sweet one; bitter things had been done
against him; bitter things he himself had done.
None the less, he turned away and wept beneath
a music-stand, as if his heart would never give
remission to his eyes. None could see him in the
dark there, only the God whose will it was, and
whose will it often is, that tears should bring us
home to Him.

" I will arise, and go home to my father. I
will cry, 'Father, I have sinned against heaven,
and against thee.' "

And so he had. Not heavily, not wilfully, not wittingly, not a hundredth part so badly as that father
had sinned against him. Yet it was wrong in him
not to allow the old man to recover himself, but,
forgetting a son's love-duty, so to leave him—hotly,
hastily, with a proud defiance. Till now he had
never felt, or at least confessed to himself, that
wrong. Now, as generous natures do, he summed
up sternly against himself, leniently against others.
And then he asked, with yearning and bitter self-
reproach, " Is the old man yet alive?"

*   *   *   *

The woods were still as rich and sweet, and the
grass as soft as in May month; the windings of
the pleasant dells were looped with shining waters;
but she who used to love them so and brighten at
their freshness, to follow the steps of each wander-

ing breeze, and call to the sun as a flower does—
now she came through her favourite places, and
hardly cared to look at them. Only three short
months ago she had returned to her woodland
home, and the folk that knew and loved her, in
the highest ·and brightest spirits of youth, conscious beauty, and hopefulness. All her old
friends were rejoicing in her, and she in their
joy delighted, when her father thought it his sor-
rowful duty, in this world of sorrow, to tell her
the bad news about her over unlucky Cradock. At
first she received it with scorn—as the high manner of her mind was—utter unbelief, because God
could not have done it. Being simple, and very
young, she had half as much faith in her heavenly
Father as she had in the earthly and fallible
parent; neither was she quite aware that we do
not buy, but accept from God.

But, as week upon back of week, and month
after tardy month, went by, Amy's faith began to
wane, and herself to languish. She watched the
arrival of every mail from the Cape, from India,
from anywhere; her heart leaped up as each
steamer came in, and sank at each empty letter-
bag. Meanwhile her father was growing very
unhappy about her, and so was good Aunt Doxy.
At first John had said, when she took it so calmly,
"Thank God! How glad I am ! But her mother
cared for me more than that." Like many
another loving father, he had studied, but never
learned his child.

Now it was the fifth day of October, the weather
bright and beautiful, the English earth and trees
and herbage trying back for the summer of which
they had been so cheated. Poor pale Amy asked
leave to go out. She had long been under Rue
Hutton's care, not professionally, but paternally
(for Rufus would have his own way when he was
truly fond of any one), and she asked so quietly,
so submissively, without a bit of joke about it, that
when she was gone her father set to and shook his
head, till a heavy tear came and blotted out a reference which had taken all the morning. As for
Aunt Doxy, she turned aside, and took off her
spectacles quickly, because the optician had told
her to keep them perfectly dry.

Where the footpath wanders to and fro, preferring pleasure to duty, and meeting all remonstrance by quoting the course of the brook, Amy
Rosedew slowly walked, or heavily stopped every
now and then, caring for nothing around her.
She had made up her mind to cry no more, only
to long for the time and place when and where no
crying is. Perhaps in a year or so, if she lived,
she might be able to see things again, and attend
to her work as usual. Till then she would try to
please her father, and keep up her spirits for his
sake. Every one had been so kind to her, especially dear Eoa, who had really cried quite steadily;
and the least thing that girl Amy could do was to
try and deserve it. Thinking thus, and doing her
best to feel as well as think it, yet growing tired

already, she sat down in a chair as soft as weary
mortal may rest in. A noble beech, with a head
of glory overlooking the forest, had not neglected
to slipper his feet with the richest of nature's
velvet. From the dove-coloured column's base,
two yards above the ground-spread, drifts of darker
bulk began, gnarled crooks of grapple, clutching
wide at mother earth, deeply fanged into her
breast, sureties against every wind. Ridged and
ramped with many a hummock, rift, and twisted
sinew, forth these mighty tendons stretched, some
fathoms from the bole itself. Betwixt them nestled,
all in moss, corniced with the golden, and cushioned
with the greenest, nooks of cool, delicious rest,
wherein to forget the world, and dream upon the
breezes. "As You Like It," in your lap, Theo-
critus tossed over the elbow, because he is too
foreign, — what sweet depth of enjoyment for a
hard-working man who has earned it!

But, in spite of all this voluptuousness, the
"moss more soft than slumber," and the rippling
leafy murmur, there is little doubt that Miss Amy
Rosedew managed to have another cry ere ever
she fell asleep. To cry among those arms of moss,
fleecing, tufting, pillowing, an absorbent even for
Niobe! Can the worn-out human nature find no
comfort in the vegetable, though it does in the
mineral, kingdom?

Back, and back, and further back into the old
relapse of sleep, the falling thither whence we
came, the interest on the debt of death. Yet as

the old Stagyrite hints, some of day's emotions filter through the strain of sleep; it is not true that good and bad are, for half of life, the same. Alike their wits go roving haply after the true Owner, but some may find Him, others fail— Father, who shall limit thus Thine infinite amnesty?

It would not be an easy thing to find a fairer sight. Her white arms on the twisted plumage of the deep green moss, the snowy arch of her neck revealed as the clustering hair fell from it, and the frank and playful forehead resting on the soft grey bark. She smiled in her sleep every now and then, for her pleasant young humour must have its own way when the schoolmaster, sorrow, was dozing; and then the sad dreaming of trouble returned, and the hands were put up to pray, and the red lips opened, whispering, "Come home! Only come to Amy!"

And then, in her dream, he *was* come—raining tears upon her cheek, holding her from all the world, fearing to thank God yet. She was smiling up at him; oh, it was so delicious! Suddenly she opened her eyes. What made her face so wet? Why, Wena!

Wena, as sure as dogs are dogs; mounted on the mossy arm, lick-lick-licking, mewing like a cat almost, even offering taste of her tongue, while every bit of the Wena dog shook with ecstatic rapture.

"Oh, Wena, Wena! what are you come to tell me, Wena? Oh that you could speak!"

Wena immediately proved that she could. She galloped round Amy, barking and yelling, until the great wood echoed again; the rabbits, a mile away, pricked their ears, and the yaffingales stopped from tapping. Then off set the little dog down the footpath. Oh, could it be to fetch somebody?

The mere idea of such a thing made Amy shake so, and feel so odd, she was forced to put one hand against the tree, and the other upon her heart. She could not look, she was in such a state; she could not look down the footpath. It seemed, at least, a century, and it may have been half a minute, before she heard through the bushes a voice—tush, she means *the* voice.

"Wena, you bad dog, come in to heel. Is this all you have learned by travelling?"

But Wena broke fence and everything, set off full gallop again to Amy, tugged at her dress, and retrieved her.

What happened after that Amy knows. not, neither knows Cradock Nowell. So anything I could tell would be a fond thing vainly invented. All they remember is—looking back upon it, as both of them may, to the zenith of their lives— that neither of them could say a word except "darling, darling, darling!" all pronounced as superlatives, with "my own," once or twice between, and an exclusive sense of ownership, illiberal

and unphilosophical.   What business have we
with such minor details ?   Who has sworn us
accountants of kisses ?   All we have any right to
say is, that after a long spell of inarticulate tauto-
logy, Amy looked up when Cradock proposed to
add another cipher ; very gravely, indeed, she
looked up ; except in the deepest depth of her
eyes.

"Oh no, Cradock.   You must not think of it.
Seriously now, you must *not*, love."

"Why ?   I should like to know, indeed !   After
all the time I have been away !"

"I have so little presence of mind.   I forgot to
tell you in time, dear.   Why, because Wena *has
licked my face all over*, darling.   Darling, yes, she
has, I say.   You are too bad not to care about it.
Now come to my own best father, dear.   Offer
your arm like a gentleman."

So they — as Milton concisely says.   Homer
would have written "they two."   How sadly our
language wants a dual !   We, the domestic race,
have we rejected it because the use would have
seemed a truism ?

*   *   *   *

That same afternoon Bull Garnet lay dying,
calmly and peacefully going off, taking his accounts to a larger world.   He knew that there
were some heavy items underscored against him ;
but he also knew that the mercy of God can even
outdo the hope He gives us for token and for
keepsake.   A greater and a grander end, after a

life of mark and power, might, to his early aspirations and self-conscious strength, have seemed the bourne intended. If it had befallen him—as but for himself it would have done—to appear where men are moved by passion, vigour, and bold decision, his name would have been historical, and better known to the devil. As it was, he lay there dying, and was well content. The turbulence of life was past, the torrent and the eddy, the attempt at fore-reaching upon his age, and sense of impossibility, the strain of his mental muscles to stir the great dead trunks of " orthodoxy," and then the self-doubt, the chill, the depression, which follow such attempts, as surely as ague tracks the pioneer.

Thank God, all this was over now, and the violence gone, and the dark despair. Of all the good and evil things which so had branded him distinct, two yet dwelled in his feeble heart, only two still showed their presence in his dying eyes. Each of those two was good, if two indeed they were—faith in the heavenly Father, and love of the earthly children.

Pearl was sitting on a white chair at the side of the bed away from the window, with one hand in his failing palm, and the other trying now and then to enable her eyes to see things. She was thinking, poor little thing, of what she should do without him, and how he had been a good father to her, though she never could understand him. That was her own fault, no doubt. She had always fancied that he loved her as a bit of his property, as a thing to be managed; now she knew that it was not so; and he was going away for ever, and who would love or manage her? And the fault of all this was her own.

Rufus Hutton had been there lately, trying still to keep up some little show of comfort, and a large one of encouragement; for he was not the man to say die till a patient came to the preterite. Throughout the whole, and knowing all, he had behaved in the noblest manner, partly from his own quick kindness, partly from that protective and fiduciary feeling which springs self-sown in the hearts of women when showers of sorrow descend, and crops up in the manly bosom at the fee of golden sunshine. Not that he took any fees; but that his professional habits revived, with a generosity added, because he knew that he would take nothing, though all were in his power.

Suddenly Mr. Pell came in, our old friend Octavius, sent for in an urgent manner, and looking as a man looks who feels but cannot open on the hinge of his existence. Like a thorough gentleman, he had been shy of the cottage, although aware of their distress; eager at once and reluctant, partly because it stood not in his but his rector's parish, partly for deeper reasons.

Though Pell came in so quietly, Bull Garnet rose at his entry, or tried to rise on the pillow, swept his daughter back by a little motion of his thumb, which she quite understood, and cast his eyes on the parson's with a languid yet strong intelligence. He had made up his mind that the man was good, and yet he could not help probing him.

The last characteristic act of poor Bull Garnet's life, a life which had been all character, all difference, from other people.

" Will you take my daughter's hand, Pell?"

" Only too gladly," answered Pell; but she shrank away, and sobbed at him.

" Pearl, come forward this moment. It is no time for shilly-shallying."

The poor thing timidly gave her hand, standing a long way back from Pell, and with her large eyes streaming, yet fixed upon her father, and no chance at all of wiping them.

" Now, Pell, do you love my daughter? I am dying, and I ask you."

" That I do, with all my heart," said Pell, like a downright Englishman. " I shall never love any other."

" Now, Pearl, do you love Mr. Pell?" Her father's eyes were upon her in a way that commanded truth. She remembered how she had told a lie, at the age of seven or eight, and that gaze had forced it out of her, and she had never dared to tell one since, until no lie dared come near her.

" Father, I like him very much. Very soon I should love him, if—if he loved me."

" Now, Pell, you hear that !"

" Beyond all doubt I do," said Octave, whose

U 2

dryness never deserted him in the heaviest rain of
tears; "and it is the very best thing for me I have
heard in all my life."

Bull Garnet looked from one to the other, with
the rally of his life come hot, and a depth of joyful
sadness.   Yet must he go a little further, because
he had always been a tyrant till people understood him.

"Do you want to know how much money, sir, I
intend to leave her, when I die to-night or to-
morrow morning?"

Cut-and-dry Pell was taken aback.   A thoroughly upright and noble fellow, but of wholly
different and less rugged road of thought.   Meanwhile Pearl had slipped away; it was more than
she could bear, and she was so sorry for Octavius.
Then Pell up and spake bravely:

"Sir, I would be loth to think of you, my dear
one's father, as anything but a gentleman; a
strange one, perhaps, but a true one.   And so I
trust you have only put such a question to me in
irony."

"Pell, there is good stuff in you.   I know a
man by this time.   What would you think of
finding your dear one's father a murderer?"

Octavius Pell was not altogether used to this
sort of thing.   He turned away with some doubt
whether Pearl would be a desirable mother of
children (for he, after all, was a practical man),
and hereditary insanity—— Then he turned

back, remembering that all mankind are mad. Meanwhile Bull Garnet watched him, with extraordinary wrinkles, and a savage sort of pleasure. He felt himself outside the world, and looking at the stitches of it. But he would not say a word. He had always been a bully, and he meant to keep it up.

" Sir," said Octave Pell, at last, " you are the very oddest man I ever saw in all my life."

" Ah, you think so, do you, Pell? Possibly you are right; possibly you are right, Pell. I have no time to think about it. It never struck me in that light. If I am so very odd, perhaps you would rather not have my daughter ?"

" If you intend to refuse her to me, you had better say so at once, sir. I don't understand all this."

" I wish you to understand nothing at all beyond the simple fact. I shot Clayton Nowell, and did it on purpose, because I found him insulting her."

" Good God! You don't mean to say it ? "

" I never yet said a thing, Pell, which I did not mean to say."

" You did it in haste? You have repented? For God's sake, tell me that."

" Treat this as a question of business. Look at the deed and nothing else. Do you still wish to marry my daughter? "

Pell turned away from the great wild eyes now solemnly fixed upon him. His manly heart was

full of wonder, anguish, and giddy turbulence.
The promptest of us cannot always "come to time,"
like a prizefighter.

Pearl came in, with her chest well forward, and
then drew back very suddenly. She thought her
fate must be settled now, and would like to know
how they had settled it. Then, like a genuine
English lady, she gave a short sigh and went away.
Pride makes the difference between us and all
other nations.

But the dignified glance she had cast on Pell
settled his fate and hers for life. He saw her
noble self-respect, her stately reservation, her deep
sense of her own pure value (which never would
assert itself), and her passing contempt of his hesi-
tation.

"At all risks I will have her," he said to himself,
for his manly strength gloried in her strong woman-
hood; "if she can be won I will have her. Oh,
how I am degrading her! What a fool-bound
fellow I am!"

Then he spoke to her father, who had fallen
back, and was faintly gazing, wondering what the
stoppage was.

"Sir, I am not worthy of her. God knows how
I love her. She is too good for me."

Bull Garnet gathered his fleeting life, and looked
at Pell with a love so deep that it banished admiration. Then his failing heart supplied, for the last,
last time of all, the woe-worn fountain of his eyes.
Strong and violent as he was, a little thing had

often touched him to the turn of tears. What impulse is there but has this end? Even comic laughter.

Pell lifted from the counterpane the broad but shrunken hand, which was on the way to be offered to him, until sad memory stopped it. Then he looked down at the poor grey face, where the forehead, from the fall of the rest, appeared almost a monstrosity, and the waning of strong emotions left a quivering of hollowness. The young parson looked down with noble pity. Much he knew of his father-in-law! Bull Garnet would never be pitied. He drew his hand back with a little jerk, and placed it against his broad, square chin.

"I can't bear to die like this, Pell. *I wish to God you could shave me.*"

Pell went suddenly down on his knees, put his strong brown hands up, and said nothing except the Lord's Prayer. Bull Garnet tried to raise his palms, but the power of his wrists was gone, and so he let them fall together. Then at every grand petition he nodded at the ceiling, as if he saw it going upward, and thought of the lath and plaster.

He had said he should die at four o'clock, for the paroxysms of heart-complaint returned at measured intervals, and he felt that he could not outlast another. So with his usual mastery and economy of labour, he had sent a man to get the keys and begin to toll the great church bell, as soon as ever the clock struck four. "Not too long apart," he said, "steadily, and be done with it."

When the boom of the sluggish bell came in at the open window, Bull Garnet smiled, because the man was doing it as he had ordered him.

"Right," he whispered, "yes, quite right. I have always been before my time. Just let me see my children." And then he had no more pain.

*   *   *   *

Amy came in very softly, to know if he was dead. They had told her she ought to leave it alone, but she could not see it so. Knowing all and feeling all, she felt beyond her knowledge. If it would — oh, if it would help him with a spark of hope in his parting, help him in the judgment-day, to have the glad forgiveness of the brother with the deeper wrong—there it was, and he was welcome.

A little whispering went on, pale lips into trembling ears, and then Cradock, with his shoes off, was brought to the side of the bed.

"He won't know you," Pearl sobbed softly; "but how kind of you to come!" She was surprised at nothing now.

Her father raised his languid eyes, until they met Cradock's eager ones; there they dwelt with doubt, and wonder, and a slow rejoicing, and a last attempt at expression.

John Rosedew took the wan stiffening hand, lying on the sheet like a cast-off glove, and placed it in Cradock's sunburnt palm.

"He knows all," the parson whispered; "he has

read the letter you left for him; and, knowing all, he forgives you."

"That I do, with all my heart," Cradock answered firmly. "May God forgive me as I do you. Wholly, purely, for once and for all!"

"Kind—noble—Godlike——" the dying man said very slowly, but with his old decision.

Bull Garnet could not speak again. The great expansion of heart had been too much for its weakness. Only now and then he looked at Cradock with his Amy, and every look was a prayer for them, and perhaps a recorded blessing.

Then they slipped away, in tears, and left him, as he ought to be, with his children only. And the telegraph of death was that God would never part them.

Now, think you not this man was dying a great deal better than he deserved? No doubt he was. And, for that matter, so perhaps do most of us. But does our Father think so?

CHAPTER XVIII.

SOFTLY and quietly fell the mould on the coffin of Bull Garnet. A great tree overhung his sleep, without fear of the woodman. Clayton Nowell's simple grave, turfed and very tidy, was only a few yards away. That ancient tree spread forth its arms on this one and the other, as a grandsire lays his hands peacefully and placidly on children who have quarrelled.

A lovely spot, as one might see, for violence to rest in, for long remorse to lose the track, and deep repentance hopefully abide the time of God. To feel the soft mantle of winter return, and the promising gladness of spring, the massive depths of the summer-tide, and the bright disarray of autumn. And to be, no more the while, oppressed, or grieved, or overworked.

There shall forest-children come, joining hands in pleasant fear, and, sitting upon grassy mounds, wonder who inhabits them, wonder who and what it is that cannot wonder any more. And haply they shall tell this tale—become a legend then—when he who writes, and ye who read, are dust.

Ay, and tell it better far, more simply, and more sweetly, never having gone astray from the inborn sympathy. For every grown-up man is apt to mar the uses of his pen with bitter words, and small, and twaddling; conceiting himself to be keen in the first, just in the second, and sage in the third. For all of these let him crave forgiveness of God, his fellow-creatures, and himself, respectively.

Sir Cradock Nowell, still alive to the normal sense of duty, tottered away on John Rosedew's arm, from the grave of his half-brother. He had never learned whose hand it was that dug the grave near by, and no one ever forced that unhappy knowledge on him. This last blow, which seemed to strike his chiefest prop from under him, had left its weal on his failing mind in great marks of astonishment. That such a strong, great man should drop, and he, the elder and the weaker, be left to do without him! He was going to the Rectory now, to have a glass of wine, after fatigue of the funeral, a vintage very choice and rare, according to Mr. Rosedew, and newly imported from Oxford. And truly that was its origin. It might have claimed "founder's kin fellowship," like most of the Oxford wine-skins.

"Wonderful, wonderful man!" said poor Sir

Cradock, doing his best to keep his back very upright, from a sudden suffusion of memory,—"to think that he should go first, John! Oh, if I had a son left, he should take that man for his model."

"Scarcely that," John Rosedew thought, knowing all the circumstances; "but of the dead I will say no harm."

"So quick, so ready, so up for anything! Ah, I remember he knocked a man down just at the corner by this gate here, where the dandelion-seed is. And afterwards he proved how richly he deserved it. That is the way to do things, John."

"I am not quite sure of that," said the conscientious parson; "it might be wiser to prove that first; and then to abstain from doing it. I remember an instance in point——"

"Of course you do. You always do, John, and I wish you wouldn't. But that has nothing to do with it. You are always cutting me short, John; and worse than ever since you came back, and they talked of you so at Oxford. I hope they have not changed you, John."

He looked at the white-haired rector, with an old man's jealousy. Who else had any right to him?

"My dear old friend," replied John Rosedew, with kind sorrow in his eyes, "I never meant to cut you short. I will try not to do it again. But I know I am rude sometimes, and I am always sorry afterwards."

" Nonsense, John ; don't talk of it. I understand you by this time ; and we allow for one
another. But now about my son, my poor unlucky boy."

" To be sure, yes," said the other old man, not
wishing to hurry matters. And so they stopped
and probed the hedge instead of one another.

" I don't know how it is," at last Sir Cradock
Nowell said, being rather aggrieved with John
Rosedew for not breaking ground upon him —
" but how hard those stubs of ash are!   Look at
that splinter, almost severed by a man who does
not know how to splash ; Jem, his name is, poor
Garnet told me, Jem—something or other—and
yet all I can do with my stick won't fetch it away
from the stock."

" Like a child who will not quit his father, however his father has treated him."

" What do you mean by that, John ?   Are
you driving at me again ? I thought you had given
it over."

" I never give over anything," John answered,
in a manner for him quite melodramatic, and beyond his usual key.

" No. We always knew how stubborn you were.
And now you are worse than ever."

" No fool like an old fool," John Rosedew answered, smiling sweetly, yet with some regret.
" Cradock, I am such a fool I shall let out everything."

" What do you mean?" asked Sir Cradock

Nowell, leaning heavily on his staff, and setting his white face rigidly, yet with every line of it ready to melt; "John, I have heard strange rumours, or I have dreamed strange dreams. In the name of God, what is it, John? My son!—my only son——"

He could say no more, but turned away, and bowed his head, and trembled.

"Your only son, your innocent son, has been at my house these three days; and when you like, you can see him."

"When I like—ah, to be sure! I don't like many people. I am getting very old, John. And no one to come after me. It seems a pity, don't you think, and every one against me so?"

"You can take your own part still, my friend. And you have to take your son's part."

"Yes, to be sure, my son's part. Perhaps he will come back some day. And I know he did not do it, now; and I was very hard to him—don't you think I was, John?—very hard to my poor Craddy, and he was so like his mother!"

"But you will be very kind to him now; and he will be such a comfort to you, now he is come back again, and going away no more."

"I declare you make me shake, John. You do talk such nonsense. One would think you knew all about him,—more than his own father does. What have I done, to be kept like this in the dark, all in the dark? And you seem to think that I was hard to him."

" Cradock, all you have to do is just to say the word; just to say that you wish to see him, and your son will come and talk to you."

" Talk to me! Oh yes, I should like to talk to him—very much—I mean, of course, if he is at leisure."

. He leaned on his stick, and tried to think, while John Rosedew hurried off ; and of all his thoughts the foremost were, " What will Cradock my boy be like ; and what shall I give him for dinner ? "

Cradock came up shyly, gently, looking at his father first, then waiting to be looked at. The old man fixed his eyes upon him, at first with some as-tonishment—for his taste in dress was somewhat outraged by the Broadway style—then, in spite of all the change, remembrance of his son returned, and love, and sense of ownership. Last of all, auctorial pride in the young man's width of shoul-der, blended with soft recollections of the time he dandled him.

" Why, Cradock ! It is my poor son Cradock ! What a size you are grown, my boy, my boy ! "

" Oh, father, I am sure you want me. Only try me once again. I am not at all a radical."

" Crad, you never could be. I knew you must come round at last to my way of thinking. When you had seen the world, Crad ; when you had seen the world a bit, as your father did before you."

And so they made the matter up, in politics, and dress, and little touches of religion, and in the depth of kindred love which underlies the latter; and never after was there word, except of migrant petulance, between the crotchety old man, and the son who held his heart's key.

All this while we have been loth to turn to Mrs. Corklemore, and contemplate her discomfiture, although in strict sequence of events we ought to have done so long ago. But it is so very painful —and now-a-days all writers agree with Epicurus, in regarding pain as the worst of evils—so bitter is the task to describe a lovely mother failing, in spite of all exertion, to do her duty by her child, in robbing other people, that really—ah well-a-day, physic must be taken.

At the time of her dismissal from the halls of Nowelhurst, Mr. Corklemore had been so glad to see his pretty wife again, and that queer little Flore, who amused him so by pinching his stiff leg, and crying " haw," and he had found the house so desolate, and the absence of plague so unwholesome, and the responsibility of having a will of his own so horrible, that he scarcely cared to ask the reason why they were come home. And Georgie—who was not thoroughly heartless, else: how could she have got on so?—thought Coo Nest very snug and nice, with none to contradict her. So she found relief awhile, in banishing her worse, while she indulged her better half.

Let me do the same by suppressing here that evil tendency to moralise. In Georgie's case, as well as mine, the indulgence possessed at any rate

the attractions of change and variety. But, knowing how strictly we are bound by the canons of
philosophy to suspect and put the curb on every
natural bias, that good young woman soon refrained
from over-active encouragement of her inclination
to goodness. Rallying her sense of right, she van-
quished very nobly all the seductions of honesty,
and, by a virtuous effort, marched from the Capua
of virtue.

She stood upon the wood-crowned heights which
look upon Coo Nest, and as the smoke came
curling up, the house seemed very small to her.
What a thing to call a garden! And the pigeon-
house at Nowelhurst was nearly as large as our
stable! And oh that little vinery, where one
knew every single bunch, and came every day
to watch its ripening, and the little fuss of its
colouring, like an ogre watching a pet babe roasting. Surely nature never meant her to live upon
so small a scale; or why had she been gifted with
such large activities?

She turned her back upon Coo Nest, and her
face to Nowelhurst Hall, and in her mind's eye
saw a place ever so much larger.

Then a pleasant sound came up the hollow, a
nice ring of revolving wheels coquetting with the
best C springs and all the new improvements.
Well-mettled horses, too, were there, stepping together sonipedally, and a footman could be seen,
whose legs must stand him in 60l. a year.

"That odious old Sir Julius Wallop and his

wizen-faced wife come to patronize us again and say, 'Ha, Corklemore, snug little place, charming situation; but I think I should pull it down and rebuild; no room for Chang to stand in it. And how is my old friend, Sir Cradock, your forty-fifth cousin, I believe? Ah, he *has* a nice place.' I haven't the heart to meet them now, and their patronizing disparagement. Heigho! It is a nice turn-out. And yet they have at Nowelhurst three more handsome carriages. And it does look so much better to have two footmen there behind; and I do like watered linings so. How nice Flo did look by my side in that new barouche! Oh, my darling child, I must not give way to selfish feelings. I must do my duty towards you."

Therefore she proceeded, against her better nature, in the face of prudence, with her attempt to set aside poor Sir Cradock Nowell, and obtain fiduciary possession of his property. Cradock was lost in the *Taprobane,*—of that there could be no doubt; and so she was saved all further trouble of laying before the civil authorities the stronger evidence they required before issuing a warrant. But all was going very nicely towards the commencement of an inquiry as to the old man's state of mind. Then suddenly she was checkmated, and never moved a pawn again.

One afternoon, Mrs. Corklemore was sitting in her drawing-room, expecting certain visitors, and quite ready to be bored with them, because they were leading gossips—ladies who gave the first com-

plexion to any nascent narrative. And Georgie
knew how to handle them. In the county talk
which must ensue, only let them take her side, and
all the world would feel for her in her very painful
position.

After a rumble of rapid wheels, and a violent
pull at the bell, which made the lady of the house
to jump, because they had just had the bell-
hanger, into her sanctuary came with a cooler than
cucumine temperature, not indeed Lady Alberta
Smith and her daughter Victorina Beatrice, but
Eoa Nowell and her cousin Cradock.

For once in her life Mrs. Corklemore was de-
prived of all presence of mind, ghostly horror being
added to bodily fear of Eoa. She fain would have
fled, but her limbs gave way, and she fell back
into a soft French chair, and covered her face with
both hands. Then Eoa, looking tall and delicate
in her simple mourning dress, walked up to her
very quietly, leading Cradock as if she were proud
of him.

" I have taken the liberty, Mrs. Corklemore, of
bringing my cousin Cradock to see you, because it
may save trouble."

" I trust you will forgive," said Cradock, " our
very sudden invasion. We are come upon a matter
of business, to save unpleasant exposures and disgrace to our distant relatives."

" Oh," gasped poor Mrs. Corklemore, " you are
alive, then, after all? It was proved that you had
lost your life upon the coast of Africa."

x 2

" Yes, but it has proved otherwise," Cradock
answered, bowing neatly.

" And it would have been so much better, under
the sad, sad circumstances, for all people of good
feeling, and all interested in the family."

" For the latter, perhaps it would, madam; but
not so clearly for the former. I am here to protect my father from all machinations."

" Leave her to me," cried Eoa, slipping prettily
in front of him, " I understand her best, because—
because of my former vocation. And I think she
knows what I am."

" That I do," answered Georgie, cleverly inter-
posing first a small enamelled table; " not only
an insolent, but an utterly reckless creature."

" You may think so," Eoa replied, with calm
superiority; " but that only shows your piteous
ignorance of the effects of discipline. I am now
so sedate and tranquil a woman, that I do not hate,
but scorn you."

Cradock could not help smiling at this, knowing
what Eoa was.

" We want no strong expressions, my dear, on
one side or the other," for he saw that a word
would have overthrown Eoa's new-born discipline;
" Mrs. Corklemore is far too clever not to perceive
her mistake. She knows quite well that any inquiry as to my dear father's state of mind can now
be of no use to her. And if she thinks of any
further proceedings against myself, perhaps she

had better first look at just this—just this docu-
ment."

He laid before her a certificate, granted by three
magistrates, that indisputable evidence had been
brought before them as to the cause and manner
of Clayton Nowell's death, and that Cradock
Nowell had no share in it, wittingly or unwittingly.
That was the upshot of it; but of course it extended
to about fifty-fold the length.

Mrs. Corklemore bent over her, in her most be-
witching manner, and perused it very leisurely, as
if she were examining Flore's attempts at pothooks.
Meanwhile, with a side-glint of her eyes, she was
watching both of them; and it did not escape her
notice that Eoa was very pale.

"To be sure," she said at last, looking full at
the Eastern maid, "I see exactly how it was. I
have thought so all along. A female Thug must
be charmed, of course, by the only son of a murderer. My dear, I do so congratulate you."

"Thank you," answered Eoa, and the deep gaze
of her lustrous eyes made the clever woman feel a
world unopened to her; "I thank you, Georgie
Corklemore, because you know no better. My
only wish for you is, that you may never know
unhappiness, because you could not bear it."

Saying so, she turned away, and, with her light,
quick step, was gone, before her enemy could see a
symptom of the welling tears which then burst all
control. But Cradock, who had dwelt in sorrow,

compared to which hers was a joke, stayed to say
a few soft words, and made a friend for evermore
of the woman who had plotted so against his life
and all his love.

Madame la Comtesse since that time has seen
much tribulation, and is all the better for it. Mr.
Corklcmore died of the gout, and the angel Flore
of the measles; and she herself, having nursed
them both, and lost some selfishness in their graves,
is now (as her destiny seemed to be) the wife of
Mr. Chope. Of course she is compelled to merge
her strong will in a stronger one, and, according
to nature's Salique law, is the happier for doing
so. Whether this union will produce a subject for
biography to some unborn Lord Campbell, time
alone can show.

From the above it will be clear that poor Eoa
Nowell was now acquainted with the secret of the
Garnet family. Bob himself had told her all,
about a month after his father's death, renouncing
at the same time all his claims upon her. Of that
Eoa would not hear; only at his urgency she promised to consult her friends, and take a week to
think of it. And this was the way she kept her
promise.

First she ran up to Cradock Nowell, with the
bright tears still upon her cheeks, and asked him
whether he had truly and purely forgiven his in-
jurer. He took her hand, and answered her with
his eyes, in which the deepened springs of long
affliction glistened, fixed steadily upon hers.

"As truly and purely as I hope to be forgiven at the judgment-day."

"Then that settles that matter. Now order the dog-cart, Crady dear, and drive me to Dr. Hutton's." -

Of course he obeyed her immediately, and in an hour they entered the gate of Geopharmacy Lodge. Rosa was amazed at her beauty, and thought very little, after that, of Mrs. Corklemore's appearance.

"For my part," said Rufus Hutton, when Eoa had laid the case before him in a privy council, "although it is very good of you, and very flattering to me, that you look upon me still as your guardian, I think you are bound first of all to consult Sir Cradock Nowell."

"How very odd! Now that is exactly what I do not mean to do. He never can understand, poor dear, and I hope he never will, the truth about poor Clayton's death. His present conviction is, like that of all the neighbourhood, that Black Will the poacher did it, the man who has since been killed in a fight with Sir Julius Wallop's gamekeepers. And it would shock poor uncle so; I am sure he would never get over it if the truth were forced upon him. And if it were, I am sure he would never allow me to have my way, which, of course, I should do in spite of him. And I am not his heiress now, since Cradock came to life again. But I have plenty of money of my own; and I have quite settled what to give him the day that I am married, and you too, my

dear guardy, if you behave well about this.   Look
here !"

She drew forth a purse quite full of gold, and
tossed it in her old Indian style, so that Rufus
could not help laughing.

" Well, my dear," he answered kindly, " who
could resist such bribery? Besides, I see that your
mind is made up, and we all know what the result
of that is.   And after all, the chief question is,
what effect will your knowledge of this have on
your love for your husband?"

" It will only make me love him more, ever so
much more, because of his misfortune."

" And will you never allude to it, never let him
see that you think of it, so as to spoil his happiness?"

" Is it likely I should think of it?   Why, my
father must have killed fifty men.   He was desperate in a battle.   And Bob has never brought that
up against me."

" Well, if you take it in that light—decidedly
not an English light——"

" And perhaps you never heard that Bob's father,
by his quickness and boldness, saved the lives of
fifteen men in a colliery explosion before he ever
came to Nowelhurst, and therefore he had a perfect right to—to——"

" Take the lives of fifteen others.   Fourteen to
his credit still.   Well, Eoa, you can argue, if any
female in the world can.   Only in one thing, my
dear child, be advised by me.   If you must marry

Robert Garnet, leave this country for a while, and take his sister Pearl with you."

"Of course I must marry Bob," said Eoa; "and of course I should go away with him. But as to taking Pearl with us, why, that's a thing to be thought about."

However, they got over that, as well as all other difficulties; Sir Cradock Nowell was at the wedding, Mr. Rosedew performed the ceremony, and Rufus Hutton gave away as lovely a bride as ever was seen. Bob Garnet spied a purple emperor, who had lost his way, knocking his head in true imperial fashion against the chancel-window, and he glanced at Eoa about it, between the two "I wills," and she lifted her beautiful eyebrows, and he saw that she meant to catch him. So, after signing the register, they contrived to haul him down, without letting John Rosedew know it; then at the chancel-porch they let him go free of the Forest, with his glorious wings unsoiled. Not even an insect should have cause to repent their wedding-day.

And now they live in as fair a place as any the world can show, not far from Pezo da Ragoa, in the Alto Douro district. There Eoa's children toddle by the brilliant river's brink, and form their limbs to strength and beauty up the vine-clad mountain's side. Bob has invested his share of proceeds in a vineyard of young Bastardo, and Muscat de Jesu; moreover, he holds a good appointment under the Royal Oporto Company,

agricultural of the vine. Many a time Eoa sits
watching with her deep bright eyes the purple
flow of the luscious juice from the white marble
"lagar," wherein the hardy peasants, with their
drawers tied at the knee, tramp to the time of the
violin to and fro, without turning round, among
the pulpy flood. Then Bob, who has discovered a
perfect cure for oidium, and knows how to deal
with every grub that bores into or nips the vine,
to his wife and bairns he comes in haste, having
been too long away, bringing a bunch of the
"ladies' fingers," or the Barrete de Clerigo, or it may
be some magnificent insect new to his entomology;
or, still more interesting prize, a letter from Pearl
or Amy, wherein Mrs. Pell, or Nowell, gossips of
the increasing cares which increase her happiness.
Yet even among those lovely scenes, and under
that delicious sky, frequent and fond are the
glances cast by hope, as well as memory, at the
bowered calm of the Forest brooks, and the brown
glamour of the beechwood.

And when they return to dwell in the Forest,
and to end their days there, even Bob will scarcely
know the favourite haunts of his boyhood—to such
an extent has Cradock Nowell planted and improved, clothing barren slopes with verdure, adding
to the wealth of woods many a new tint and tone,
by the aid of foreign trees unknown to his father.
In doing so, his real object is not so much to improve the estate, or gratify his own good taste, or
even that of Amy; but to find labour for the

hands, and food for the mouths, of industrious
people. Sir Cradock grumbles just a little every
now and then, because, like all of us Englishmen,
he must have his grievance. But, on the whole,
he is very proud of what his son is doing, and
thoroughly enjoys his power of urging or repress-
ing it.

And if on theoretic matters any question chances
to arise between them, when one says "no" to the
other's "yes"—as all true Britons are bound to do
upon politics, port wine, and parsons,—then a
gentle spirit comes and turns it all to laughter,
with the soft and pleasant wit of a well-bred
woman's ignorance. For Amy still must have her
say, and still asserts her privilege to flavour every
dull discussion with lively words, and livelier
glances, and a smile for both the disputants.
Then Cradock looks at his dear young wife with
notes of admiration, and bids her keep such
piquant wisdom for the councils of the nursery.
Upon which pleasant reminder, the old man
chuckles, as if some very good thing had been
said; then craftily walks with a spotted toy, capable of barking and exactly representing Caldo
or Wena, whichever you please, to the foot of certain black oak-stairs, where he fully expects to hear
the prattle of small Clayton.

To wit, it has been long resolved, and managed
with prospective wisdom down the path of years,
that the county annals shall not be baulked of a
grand Sir Clayton Nowell. And a very grand

fellow indeed he is, this two-year-old Clayton
Nowell—grand in the stolid sageness of his broad
and steadfast gaze, grand in the manner of his legs
and his Holbein attitude, grander still in stamping
when his meat and ale are late, but grandest of all,
immeasurably grand, in the eyes of his grandfather.

Hogstaff, whose memory is quite gone, and his
hearing too of every sound except the voice of this
boy, identifies him beyond all cavil with the Clayton of our story.   Many a time the bowed retainer
chides his little master for not remembering the
things he taught him only yesterday.   Then Cradock smiles at his son's oblivion of the arts his
uncle learned, but never reminds old Hoggy that
the yesterday was rather more than five-and-
twenty years ago.

Is it true or is it false, according to the rules of
art, that the winding-up of a long, long story,
handled with more care than skill, should have
some resemblance to the will of a kindly-natured
man?   In whose final dispositions, no dependent,
however humble, none who have helped him in the
many pages of his life, far less any intimate friend,
seeks in vain a grateful mention or a token of
regard.

Be that as it may, any writer who loves his work
(although a fool for doing so) feels the end and
finish of it like the signature of his will.   And
doubly saddened must he be, if the scenes which
charmed him most, and cast upon him such a spell

that he could not call spectators in,—if these, for want of skill, have wearied eyes and hearts he might have pleased.

For surely none would turn away, whose nature is uncancelled, if once he could be gently led into that world of beauty. To rest in the majesty of shade, forgetting weary headache; to let the little carking cares, avarice and jealousy, self-conceit and thirst of fame, fly away on the wild wood, like the piping of a bird; to hear the rustle of young leaves, when their edges come together, and dreamily to wonder at the size of things above us.

Shall ever any man enclasp the good that grows above him, or even offer to receive the spread of Heaven's greatness? Yet every man may lift himself above the highest tree-tops, even to the throne of God, by loving and forgiving.

And verily, some friends of ours, who could not once forego a grudge, are being taught, by tare and trett, how much they owe their Maker, and how little to themselves. First of these is Rufus Hutton, quite a jolly mortal, getting fat, and riding Polly for the sake of his liver and renes. And all he has to say is this : first, that he will match trees and babies with those of any nurseryman; next, that as I have a knack of puffing good people and good things, he begs for reciprocity on the part of superior readers. And if this should chance to meet the eye of any one who knows where to find a really first-rate Manilla, conducted on free-trade principles, such knowing person, by address-

ing, confidentially under seal, " R. H., Post-office,
Ringwood," may hear of something very greatly
to his own advantage.

Now do we, without appeal to the blue smoke
of enthusiasm, know of anything to the advantage
of anybody whatever? Yes, I think we do. We
may highly commend the recent career of the
Ducksacre firm, and Mr. Clinkers, and Issachar
Jupp the bargee. Robert Clinkers and Polly his
wife are driving a first-rate business in coal and
coke and riddlings, not highly aristocratic perhaps, but free from all bad debts. You may see
the name on a great brass-plate near the Broadway, Hammersmith, on the left hand, where the
busses stop. But Mr. Jupp flies at higher game.
He has turned his length of wind, that once se-
cured the palm of victory in physical encounters,
to a higher and nobler use. In a word, Mr.
Jupp is a Primitive Christian upon and beside
the waters of Avon. There you may hear him
preaching and singing through his nose alternately
—ah, me, that is not what I mean—for either
proceeding is nasal—every Sunday and Wednesday evening, when the leaks in the punt allow
him. He gets five-and-thirty shillings a-week, as
Sir Cradock's water-bailiff, and he has not stolen
twig or catkin of all the trees he convoys down
Avon. In seven or eight more summers, little
Loo Jupp will probably be the prettiest girl in
the Forest. May we be there to see her!

The best and kindest man of all who have said

their say in my story, and not thrust their merits forward, John Rosedew, still leads his quiet life, nearer and nearer to wisdom's threshold, nearer and nearer to the door of God. His temper is as soft and sweet, his memory as bright and ready, and his humour as playful, as when he was only thirty years old, and walked every day to Kidlington. As for his shyness, that we must never ask him to discard; because he likes to know us first, and then he likes to love us.

But of all the people in the world, next to his own child Amy, most he loves and most he honours his son-in-law, Cradock Nowell—

Cradock Nowell, so enlarged and purified by affliction, so able now to understand and feel for every poor man. He, when placed in large possessions and broad English influence, never will forget the time of darkness, grief, and penury, never will look upon his brethren, as under another God than his.

It is true that we must have hill and valley, towering oak and ragged robin, zenith cloud overlooking the sun, and mist crouching down in the hollows. And true as well that we cannot see all the causes and needs of the difference. But is it not still more true and sure, that the whole is of one universal kingdom (bound together by one great love), the high and low, the rich and poor, the powerful and the helpless? And in the spreading of that realm, beyond the shores of time and space, when at last it is understood what the true aim of this life has been, not greatness, honour, wealth, or science, no, nor even wisdom—as we unwisely take it—but happiness here and here-after, a flowing tide whose fountain is our love of one another, then shall we truly learn by feeling (whereby alone we can learn) that all the cleaving of our sorrow, and cuts into the heart of us, were nothing worse than preparation for the grafts of God.

THE END.

LONDON:
PRINTED BY C. WHITING, BEAUFORT HOUSE, STRAND.